LOVE TO HATE YOU

T0349073

ALSO BY MARINA ADAIR

Revved-up Romance series

ALWAYS A BRIDESMAID

Sierra Vista series

FAUX BEAU

SECOND FIRST KISS

The Eastons series

CHASING I DO

DEFINITELY, MAYBE DATING

SUMMER AFFAIR

SINGLE GIRL IN THE CITY

FOUR DATES AND A FOREVER

Romcom novels

YOU'VE GOT MALE

SITUATIONSHIP

ROMEANTICALLY CHALLENGED

HOPELESS ROMANTIC

ROMANCE ON TAP (novella)

Sweet Plains, Texas series

TUCKER'S CROSSING

BLAME IT ON THE MISTLETOE (novella)

Nashville Heights series

PROMISE ME YOU

Sequoia Lake series

IT STARTED WITH A KISS

EVERY LITTLE KISS

Destiny Bay series

LAST KISS OF SUMMER

LIKE THE FIRST TIME

Heroes of St. Helena series

NEED YOU FOR KEEPS

NEED YOU FOR ALWAYS

NEED YOU FOR MINE

St. Helena Vineyard series

KISSING UNDER THE MISTLETOE

SUMMER IN NAPA

AUTUMN IN THE VINEYARD

BE MINE FOREVER

FROM THE MOMENT WE MET

Sugar, Georgia series

COMING HOME TO SUGAR LAKE

SPRINGTIME IN SUGAR LAKE

REUNION AT SUGAR LAKE

LOVE TO HATE YOU

a novel

MARINA ADAIR

Published by 8th Note Press
Text Copyright © 2025 by Marina Adair
All rights reserved.

ISBN: 9781961795464
eBook ISBN: 9781961795457
Audiobook ISBN: 9781961795471

Manufactured in the United States

Cover design by Lucy Rhodes/Pixel Goose Design
Cover art by Valentina Damato
Typeset by Typo•glyphix

To Barb Haliday
for sharing your stories and
being vulnerable so that
this book could be possible.

Chapter 1

THE MEET-CUTE

Summer Russo believed in destiny, true love, and chocolate cake. She also believed that her perfect meet-cute was right around the corner. Or maybe right in front of her, she thought giddily, while staring up at her very own romance hero.

After months of watching Dr. Dashing from afar, Summer had finally snagged her man. Well, their leashes had snagged and, in trying to free their dogs, they'd become entangled. Thigh to thigh, chest to chest, their personal space bubbles completely merged. Then he'd asked for her number. Which was how she now found herself, on a cool May evening, outside her bookshop, All Things Cupid, staring into the eyes of a man who could possibly be her soulmate.

"Sorry about the dry-humping situation," Dr. Daniel said with a half-cocked grin.

Summer waved a dismissive hand. "These things happen."

"Well, I'm hoping after the . . ."—Daniel leaned down and used his hands as earmuffs for Freckle, his Dalmatian—"snip-snip, this won't happen again."

"He's still a puppy. Think of when you went through puberty."

"I didn't go around humping random women."

The word "random" made her cheeks heat with uncertainty. Sure, they'd only officially "met" a few months ago, and this was their first date, but the kind of rom-com-worthy meet-cute they'd shared didn't seem to fit the word. Had it been love at first sight? No, but Cupid had been working his magic, because on that February-in-Connecticut day all those months ago, the sun had been out, the sky a brilliant blue, and romance had been in the air. Surely if your eyes met across a crowded dog park on Valentine's Day, Fate had her hand in the mix.

"Today was nice," Summer said.

"We should do it again sometime," Dr. Daniel said, stepping closer. His eyes were the color of melted chocolate—and Summer loved chocolate. He had thick, dark brown hair, a strong jawline, and nice full lips. He was tall-*ish*—five-nine on a good day—and handsome in that I-love-science kind of way. He loved books—mainly medical journals—and dogs, and was a great conversationalist. He believed in science over fate, but nobody was perfect.

"My shop is closed on Mondays," she offered, and then remembered the promise she'd made to herself when she was sixteen and her secret crush asked her twin to the prom.

Be bold. Be the heroine of your own story.

Summer had spent most of her life between the pages of a book—her heart was safer there. But she hadn't given up on love. In fact, finding the kind of head-over-heels romance her parents shared was at the top of her list, only she had an embarrassing habit of turning her meet-cutes into meet-uglies. Like dumping hot coffee on Sexy Stockbroker's shoes, or the time on the bus when she fell onto Handsome Handyman's lap and elbowed him in his tool. But it hadn't diminished her desire to find her person.

And the dashing Dr. Daniel might be that person.

He must have thought so too, because Dr. Daniel was checking out her boobs. He wasn't ogling, but every so often his eyes would dart down for a little sneak peek of what was hopefully to come—a passionate kiss beneath the porchlight. Not surprising since the girls were on display tonight, and she'd made a strategic decision to leave the top two buttons of her sexy but Sandra-Bullock-subtle red dress undone. It didn't show everything, but hinted at what was beneath curtain number one. And it was a showstopper.

"Or we can go across the street to The Distillery and get a drink now," she amended boldly, hoping her smile translated into more of a Cool Girl vibe than the Concerned Family Member vibe she normally gave off. "They're dog-friendly."

Summer had never thought that a smile could be sensitive, but Dr. Daniel seemed to have a delicate touch. It probably came from years of helping patients navigate their best and worst days. She needed to compliment him on his work ethic because this was fast becoming one of her best days.

A romantic date at the park, where Princess Buttercup and Freckle had frolicked in a field of dogs, followed by this sunset walk along the lamp-lined Main Street, which was overflowing with spring flowers set against a sea of quaint brick-fronted shops, with yellow and white awnings and a history dating back to the late 1800s.

A cool spring breeze came off the coast, wrapping around them like a comforting blanket.

Old-town Ridgefield had rolled up its doormats before the sun went down, leaving Summer and Daniel alone in the night air. The sun was still setting, so the stars had yet to come out, but the million twinkling lights strung overhead, zigzagging across the street, were creating a ready-made, picture-perfect moment for a kiss.

"Or we can go back to my place." She pointed at the upstairs window of her apartment, which sat atop her bookshop. "My sister's away on business, so I've got the place to myself. I've got some wine in the fridge and homemade dog treats."

At the word "treats," Princess Buttercup, Summer's French bulldog, stood to attention, one ear cocked, head tilted as if trying to read the room. Something Summer was trying to do herself, since Daniel's answer was to look at his watch with a furrowed brow.

He glanced across the street at the upscale bar and sighed. "I wish I could, but I'm presenting at TEDMED this weekend and I still need to finish my presentation. Between rounds at the hospital and my podcast, I've barely had time to focus on my speech."

Not only was Daniel a renowned fertility doctor, and a Doctors Without Borders frequent flyer, he was also the host of a successful podcast—another thing they had in common. Where Summer's was called *All Things Cupid* and talked about romance, cake recipes, and book recommendations, Dr. Daniel was the host of *Scrambled Eggs*.

"What's the speech about?"

"Ovulation Foreplay and the Miracle of Masturbation."

Okay. Wow. That was a lot to unpack. "That sounds interesting."

His eyes lit up. "I want to destigmatize the process of egg recovery. In vitro can be sexy and strengthen marriages if framed in the right way. Just the image of a wife assisting her partner to come to a climax for the sole purpose of fertilization is what love stories are made of. Don't you think?"

Summer didn't want to think about that image. As the book buyer for her shop, she'd read a lot of spicy stories. To her recollection, not a single one had involved sperm collection.

What she did find sexy was his passion for his profession. Plus, what kind of man dedicated his life to helping create families? Hubby material, that's who. She could already hear them laughing to her friends about their first date. Bookstore girl meets sexy doctor, they fall in love, have test-tube babies, and live happily ever after. It was suddenly one of Summer's favorite romance tropes. Pair that with their chance meeting on Valentine's Day, and it was as if it had been written in the stars.

"Which brings me to something I've been wanting to ask you all day." He moved closer, his voice lowering until it was as rough as tossed gravel, and her belly bottomed out. Anticipation had been coursing through her body since that day at the dog park when they'd laughed about their game of leash-Twister and he'd started asking the kinds of questions men ask when they're interested. "I know this is late notice, so there's no pressure to say yes, but TEDMED is in Hawaii this year."

"Hawaii?" Summer could picture Dr. Daniel on the beach, shirtless and smiling as he rubbed lotion all over her body.

God, how long had it been since she'd had a man's hands on her?

"That sounds amazing." With her knuckle, she pushed her glasses up the bridge of her nose. "A few days on the beach sounds like just what the doctor ordered."

"Exactly. I mean, there will be a lot of time spent in an unknown number of conference rooms, which is why I'm staying an extra day to relax, snorkel, unwind."

Man, after the past three years of working nonstop on growing her bookshop and podcast, Summer could use a little unwinding. She could also use a man-made orgasm.

"So, I was wondering . . ."

She blinked up at him, her eyes dropping to his lips, mesmerized as he spoke. Dreaming of how it would feel when he hauled her up against his better-than-mediocre, shirtless chest, wet with the ocean, and then asked if they could do a little tangled-sheets snorkeling of their own.

It would be difficult to take a weekend off during one of the busiest weeks of her month, but she could make it happen. For the right man, she could definitely make it happ—

". . . if you could doggie-sit Freckle?"

"I'd love to," she breathed, then suddenly felt a proverbial cold bucket of water crash over her head. "Wait. What?"

"I know it's a big ask. But he gets this preposterous separation anxiety and doggie daycare isn't his thing. I'd leave him at my parents', but my mom's allergic."

For a heartbeat, Summer contemplated gently squeezing his hand in that teasing aren't-you-a-jokester kind of way. He'd squeeze back and say, "Joking! In fact, I've been thinking about you in a swimsuit all night."

"I mean, Freckle and Princess Buttercup get along so well," he went on, and this time the bucket was filled with ice. "I was just hoping he could stay with you for the weekend."

"The weekend?" she croaked.

"Four days tops." Finally, she got that hand squeeze. "I'm desperate."

"Something I can relate to," Summer said brightly.

"God, Summer. You're a lifesaver."

"I'm something." The word "pushover" came to mind.

"No, seriously, I don't have any other friends I'd trust with Freckle."

And there was the nail in this meet-cute coffin. That F-word heard around the world which seemed to follow her everywhere.

Romance was her life and her profession, so she knew how this story would end. With a new guy friend looking for a woman's perspective on dating, while Summer was looking for love. It was a tale as old as time. Girl meets boy, boy flirts with girl, then he asks her to spend the weekend picking doggie poop up off the sidewalk, while boy goes on an exotic vacation and meets his one true love, to whom he becomes engaged. The epilogue would be their wedding, with the first girl invited to sit at the singles' table.

Maybe Summer should just RSVP now, put in her request for the roasted chicken—which would likely be as dry as the other single men at the table.

"Humping aside, Freckle is a great dog. Easy, quiet"— Freckle barked—"friendly and very social. Look at how good he is with Buttercup."

A sneeze exploded out of Buttercup's nose, spraying liquid all over Summer's thighs and dress hem. Then she stood up on her Q-tip legs—a hard feat since she had the body of a bowling ball and the feet of a rhino. After a long moment of mutual adoration, Buttercup let out a single bark, the one that always had Summer caving, then flashed those doggie eyes at her expectantly.

Maybe it was fate. Summer had a long weekend ahead. Preparing for a local author to come do a signing, and looking ahead to her first podcast interview, about intergalactic love, then there was the annual Russo family reunion just a month away, and payroll, inventory, and making a new spring window display. Having a playdate around for Buttercup might be a good thing.

With a resigned sigh, Summer bent down to give Freckle a ruffle behind the ears. He panted in ecstasy, then rolled over to show off his doggie bits. "When do you want to drop him off?"

"Does Friday morning work?"

As the fixer in the family, a characteristic that had bled over into her personal and professional life, Summer had developed a finely tuned facility for being a human pacifier.

"Sure," she said, her cheeks hurting from the weight of her smile. "Why not."

It wasn't like a cute dog with attachment and humping issues would scare away her customers.

God, what was she thinking?

She should say no. Stand her ground. Tell her inner people-pleaser to shut up. Remind that stubborn witch that she wasn't looking for a friend, she was looking for her forever. And, for a moment there, she'd thought she'd found him. Maybe Summer could salvage the situation, keep herself open to a friends-to-lovers kind of situation. Or maybe she was looking for love in the wrong place.

Her sister would know how to turn this date around. How to get out of the friend zone. Autumn had this magnetic and sensual confidence about her that drew people in, especially men. She made being popular look easy, and there wasn't anyone she couldn't win over.

Unless it was about books or movies, Summer had a hard time striking up a conversation with strangers. It was a left-over from a quiet childhood spent watching people through the lens of her insecurities. Insecurities she could no longer afford if she was to stand any chance of finding her person.

Even as babies, Autumn had demanded center stage: walking first, talking first, being the right amount of snuggly and independent. Summer would rather be behind the spotlight, shining that beam on anyone but herself. For the most part, it worked. But there were times, like tonight, when Summer wondered what it would be like to have that easy confidence her twin sister possessed. How different would her life be? And how many things about herself would she have to alter to become the kind of woman a man like Dr. Daniel, or her ex, saw forever in?

Autumn flew by the seat of her pants, always landing on her feet. She could step through dog poop and come out smelling like roses, leaving the poop for someone else to clean up—someone like Summer. But Summer was tired of being on poop duty; she wanted to smell the roses with someone who saw her as spotlight-worthy.

Before she could retract her offer, Daniel pulled her into an awkward side-hug. "I'll pay you back. You need a handy-man, a wedding date, a wingman, I'm your guy."

He was most definitely not her guy. He was just another in a long line of misshaped meet-cutes.

"Couldn't ask for a better wingman."

On cue, Freckle jumped in on the action, or the non-action as it were. She could feel his hips undulating against her calf and his claws digging into the fabric of her too-much-for-her-budget-but-looks-fabulous new sundress.

"Freckle, down," Daniel ordered. Before he could get a hold of the pup's collar, a loud rip tore through the evening breeze, leaving Summer with a slit she felt from her waist to her toes. Not to mention the sudden gust of crisp air.

It was as if someone had plugged in an air conditioner and aimed it at her butt.

"Oh my god." Summer plastered her hands on her ass and looked over her shoulder to check out the extent of the damage. "Oh my god."

It was even worse than she'd imagined. Her entire back-side was on full display. No amount of tugging could close that hole. A hospital gown would have been less revealing.

At least she had on her sexiest pair of panties. Not that Daniel was looking. He kept his eyes front and center and his hands to himself.

Summer waited for him to say something quippy to lighten the mood and make the embarrassment flooding her cheeks subside. A real hero-to-the-rescue kind of banter, straight from the pages of a Nora Ephron screenplay. Instead, he simply said, "Uh-oh."

Uh-oh. A real heartstopper there.

"Summer, I am so sorry. We're still working on commands like 'down' and 'sit.'"

And "no humping," she thought.

Humiliation hitting her like a cannonball to the chest, Summer gripped the tattered edges of her dress and backed away, wishing she could disappear into the wall. "It's okay. It was an accident."

Daniel cataloged her from head to toe and then chuckled—and it was not a you-look-beautiful-even-if-the-dress-is-ripped chuckle. "You know, when you first approached me at the park—"

"I didn't approach you. Our leashes got tangled."

"—I thought you were Autumn. But after tonight, I can totally see the difference."

Summer's pride took a direct hit. "You mean when I tripped over my words, or when your dog ripped my dress?" Because neither of those things would have happened to Autumn. She wouldn't allow it.

"I didn't mean—"

"What did you mean? That when you said yes to the date you thought you were going out with my sister?"

Daniel ran a hand over his face. "You guys look exactly alike. It's a trip."

"It's called being twins."

"But I should have noticed the difference right away. I mean, Autumn's loud and laugh-a-minute and she's got this mysterious quality to her. And you're more—"

"—reserved and predictable."

"Predictability is a good thing," he said vehemently. "Guys might want a little mystery, but after a while they just want something comfortable, loyal, and warm."

"You just described your dog." Summer told herself that it didn't matter, it would only add insult to injury, but she couldn't stop herself from asking, "Would you have said yes if you'd known it was me?"

"I was relieved it was you," he said with no hesitation, and her bruised ego recovered just enough so she could take in a breath without inflicting too much pain. "I'm not looking to date right now. Between work and my research, I don't have the energy for anything more than friends."

"So you knew I'd be a friend right off the bat?"

"Didn't you? I mean, you asked me to meet you at the dog park. We talked about books and medical journals, and our dogs' gastrointestinal systems. That doesn't really scream 'date.'"

She crossed her arms over her chest, flashing the public be damned. "I wore a new dress. A red, hot-date kind of dress."

"Maybe, but your energy is dialed to 'waiting for someone else to come along.'"

Was it?

Summer liked to think of herself as open and responsive, genuinely looking for that right connection. Maybe she'd been so busy looking for the insta-love that she'd missed out on a slow burn with a great guy. But she'd tried the slow burn with Ken, and the embers had been so contained that he'd walked away to start over, three thousand miles away—where, according to a social-media deep dive on her part, he'd found his flame.

Daniel stilled, his eyes going soft with something that made Summer nauseous. "Did you think this was a date?"

Yes! Of course I thought it was a date. Any woman would think so! Then again, she wasn't any woman. Summer Russo was Ridgefield's honorary bookworm and shy girl with a penchant for chasing away great men. "I've got to go."

He stuffed his hands in his pockets and rocked back on his heels. "So we're still good for Friday?"

Summer gave a lame two thumbs up and Princess Buttercup barked. "So good."

She waited until Dr. Daniel and Freckle had disappeared around the corner before she leaned back against the wall and closed her eyes.

Why was this her life? This was the seventh failed meet-cute just this year, and it was only May.

"Upward and onward," she said to Buttercup.

Buttercup looked at her with those big doggie eyes and cute wrinkly jowls and farted.

"Pretty much sums it up." She straightened and led Buttercup through into the shop, the jingling bells welcoming her and bringing her back to the first time she'd stepped through that door.

She was immediately greeted by the musty smell of ink on paper, glue from the bindings, and a hint of the aroma of the hand-pressed Italian espressos that had been served to customers earlier that day. She was also greeted with the many memories she'd made there. Huddled on her grandmother's lap, both in their pajamas, reading *The Secret Garden* or *Little Women*. She could almost feel her nonna's arms around her, whispering in her ear the words that one day this shop would be hers.

Summer wasn't a storyteller like her father or a shining star like her twin. But in this bookstore, she could become anyone she wanted to be. A fair maiden, a deadly assassin, or even the sometimes awkward but endearing girl who, through self-exploration and pluck, got the boy of her dreams.

Summer took it all in and found herself smiling. So the date hadn't gone as planned. So what? She was living her dream.

Spending her days at All Things Cupid, using her superpower of pairing the right love story with the right person.

After unleashing Buttercup, who immediately waddled to her food bowl and then plopped down in front of it like one of Her Majesty's Guards protecting the Crown Jewels, Summer unbuttoned her dress and slowly made her way back toward the counter, where she kept a spare change of clothes. She looked at herself in the mirror that hung behind the register and let out a sigh that came from the depths of her soul.

Normally, being in her nonna's shop, surrounded by all the beautiful books and endless adventures, could erase even the worst of days. Owning All Things Cupid was every bookworm's dream and every booklover's escape from the daily grind of life.

But not tonight, she thought as she looked at her reflection. Tonight, she felt like a big red fire hydrant in a dog park. She was covered in fur, snot, and possibly had dog poop stuck to the underside of her heels.

"You never know, this may end up being a friends-to-lovers situation," she told herself, pulling her dress over her head and inspecting the gigantic rip. The dress was ruined, but her night hadn't been a total disaster. She'd gone on a date with a charming man, gained some new experiences, and come out one failed meet-cute closer to her soulmate.

Her ability to see the romance in everyday life was another of her superpowers. She lived her life like that quote from the movie *Love Actually*: "Love is actually all around us."

Summer believed that, with all her being. Just look at her family. They were crazy and loud and intrusive, but they loved as fiercely as they nosed into each other's business. It was the kind of love and passion her parents had that Summer was craving in a partner.

"One more trope down, a hundred to go," she said, dropping her dress to the floor.

"You know," someone said from behind her, "if you'd gone at him in those, you'd have probably gotten a kiss. Maybe even some two-legged action."

A scream stuck in Summer's throat as she grabbed her work shirt and hugged it against her chest. In the mirror, she could see a tall, broad, axe-murdering shadow.

Never a fan of the damsels in distress, Summer tapped into her best heroine-saves-herself confidence and grabbed the heaviest thing within reach—a signed first edition of *Anna Karenina* that her nonna had hand-carried from Italy. It weighed as much as a concrete slab and had edges as sharp as a fileting knife.

On instinct, she spun around and launched the literary grenade at her intruder. Only, Summer had never been the most coordinated twin—that title went to Autumn—and so the book flew into left field, crashing into a shelf housing Bigfoot erotica.

"Should I call foul, love?" the clipped and precise British voice said from the buttery leather couch in the reading area that he'd completely overtaken.

She'd know that pompous, entitled voice anywhere. The evenly stressed syllables, the slight trill on the r's making the words almost musical—not in a good way like Prince Harry, but in an entitled way that grated on her every nerve. To think she'd once found him a bit dashing and charming.

A slow smile spread across his face as he leaned over to pick up the book and lazily thumbed through it. She growled in frustration. Of all the people to witness her botched date, why did it have to be the all-around book snob and corporate raider who gobbled up mom-and-pop shops for breakfast? Not to mention that he was dead set on putting Summer out of business.

Evil incarnate—Wes Kingston.

Chapter 2

THE CHEMICAL EQUATION

"Who said I wanted a kiss?" Summer snapped—and, man, was she ticked.

Wes's gaze dropped from her bra to her stilettoes, admiring the complete package that was Summer Russo, and grinned. "Those peek-a-boo panties you have on."

Her cheeks went red, but he didn't think it was from embarrassment. Unlike a moment ago with Dr. Dildo, there wasn't a trace of sweet or nice; she was all fire and brimstone.

She looked him square in the eyes. "Maybe I wore them for me."

"Then, by all means, you do you." He let his gaze lazily catalog her every inch. The way the pastel pink looked against her olive skin, the way the strap of those cheeky-cuts hugged her generous curves. If she weren't such a pain in his ass, he'd take the time to appreciate that ass.

But after weeks of her being a burr in his side, for example starting a petition to close his bookstore down, he shrugged as if unimpressed.

He heard her mumble "Dick" under her breath. For some reason, that made him smile.

"I can't now that you've invaded my personal space, not to mention broken into the shop." She circled her finger. "Do you mind?"

He turned around. "I'll give you some privacy."

"It's PRI-vuh-see not PRIV-uh-see."

"Since my country was essentially the birthplace for your language, it's PRIV-uh-see."

"*For* my language? It's the birthplace *of* my language."

"Do you like to argue for argument's sake?"

"Only with you."

He could hear the rustling of fabric, the sound of a zipper echoing throughout the bookshop.

"Then I shall count myself lucky." When she didn't answer, he asked, "So I guess you won't be seeing Dog Boy again." He didn't know why he cared, but on some sick level he did.

"He's a doctor."

"He doles out *Playboy* and little plastic cups all day."

"He's making babies."

"There are better ways to make babies."

He heard a sharp intake of breath, followed by a weighted pause that seemed to grow and crackle.

"You can turn around now."

He did and couldn't hold back a smile. She was wearing a pair of distressed jeans and a TEAM CUPID shirt that fit her to a tee, placing the T and D in a losing battle with her breasts. Her hair was twisted into a messy knot on her head, secured by a pencil. Then there were those glasses that made her look like a coed clashed into a wet dream of a librarian. Couldn't forget her attitude—always dialed to "nut-crusher" around him.

"What are you doing here?" she asked, and some of her earlier flames had been snuffed out. She looked tired and worn down, and his chest gave an annoying pinch.

"I came to tell you to move your car."

"It's a free country. I can park where I please."

"As long as it's not blocking the entrance to the parking lot. The construction guys are done for the day and can't pull out."

"Sounds like a personal problem."

"I'm paying them for every minute they sit there."

"Maybe they shouldn't park in my parking lot. There are signs specifically stating that the spaces are for customers only."

"The signs are hand-painted on foamboard."

She ignored this. "Why are you in my shop?"

"The door was unlocked, and I didn't want anyone breaking in."

"Said the B&E asshole. My door was definitely not unlocked. The sign was definitely flipped to CLOSED. I should call the cops and report you for breaking and entering."

He watched her slide a covert glance at the door, and when she looked back his smile conveyed all she needed to know. He'd caught her.

"Made myself an espresso, hope you don't mind." He jerked his chin toward a cup of steaming coffee sitting on the end table next to him. He picked it up, burying his nose in the rising steam, and gave a sigh.

"I mind." Summer marched over and snatched it out of his hands, then polished it off in a single gulp. Her eyes watered from sucking down such hot liquid, but she put on a brave face. "This has been fun. Don't let the door hit you in the ass on the way out."

"That's your best comeback? A cliché? I'm disappointed, love."

"I added the ass part, making it a twist on a well-loved cliché, *crumpet*." She walked over and opened the door and stood like one of the yellow Sphinxes from *The Neverending Story*, ready to shoot lasers at him. This was not going as planned.

"I'm sorry that I invited myself in." It wasn't the first time he'd had to invite himself in. In fact, he'd had an entire life of being on the outside waiting for someone to open the door. After a while, he'd gotten tired of waiting and instead became assertive. Blunt, concise, to the point—that was how he now lived his life.

Summer blinked as if genuinely shocked at his apology. Almost as shocked as he was. Apology stemmed from regret, and Wes was too strategic about his every move to form regret. But if his project were to come in on time, he needed to call a truce. It was imperative that the Ridgefield BookLand location opened without a hitch.

Now who was using clichés?

"I'm not sorry to show you out," she said.

He let out a long, tired breath. Anger was exhausting and he was angry. At his dad for dying and leaving him a business he'd never asked for nor wanted. At his half-brother, Randy, for being inept at running a billion-dollar enterprise. And at himself for agreeing to the terms of his father's will. He should have walked the moment the lawyer had explained that Wes and Randy only had a year to grow the company, or it was forfeited to the board. Just like Wes had been forfeited the moment his father had found out that his mistress, Wes's mother, was pregnant with his bastard son.

Wes felt as if his life had been full of being forfeited. Which was why he always led with his head instead of his heart. If he even had a heart anymore.

"I have a proposition that I think will solve both our problems."

"If you say it's in your pants, I don't feel like being underwhelmed tonight. So that's a hard pass."

God, she was prickly.

"If you let my guys park in your lot, I'll rent the space until construction is complete."

She paused, and he could hear her mental calculator clicking away, see the dollar signs in her eyes. Not that he was surprised. In his experience, money was like catnip and women were tigers ready to pounce. Summer though, she was more of a bobcat. Short in stature, but vicious if provoked. And he loved provoking her.

"What about after?" she said. "When your customers use my lot, making it impossible for my customers to park?"

She wanted to play hardball—fine. He knew that everyone had their number. "A thousand dollars a day for each spot taken."

She didn't even balk. "No deal."

"You don't mind if customers from Drip and Sip or Critter Couture park there."

"Drip and Sip and Critter Couture are allies. You, Mr. British Bully, are not."

"Are you saying we're at war?" he asked.

She placed her hands on his chest to push him out the door, but that didn't stop the warm sensation from moving through his body like he'd been struck by a live wire. Then she shoved him hard and there he went—stumbling over the threshold and into the cool evening air.

"May the best bookshop win!" she said, then slammed the door in his face, the jingling bells mocking as she flipped the signed to CLOSED—but not before flipping him the bloody bird.

Chapter 3

ESCALATING COMPLICATIONS

Monday couldn't have come fast enough. Freckles was finally gone, and talk about what an awkward drop-off that had been, but it was done and behind her. Now she was dealing with a romantic mishap of an entirely different kind.

"I'm telling you, Cupid is a standup comedian," Autumn said.

Summer took in the stylized lettering and elegant embossing, and couldn't find a trace of humor in the ecru, 220-pound weighted cardstock. Usually, getting a wedding invitation was like Christmas morning, but today it felt more like April Fool's Day.

"Please tell me you aren't going to go," Autumn demanded, her expression fierce on Summer's phone screen.

"I haven't decided." Just like she hadn't decided how it felt to be invited to her ex's wedding in the first place.

Just ten months ago they'd been talking about their own wedding, because that was the next logical step and Ken was nothing but a logical man. And now he was marrying someone else—she looked at the "MD" after Ken's fiancée's name and groaned.

Of course her replacement was a doctor.

She'd known this moment would come, had anticipated it for months, but seeing the proof that her ex had officially moved on so quickly was different. In her heart she'd known Ken wasn't the one and—as one of Cupid's Devoted Fans— she was happy for him that he'd found his person. But why couldn't she have found hers first?

She dropped the invitation on her nightstand and walked to her closet.

"What?" Autumn's voice was loud enough to reach through the apartment floor and echo off the walls of the bookshop. "I must have heard you wrong, because there is no way you're considering going to that asshat's wedding. Look me in the eye and tell me you are RSVPing a big fuck off." Summer did not look her sister in the eye. She was too embarrassed to see the disappointment lying there. "I can help you draw the middle finger if you want."

"We parted on good terms," Summer said.

"He parted. You allowed it to be good terms."

Summer didn't see the point of ending things badly. It wasn't like Ken had purposefully set out to break her heart. He'd been following his own, which had led him to Los Angeles for his dream job. And apparently his dream girl.

"You're right. I'm not going. In fact, I'm dropping the invitation in the trash right now."

"Good!"

"On to more important things." Summer leaned her cell phone against the wall, using a book to hold it upright while she rifled through her closet. She pulled out a dress and held it up to her chest. She looked at her reflection in the mirror. It was simple, sophisticated, and professional. Exactly the vibe she was hoping for. "How about the dress I wore to Mom and Dad's anniversary party?"

A long, unwelcome tension stretched wider between them. Summer could feel her sister's judgment smother her through the phone. "The black one with the scalloped collar?" Autumn asked, right as Summer slipped it over her head and stood in front of her phone, giving a little cock of the hip. "Absolutely not. You look like Morticia."

"When I bought it, you said it was a universal dress." Otherwise, Summer wouldn't have purchased it. Admittedly, she was fashion-challenged, while Autumn was the fashion queen. They were the complete reverse of each other, after all.

Summer and Autumn weren't normal twins. They were mirror twins, which meant that they were asymmetrical. The same but opposite. Autumn's heart was on the left side of her body and Summer's was on the right. Autumn's dimple was in left field and Summer's the reverse. They were truly two peas in the same pod.

Even their personalities were polar opposites. Autumn hadn't met a person she couldn't befriend. She looked like a model, acted like a coed, and lived like an influencer—was even a social media content creator for a midsized advertising company. Her outgoing and bubbly personality—not to mention boobs—attracted men like flies to honey.

Summer was the reliable and introspective one and Autumn was spontaneous and charismatic. Bottom line, Summer was the ying to Autumn's yang, the Laverne to her Shirley—an unexpected pairing with an unbreakable bond.

"You bought it without my input and then told me it was nonreturnable. What was I supposed to say?" Autumn asked.

"That I looked like Morticia."

"It isn't Morticia-bad, but also isn't podcast-appropriate."

"That's the point of a podcast, no one can see me."

"But *you* can see you, and how you dress influences how you come across to your listeners. You're supposed to be a romance guru, not look like you're going to Auntie Cecilia's funeral."

"Auntie Cecilia probably felt that energy you just put out into the universe." Their aunt was not only a brilliant businesswoman, she also fancied herself a bona fide psychic.

"Hang on, I have a text coming in." Autumn's face went pale. "Oh my god," she whispered. "It's Auntie Cecilia."

"Told you." Summer hid her smile. Cecilia had texted Summer a bit ago asking what their mom wanted for her birthday. Since Autumn and her mom were the most alike, she'd told Cecilia she'd contacted the wrong twin. "How about that blue and white maxi-dress I bought when we went to Mystic?"

"And look like a sailor?" Autumn's face filled the entire screen now. "Summs, you are gorgeous and genuine and believe in romance the way Mom believes that the key to flawless skin is sunscreen and hats. And the way I believe in you."

It took Summer a moment to gather herself at her sister's words, but even then, as she spoke, her voice was thick with emotion. "You have to say that. You're my sister."

"And I'd never bullshit you. You have the most beautiful and gentle soul of anyone I've ever met. We need an outfit that showcases that."

"That's a tall order." Plus, tomorrow wasn't just a regular podcast. Tomorrow was Summer's first podcast where she was interviewing a guest, to discuss May's most anticipated romance book. With Autumn's help, Summer had grown her following to over ten thousand and she wanted to impress.

Summer looked at the time, then her sister's face, and a bad feeling settled in her belly. "How are you calling me? Aren't you supposed to be mid-flight, somewhere over the Atlantic?"

"About that . . ."

Summer picked up the phone and held it to her face. "No, no, no. I know that voice. That's the don't-hate-me voice, and I swear on my entire and complete, first-edition J.D. Robb collection that if you say what I think you're about to say, the hate will be real."

"My trip was extended, and it looks like I won't be home for another couple of days."

"But my event is tomorrow. The event, I should remind you, that you said was necessary to grow my brand."

"And it will."

"You promised we'd do this together. That's why I agreed to do this, because you had my back."

No matter where they were in the world, to Summer it always felt as if they were in their nine-hundred-square-foot apartment above the shop. Finishing each other's sentences, sharing in each other's successes and hardships as if they were their own. But lately, they'd been like two ships passing in the night.

Summer had felt this slight shift in their usually aligned planets as deeply as the loss of a limb. She'd lost the everyday bonds with many people in her life over the past few months; she couldn't bear to lose another.

First, she'd lost Ken to his career. Then, six months ago, her parents had moved from Ridgefield to Boca Raton, retiring in the Florida sun in a house next door to Summer's auntie and uncle. It was difficult to go from seeing her large family every day at the shop to being a business owner of one. No more Friday family dinners or Boardgame Wednesdays to get her through the week. All that was left in Connecticut was her twin. And she really needed her support right now.

"I do. I'll tune in and everything. Be there remotely. You won't even notice my absence. I do this all the time with creators. It's my thing."

Summer's stomach shifted queasily. "But it's not *my* thing."

"You've got this," Autumn assured her, but Summer didn't feel assured. "And if this trip wasn't a possibly life-changing one, I would be there. I swear. But the content I made about Swifties," she said, referring to Taylor Swift superfans, "was so good that I'm, uh, being flown from London to Paris tomorrow morning. Paris, Summs! In the spring. How could I pass that up?"

Easy. You say no. That's what Summer would have said if the situation were reversed.

"Tell me you understand." Autumn's eyes were so uncertain that Summer felt her sister's unease as if it were her own. Summer was a giver by nature, and Autumn tended to be a bit of a taker—but her huge heart made up for it. And having a big heart sometimes meant that you had to follow it.

"I get it. I mean, Paris," Summer whispered.

"I know, right!" Autumn said, and their through-the-ether twin thing must have been one-way right then because her sister clearly wasn't reading the room. "Which brings me to a little favor."

"How little?"

"Depending on how this thing goes, I might need to borrow some money for the trip."

Summer flopped on her bed. "How much?"

Autumn rattled off some insane amount and Summer sat straight up. That bad feeling turned acidic. "You said just a couple of extra days. Why do you need that kind of money?"

"If Paris goes well, I might end up going to Prague, and then Berlin, and I'm a little short on cash."

"So am I." Summer had spent a huge chunk of her savings buying the bookstore from her mom and auntie. Then there was the remodel she'd done to the shop, not to mention the small business loan she'd taken out. "All that I have is my wedding fund." A fund that had taken her a lifetime to accumulate.

"Which is why I'll pay you back with my end-of-quarter bonus. Please, Summs. I'll even tack on interest."

Summer felt herself caving. It wasn't like she was getting married anytime soon, and her sister might be a little flaky when it came to the little things, but she never broke a promise. And while Summer was cash-poor, she was passion-rich. So if she could help her sister fulfill one of her dreams, then she was all in.

"How about you let me borrow something romance-worthy from your closet and we'll call it even?"

Chapter 4

THE BEAST

"Are we talking Gumball Pink or Cotton Candy Pink on those cheekies?" Summer's best friend, Cleo, asked. She was sitting on the checkout counter handing Summer novels for the bookshop's new front window display.

"Does it matter?"

It had been six days since her run-in with the brooding British villain and she was still irate. Sure, his workers no longer parked in her lot. Instead, they were taking up all the street spaces, their big, obnoxious trucks blocking her storefront from passersby.

Still, the bookshop was full of customers, some perusing the shelves, others relaxing with friends in the reading area over espressos while talking about their latest reads. In the far corner was the Smut Club, who were engaged in a hot debate over how many chili peppers their latest book pick should receive.

"Definitely a five," Mable, the club's fierce leader, said.

"Just because they used C-O-C-K over M-A-N-R-O-O-T doesn't make it a five, Mable," Claire pointed out.

"If you're spelling out the words, it makes it a five-chili-pepper read," Mable shot back.

Mable was a grandmother and nine-time bass fishing champion. Claire was a college student getting a degree in botany. Yet every month the two came together, with a group of other erotica enthusiasts, to talk about a shared passion. They bickered and hugged it out like they were family.

That's what this was, Summer marveled. A family. Started by her grandmother, nurtured by her mother and auntie, and now blossoming under Summer's watchful care.

"It absolutely matters!" Cleo said, bringing Summer back to the conversation at hand. "When it comes to men, details matter. See, Gumball Pink means you're playful in bed and you don't mind a little blow action. Wild Orchid hints at the fact that you own a red room and there's a ninety percent chance you have a hidden runway behind your lace that's ready for takeoff. Tickle Me Pink, well, that's self-explanatory. Fun fact. Did you know that ninety-five percent of women find that ear play is as erotic as rear play? It gives the whole 'little tickle behind the ear' new meaning. By the way, my secret tickle place is—"

"Not important to this conversation."

"I forget you're a prude."

"I sling some of the best smut on the East Coast. We're talking reverse harems, BDSM, shapeshifting unicorns with unearthly large and magical horns. That sounds pretty Wild Orchid to me."

Cleo snorted, so Summer went back to her window display. She took her displays seriously. It was a customer's first impression, and she worked hard to showcase every author in a way that captured the uniqueness of their works. The way the words intertwined, the subtle rhythm of the sentences, the lyrical quality of each paragraph—every author approached writing in their own special way. Then there was how each story was woven together, the careful balance between humor, heartache, and hope.

Hope was what had gotten Summer through some of the hardest times of her life, and encouraged her to shoot for the sky and reach the stars. When Summer was little and her family had lost their home, and Summer had to leave her school and friends behind, her dad had told her that the universe had something even better in store for her—and that year she'd met her soul-sister, Cleo.

Years later, when Summer was a junior in college and her mom had told her the heartbreaking news that the bookstore was in trouble, Summer had quit college, taken out a loan, and revived All Things Cupid, making it the center of the book community in Ridgefield. Last year, her little shop had been named one of the best bookstores in Connecticut.

In her heart, she knew her nonna would be so proud. And if she lost sight of that or the doubt crept in, all she had to do was look at the photo of her grandparents, fresh off the boat from Italy, sharing a kiss that had sparked a tradition of love and romance for the generations to come.

Summer was a quiet dreamer by nature, but a big dreamer in her heart—a trait she'd inherited from her dad and a trait she hoped to pass down to her own children someday.

All Things Cupid might look like a traditional bookshop with its floor-to-ceiling stacks, antique rolling ladders, and plush leather couches and barrel chairs situated in several intimate reading areas, but it was an independent bookstore that specialized in romance and beach reads. And hanging behind the checkout counter were several black-and-white photos of her family commemorating all the special moments in this shop. Her favorite picture was the one of Nonna and Papa Russo standing in front of the shop for the store's grand opening, sharing a kiss that was the pure embodiment of victory and romance: two things Summer wanted to uphold. She'd achieved it in her work and was now searching for it in her personal life.

"Just for curiosity's sake, what does Cotton Candy Pink imply?" Summer asked.

Her best friend crossed her arms smugly. "Let me guess. Asking for a friend?"

Summer lifted a defiant brow.

"Fine. Ballerina Pink, Carnation Pink, all the pastels, tell a guy that you stream a lot of Hallmark movies and do your own lady-scaping. Pretty much, romance on a budget."

Summer refused to cover her face, but she did feel it flush with embarrassment.

Cleo was a welder by trade, a ballbuster by choice, and the part-time manager of All Things Cupid because she'd known Summer needed the help and in her loyalty had stepped up. Crafted from steel, street smarts, and questionable choices, she was a romantic hiding behind realist armor. Which was why she wore steel-toe boots with vampire-red hearts on them.

"What about Quartz Rose?" Summer asked casually, pretending all her focus was on the window display she was revamping to make room for the latest releases. "Understated sexy with a magical-mystery twist?"

"Depends. Does your LadyLand give magical orgasms, or is it a mystery like in *Romancing the Stone* where they need a treasure map?"

"Can we stop calling it that?"

"How about Vagayjay?"

"What? Are we in high school?"

"Bajingo?"

"Middle school?"

"Right, I'm talking to a romance expert. How about something more novel?"

"Har-har."

"Slit," Cleo said in her best sex-operator voice. "Heat. Core. Depths. Meat curtains. Femininity. Womanhood. Oh—I know—her *portal*."

"Is it going to take him to another dimension?"

"If you were wearing Wild Orchid it would."

A chuckle rattled out of Summer. "I doubt that Screw Me Scarlet would have helped with Dr. Daniel. He friend-zoned me even before he saw my panties."

Regardless of what Daniel had said about his current lack of interest in dating, his lack had something to do with the fact that Summer wasn't Autumn. There had been over-flowing interest on his side that first day they met at the park, even some flirt and banter on the walk, but when he'd complimented her eyes, Summer had stumbled over her words and his expression had shifted ever so slightly. That was the moment Summer had been moved from the GIRL-FRIEND POTENTIAL LANE across NO POTENTIAL HIGHWAY and straight to FRIEND ZONE JAIL—she did not pass go and nor did she collect her kiss.

"Panties? God, you need an intervention. Life isn't a Nora Ephron movie, Summer. It's loud and messy with lots of twists and unexpected turns. And it involves thongs and G-strings."

"That's what romance is all about," she said defensively.

"G-strings?"

"A chance first encounter with a charming man where amusing and canny antics ensue, followed by witty banter and, of course, a first kiss under the stars."

"Look at *Jane Eyre*. The typical governess-falls-for-a-nobleman trope. Only said man has his first wife locked in the attic just because she fought back against the patriarchy. It's a meet-cute turned Stephen King."

"Which is exactly why I don't go on dating apps. It's easier to spot serial killers when you can see the whites of their eyes."

"Bertha met Mr. Rochester IRL. Meg Ryan met Tom Hanks over the internet. Which seems safer?"

Summer let out a semi-defeated sigh. "Going on Tinder would feel like giving up. I don't want a hookup. I want a connection."

"I met Hunter on Tinder and we connected. All over the kitchen, workout room, and patio. We're going out again this Saturday and I'm hoping we connect multiple more times." Cleo stared at Summer. "When was the last time you *connected* with someone else physically in the room?"

Without looking up from her window display, Summer flipped Cleo off. "I don't need an app to help me find a date. I do just fine on my own."

"Maybe, but you need help landing a second date."

"That's not true. I went out twice with, uh, what was his name? The podiatrist."

"And he started talking about proper foot care and parenting methods."

"Parenting is an important topic."

"Yeah, if he already had kids." Cleo picked up a steampunk romance from the stack and handed it to Summer. She lovingly placed the book on a stand that was covered in metal gears and had a pocket watch hanging from the corner. She'd been inspired at three in the morning when she'd finished rereading *Shadow and Bone*.

"You know what your problem is?" Cleo asked.

"Probably, but I know how much you like to be right, so go on."

"You date guys who are exactly like you. Studious, house-bound, who live in a book and have companions with four legs that tend to drool when in the vicinity of bacon."

Summer shrugged. "So I date guys I'm compatible with."

"You date boring guys, who think banter is asking about your favorite color."

As Summer met her friend's gaze, her own narrowed. "Great, so you're saying I got friend-zoned by a boring doctor who thinks I'm a dog sitter?"

"You got friend-zoned because you think with your head and not your heart. For a romantic, you're pretty slow when it comes to relationships," Cleo said. "You have to ask your-self, what do you really want? A funny story to tell at parties or someone who lights your fire?"

Summer wanted all the things every hopeless romantic wanted—a perfect meet-cute, followed by insta-love, and finally the dream wedding, ending with a honeymoon in Paris. She wanted two kids, twins—like her and her sister—a house in the suburbs, and the kind of marriage romance novels were made of.

First though, she needed to find herself a qualified candidate. She thought she'd found the one once, a gentle, caring fellow booklover who worked as an editor for a Los Angeles paper. They had similar habits, so much in common, and were perfectly compatible. He'd checked all the boxes—except the passion box.

Gah, she hated being incorrect, but Cleo had a point. Maybe she was going about this all wrong.

"Fine," she said, handing over her phone. "You get one app and not Tinder. Make it one where people aren't just looking for meaningless hookups."

"Meaningful hookups. Got it." Cleo snatched up Summer's phone like it was a slice of chocolate cake. "I know just the app. RoChance. There's this extensive questionnaire to ensure you're paired with compatible people who share the same hobbies and interests."

Compatible. Hobbies. Interests. That didn't sound so scary.

"Plus, there are photos so you can accept or reject from the comfort of your own couch."

"No dick pics."

Cleo rolled her eyes. "I don't see how you can adequately vet a guy without a proper dick pic, but it's your love life so I'll check the No Dick Pic box. Whenever a potential soulmate is in the vicinity it will ping you, and then you have the choice to approach him or not." Cleo's finger flew over the screen of Summer's phone, and a few minutes later she handed it back. "Done."

"I thought you said it was extensive."

"I didn't overthink it. I just went with the first answer that came to mind." Cleo wiggled her fingers like exploding fireworks. "Plus, these babies are like lightning. Give it a few minutes and then you should start getting some matches. I give it a day tops before your DMs are overflowing."

"I'd be happy with a nice, sweet, local guy."

Cleo made the sound of a buzzer. "You've done nice, sweet locals. You need something different. Maybe a caveman type or a mafia boss who is set on making you his bitch because your baby brother wronged him."

"I don't have a brother. You do."

Cleo smiled. "Right, so I get the mafia boss. You get the billionaire bad boy who falls for the small-town bookshop owner and is into ear play."

Summer was about to argue that she preferred betas to alphas and that ear play wasn't a real thing, when something out the window caught her eye. "What the hell!"

"It's just an opinion," Cleo said, but Summer wasn't listening.

Because there, sitting innocently on the main strip of road that went through the heart of Ridgefield, parked between The Codfather and Thai Titanic and directly in front of the soon-to-open BookLand, sat her 1955 Sunbeam Alpine Mark III replica—that was a dead ringer for the car Cary Grant and Grace Kelly had driven in *To Catch a Thief*, and was the car she and her dad had built from the engine up—about to be accosted by a dirty yellow tow truck. And next to the curb, holding a coffee-to-go, was Satan's younger brother.

"Oh no you don't!" Summer dropped the stack of books she was holding and made a mad dash out the door and across the street, the bell jingling angrily behind her as the door slammed. She arrived just as Merle, of Merle's Tow &

Tune-up, was attaching the winch to her baby's bumper. "What the hell is going on?"

Merle lifted his trucker's hat to swipe the sweat from his forehead, and replaced it before talking. "I'm really sorry, Miss Russo, but when I get a call, I have to come."

"Who called?"

"That would be me." Wes's usual frown was replaced by a tummy-flipping grin. Stupid tummy. "Seems parking in a green zone for more than the allotted time is a violation in this country."

"This is not a green zone." Summer stormed around the car and—

"What the hell?" she found herself repeating. The curb was painted a fresh, shiny, parakeet green. She looked at Merle. "It wasn't like this when I parked here."

"My guys finished it, oh, about"—Wes looked at his watch, which probably cost more than her 1955 Sunbeam Alpine Series III replica—"twenty-one minutes ago." His voice was steady, not a hint of smartass, but Summer could see that behind those luxury-brand sunglasses his eyes were crinkling at the corners, fully aware that he was pushing every button she possessed. And enjoying it.

Refusing to give him the pleasure of seeing her squirm, she turned her attention to Merle, who was fiddling with the winch. "Then how did you get here so quickly?"

"As a concerned citizen, I called the police the moment I learned of the twenty-minute zone rule," Wes said. "I explained that a car had been illegally parked in front of my store by someone who seemed like a rule breaker. They sent Merle."

Merle remained mute on the topic.

"Merle, you make one more move with that hook and I will stop selling erotica to your wife," Summer said.

Merle paled, then immediately started unhooking her car. "Sorry, man. But my sex life depends on those books. They were the inspiration behind all three of my kids."

Summer crossed her arms, victorious. "Well, I guess that settles that."

"It settles one topic of conversation," Wes said, his smile obnoxiously self-satisfied.

Just like the other night, a bad feeling settled inside her belly. He looked like he was high-fiving himself. As if he'd already won the next battle. Too bad for him—she knew everyone in this neighborhood, and they were as loyal as they were nosy. They would have Summer's back over his any day of the week.

"Turns out those little online-purchase CUSTOMER PARKING ONLY signs of yours are nothing more than decoration."

Oh god, he knew, and now she was one step closer to going under.

"According to the planning commission, only two spots are designated for your shop. The rest are public parking, so starting tomorrow my crew will be parking there."

"You have a gigantic, brand-spanking new parking lot on the other side of the building."

"Which is for customers only. My crew aren't customers. Therefore, I have suggested that they park here. In this very public lot."

"I'll sue!"

"Love, I have a team of lawyers that can get me out of anything, and they will shred you."

"You jerk!" she exploded. "That whole nice-guy act about offering to pay for the spots was a part of your plan all along."

He stepped off the curb and into her space. He was so tall she had to crane her neck to meet his eyes. She'd never felt so petite or turned on in her entire life.

He was dressed in black slacks, a blue button-up which, annoyingly, she knew matched his eyes. The shirt was starched, the slacks Italian wool, and the expression dialed to "prepare your battleships." He looked like a corporate raider ready to put the poor little shopgirl's head on a pike.

"If you remember correctly, I did offer you reparation."

"Reparation? Who even uses that word?"

"The guy who now gets those spaces for free."

"Shit!"

She grunted and stomped her foot. Merle's brows disappeared beneath the bill of his hat as he took in Summer's tantrum. Not that she blamed him. To most of Ridgefield, Summer was the sweet, if not a bit shy, bookworm who preferred glasses to contacts and paperbacks to a tablet. She was always cordial, had a smile for everyone, and never lost her shit—at least publicly. She was as steady and even-keeled as they came.

Yet, around Wes, all that cool and calm seemed to evaporate.

Morning after morning, she'd called the police to file a noise complaint against him when his crew started work before seven. Officer Joe had told her that the owner was just paying the fines, so he stopped showing up. She'd complained to every city official she knew, but everyone was too excited by the kind of commerce the new store would bring to the neighborhood. Even her fellow shop owners had allowed themselves to be charmed by the book-wielding charlatan, who'd promised that BookLand would raise the value of every business in this historic part of downtown.

He'd failed to mention that it would also raise the rent. So when these small business owners went to re-up their lease, they'd find themselves looking at a fifty percent increase. Summer had done her research with comparable communities, crunched the numbers, and fifty percent was a optimistic estimate. Luckily, she owned her building, but few of the others did.

Then there was her shop, which would be lost in the shadow of the giant. She had rocks to throw; she just wasn't sure she could aim high enough to take down Goliath.

"Is this some game?" she asked.

His smile vanished and he seemed almost confused by her comment. "It's business, love. You're the one who started the war, and the first rule in war is know your enemy's weakness."

"I thought the first rule of war was to keep your friends close and your enemies closer. I guess that would be hard though, since Satan doesn't have friends."

"And that's your weakness."

She blinked. "What? Having friends? You should try it. It might soften the Goliath complex you have going on."

And the scowl was back. "No—believing in the good in people."

"That's a weakness?"

"It is in business."

Just then, a double ping sounded. They both looked at Merle, who shrugged. "It's not me."

Their eyes met again as they each fished their phone from their pocket. Summer's mouth went slack when she saw the notification from RoChance. She had her first match. Not wanting to betray the fact that she was on a dating app, she casually pretended like it was an incoming text. Only, when she swiped open her phone and saw the little cupid arrow above the picture of her soulmate, she practically dropped her cell. Horror. Sheer horror coursed through her at the picture filling her screen.

She looked up to find Wes looking back, a superior smile on his face. "Did you just swipe right on me?" he asked.

"There is RoChance in hell that I'd ever swipe right on you. And this isn't a swipe-right kind of app." Cleo had told her as much. "It's more of an AI Cupid at play. It pings every time a potential soulmate is in the vicinity."

"I wouldn't know," he said. "My brother signed me up as a joke."

He said it as if only a romantically challenged idiot would be on the app. "For the record, I didn't sign up either. My friend did," said Summer.

"That would be me," Cleo said, and Summer nearly jumped. She'd been so distracted by the pompous ass in front of her, she hadn't even realized Cleo had joined them or that a crowd had gathered. A crowd who was watching them like they were an episode of *Days of Our Lives*. "I am the friend in question."

"'Friend' is a strong word," she hissed at Cleo, who just smiled. "And clearly the algorithm is broken!" She shoved her phone back in her pocket, watching as Wes did the same. They stared each other down, neither willing to give in.

"So, about the price of the tow . . ." Merle began.

"I'll get it," they said in unison, and the crowd fell silent.

"Fine, you pay," Summer finally said. "Think of it as the cost of war."

"It's just one battle, love. The war is far from over." With that, Wes spun on his thousand-dollar dress shoes and disappeared into his store.

"Well," Cleo said with a smile. "That was different."

Chapter 5

FAMILY TIES

"Home sweet home," Summer said, pulling onto the winding gravel drive.

Head out the window, cheeks puffed out like a blowfish, Buttercup was too busy gobbling up the wind to respond. But when Summer pulled up to the house and stopped the car, the pooch barked with excitement.

"You already dreaming about morning beach runs and naps in the sun?"

She opened the door and had to help Buttercup down—again, Q-tip legs—and took in the warm-grey shake siding house, with its white trim and round captain's window that Summer and Autumn used to pretend was a porthole when they played pirates. The expansive deck Summer would lay on so she could read with the sun on her back and the warm planks on her belly.

She could be blindfolded and still recall every detail of the beach house, which sat on a bluff overlooking the inlet where the Mystic River and the Atlantic Ocean married. Her family had been coming to Mystic, Connecticut, since the summer she'd turned eight and they had suffered a devastating hardship, with her father losing his business and in turn the family home. Summer and Autumn had been uprooted from their friends and her dad had been devastated. Fifteen years of struggle and sacrifice and working toward his dream of owning his own business had been stolen in one fell swoop.

This house, the house on the bluff overlooking the sapphire waters of the ocean, had become their haven. It was a place where her family could come together over clam-bakes and grill-offs. Pancake breakfasts made while singing The Supremes into whisks; movie nights with the projector lighting up the backyard, watching Gregory Peck and Audrey Hepburn fall in love on the big screen in *Roman Holiday*. Lazy days by the beach, thumbing through one of the many second-hand books left by previous holiday-goers. But Summer had never felt like a guest. She'd felt like she belonged here more than anywhere in the world.

And after the month she'd had, she needed to feel like she belonged. It had taken every ounce of pride she possessed not to collapse in a weepy mess whenever a customer asked how she felt about BookLand being in her backyard. "Oh, you know, there's room for everyone." If she knew when BookLand was going to open. "Last I heard, in a few months." Or how nice it was going to be to have a big-box bookstore in town that sold cookbooks or children's books or . . . fill in the blank with any and every genre of book on the planet. "I do love me a good fantasy read."

Her fear was that "romance books" would eventually fill that blank. That it would be easier for her customers to fulfill all their literary needs in one convenient, if sterile, spot—especially when she couldn't compete with the big-box discounts.

She'd worked hard to stay upbeat and appear unaffected by how much Wes Kingston and his behemoth bookstore had affected her. It affected her mood, her bottom line, even her belief that she could survive this.

All she had to do was catch a glimpse of Weston Kingston—who gave their kid rhyming names, anyway?—and anxiety would set in. Her heart would race, her palms would sweat, and she'd get this intense pressure behind her breastbone. Then there was the fact that she hadn't had a decent night's sleep since he'd nearly had her baby towed. Now two crews were working around the clock, hammering and drilling and driving her slowly out of her mind.

She'd tried to leave her problems back in Ridgefield, but as she walked up the cedar steps of the beach house she could still feel the weight of uncertainty. She took in a deep, grounding breath. It smelled like sea salt, beachgrass, and long-ago memories. Another deep breath and she felt her pulse begin to slow. By the third, the world didn't seem so precarious.

The house was quiet, save for the coffee percolating in the corner of the kitchen. The soft glow of a lamp flickered in the family room, making her smile. Her dad had awoken to greet her.

God, she needed some advice, not to mention a hug. Francesco Russo gave the kind of hugs that made the world feel safe. And, right then, Summer needed to feel safe.

Setting her suitcase by the door, she tiptoed across the hardwood floors that had been battered by generations of kids, Buttercup hot on her trail, her nails echoing in the empty kitchen. Suddenly out of steam, her pup flopped down in the kitchen and fell instantly to sleep, so Summer filled up two mugs of coffee and carried them into the front room.

Resting his knitting needles in his lap, her dad looked up, a wide smile spreading across his face. "Hey, Sunny Bunny."

At sixty-seven years old, Frank Russo still had the boyish grin he'd had Summer's entire life. It reached from ear to ear, and curled up at the corners like he had a secret to hide. But there weren't any secrets between Summer and Frank. Maybe it was because he'd had kids later in life, or maybe it was because Summer idolized her dad, but the two of them had always had this special bond that left no room for secrets.

"Hey, Dad," she said, and felt the heaviness of the loneliness that had been following her around for the past month soften.

Autumn's week-long work trip had turned into a month of traipsing across Europe, fangirling and living the life of a Swiftie. "Twenty-two countries in thirty-one days," Autumn had marveled last night before she'd boarded a plane headed for Connecticut. Which was why this reunion meant so much to Summer. Being away from her family was hard. Being away from her twin was like missing a limb. And lately, that limb had been giving phantom pangs.

She was looking forward to a week of uninterrupted Russo time.

"Whatcha working on?' she asked, tilting her chin toward his work-in-progress.

"Neighbor's daughter is having twins. Girls. So I thought I'd knit them a couple of baby dolls like you girls had. Nearly done with the parts. All I need to do is knit them together and fill them with some stuffing."

Summer plopped down on the sofa and smiled. While her dad used to rent out tractors and bulldozers to construction crews for a living, he was also a master knitter. He also quilted, did needlepoint, and wielded a glue gun like he was Susie Soccer Mom. Her mom was the golfer and handyman of the family, and her dad was the homebody hobbyist.

"You used to carry that thing everywhere."

"Lu Lu," Summer said fondly. "I still have her. She looks like she's got a few too many miles on her but she's rocking her retirement."

Frank reached over and patted Summer's knee, giving it a gentle squeeze, then cleared the emotion from his throat. "Now, where's my grand-doggie?"

"In the kitchen, sleeping off her nap." Summer looked down at the half-eaten plate of cookies. "Does Mom know that you're eating a stick of butter for breakfast?"

"That's why I have a plate of celery next to it."

She broke into a leisurely smile. "After forty-five years, she knows that trick."

"After forty-five years she knows all my tricks."

And after forty-five years her dad's eyes still lit up with love whenever he spoke about his wife. If that wasn't relationship goals then Summer didn't know what was.

"Now, why don't you sit next to me and tell me why you're arriving before the sun's awake."

Summer rested her head on her dad's shoulder. She had so many questions, but she knew that they would only bring up buried hurt, and the last person she wanted to have to relive that time in their lives was her dad.

"I can hear you thinking in that big noggin."

"When did you know that your business was going to go under?" she asked, and she felt her dad still. She looked up. "We don't have to talk about it if you don't want."

"I've always told you girls that no question was off limits."

"Not even that one?"

"Especially not that one," he assured her.

"I just know you don't like to talk about it."

"I don't mind talking about it. As difficult of a time as that was, it was also one of the defining moments of my life. Aside from marrying your mom and having you girls."

"Why?"

"Because it reconfirmed just how lucky I am. I figured if your mom and I could be as happy and in love in a nine-hundred-square-foot apartment with bills piled sky-high, then nothing could beat us."

"Families who dance together thrive together," Summer said, referring to their family's motto.

"And I've still got some dancing left in these shoes. So why don't you tell me what this is all about, so your dad can impart some very impressive wisdom."

"I think I might have taken on too much debt for the remodel, and now with BookLand opening up next door I'm afraid that my income won't match my overhead."

"Do you need money?"

Because while the Russos had been bankrupt once upon a time, Frank had paid off every debt, and then earned back every penny he'd lost when his equipment rental business was gobbled up by a larger corporation. Her parents weren't rich by any means, but they had a nice little nest egg that allowed them to travel and enjoy their retirement.

"No, I guess I just needed a reminder that when I set my mind to something, even with two left feet, I'm a pretty good dancer."

Chapter 6

THAT WTF MOMENT

Summer blinked up at the clock over the fireplace and rubbed her eyes. It was nearly noon. Her twenty-minute nap had turned into a three-hour marathon.

She could hear muffled voices in the distance. It sounded like her auntie and mom arguing about how to properly pinch the gnocchi dough so that the potato dumplings were fluffy. She could also hear Buttercup snoring at her feet.

"Time to get up and take a walk," she said, but Buttercup didn't move. "I know you're faking." When Buttercup merely squeezed her eyes tighter, Summer said, "I think Nonna has some bacon in the fridge."

Like a bull out of the pen, Buttercup was off the couch and halfway to the kitchen before her feet touched the floor.

Summer sat up and rolled the kinks out of her neck. After a heavy breakfast of bacon and cheese frittatas, homemade shortbread with a jam shop's supply of options, and espresso, she had succumbed to a food coma. Thanks to her inconsiderate neighbor, even the power of two espressos couldn't combat the sheer exhaustion from too many sleepless nights. But she wasn't going to waste another second of her vacation thinking about Wes Kingston and his empire, not when there was a beach chair and rolling waves calling her name.

With a yawn, she stood and shuffled to the kitchen.

"There's my summer breeze," her mom said.

Even with an apron on, Blanche Russo looked fashionable in a pair of white linen palazzo pants and a navy-and-white striped shirt. Her hair was pinned up, her makeup was flawless, and her face was warm with love. Blanche might be sixty-eight, but she didn't look a day over fifty.

"How was the nap?" Aunt Cecilia asked.

After four decades of being married to the Russo brothers, Aunt Cecilia and Blanche acted more like sisters than in-laws. They were competitive, gossip hounds, and pranksters. One year both families had rented separate houseboats on the Connecticut River. On day two an argument had ensued over whose pesto was superior. Blanche had secretly swapped out the olive oil in Cecilia's houseboat for canola, and Cecilia had retaliated by hiding two trout in Mom's cupboard. It took three days to find where the stench was coming from.

"I didn't mean to sleep so long. You should have woken me." Summer didn't hesitate, just walked over to the cutting board and began rolling out the dough. The three women fell into an easy rhythm, but something still felt off.

"Did Autumn mention when she was supposed to arrive?" Summer tried to hide the hurt in her voice over her sister deciding to drive herself. In all the time they'd come to Mystic they'd never driven separately.

"She's arrived," came a singsong voice that was exactly like Summer's but somehow sultry.

Two arms came around Summer's waist and her sister planted her cheek between Summer's shoulder blades. And just like that, her chest which had been slowly seeping air for the past month filled back up.

She turned in her sister's arms and hugged her fiercely, and a bottomless peace and contentment swept through her. While Frank might hold the title of Best Russo Hugger, nothing beat the feeling of being with her twin.

"What did I miss?" Autumn asked, hoisting herself up on the counter.

Today she was dressed casual-chic, in an off-the-shoulder, sage green sundress paired with strappy heels and sunglasses on top of her head. Her golden, glossy hair was longer than Summer's and her skin was the perfect balance of matte and dewy. She looked like she was heading off to a photo shoot.

Summer, on the other hand, looked like she'd just woken up from sleeping on the couch. Her hair was sticking out of its ponytail holder, her bottoms were pajamas, and she was pretty sure she had a little drool dried in the corner of her mouth.

"That your aunt didn't knead the dough enough," Mom said.

"Too much and it's tough, too little and it won't hold together. It was the right amount of pressure. You just wait and see." Cecilia tapped her forehead, leaving behind a light dusting of flour. "I have a feeling about these things. It's my—"

"Third eye," everyone said in unison.

Aunt Cecilia had spent thirty years running her own homemade pasta company and a lifetime telling people she could see the future. Blanche called it intuition. Cecilia called it "The Sight." When Summer was young, she used to believe that her aunt could see the future—and sometimes, when she was feeling wistful, she still did.

"What do you see in Summer's future?" Autumn asked,

and Cecilia closed her eyes and began to hum. "A man. A good Italian man. Maybe a tall, dark, and sexy suit."

The last thing Summer needed was another stuffed suit in her life. "Hard pass. Maybe a firefighter or a paratrooper."

"Firefighters are too clichéd for you and paratroopers are notorious for having bad knees," Autumn said. "You don't want some guy hobbling behind you your whole life. You need someone sophisticated and steady, who is passionate."

"Have you been talking to Cleo?"

"My guides are telling me that your sister is right," Cecilia said. "He's not what you expect but he's more than he appears. And he's right around the corner."

Autumn pinched off a piece of dough and Summer smacked her hands.

"Ow!"

"These are for dinner."

"Your sister's right," Mom said. "If you want something to eat there's leftover spaghetti in the fridge."

"Tattletale," Autumn whispered, then suddenly her eyes went wide. "I have a surprise for you."

Summer's heart bubbled up with delight and she clapped her hands with excitement. She loved surprises. The anticipation, the not knowing, the unexpectedness of it all. Surprises were like sitting down with a new book where the buildup ended with a satisfying and heartwarming conclusion.

"What is it?"

"I can't tell you. I have to show you." Autumn hopped off the counter and looped her arm through Summer's, and led her to the front door and out onto the porch just as a car parked. "I brought him all the way back from Europe."

"Him?" Summer asked, squinting to see through the front window of the very expensive Aston Martin. "You've never brought a 'him' home before. Especially not to our family vacation, where your last name has to be Russo to get an invite."

Autumn bounced on her toes, her smile so bright it warmed the entire space. "He's special. Wait till you meet him."

Before Summer could ask who "him" was, her sister was bounding down the wood-flanked stairs and tossing herself into the arms of a hot guy. Not Summer's kind of hot, more of a thirst-trap, frat-bro kind of hot. But the smile on Autumn's face said everything Summer needed to know.

She was in love.

Which made not one iota of sense. Summer was the one who wanted marriage and forever. Autumn was the queen of the four-week fling.

After a long and inappropriate show of PDA, Autumn took the guy by the hand and guided him up to the porch. "Summer, this is Randy. Randy, this is the best sister in the whole world."

Summer stuck out her hand but Randy pulled her in for a big hug, really getting in there with the back pats and twisting side to side. Finally, he pulled away. "Cool to meet you, Best Sister in the World."

"Ditto," Summer said, a bit overwhelmed that Autumn was in love with a guy Summer knew nothing about. They shared everything, even their cycles. Why would Autumn keep something so big as a "him" from her this long?

"And here's the best part," Autumn whispered to Summer. "He comes with a sexy plus-one."

Summer watched in awe as the driver's-side door opened and out folded a fine specimen of a man. He wasn't just tall, he towered. Then there were those broad shoulders and the dark hair that was perfectly styled. His jeans clung to his thighs, a button-up that was rolled at the sleeves was in a losing battle with his biceps, and he had—

Summer's phone pinged in her pocket with a RoChance match.

"Bollocks," said the man with the coldest blue eyes Summer had ever seen.

"You!" she said to her nemesis, who was grinning like Napoleon right before he conquered Italy.

"Hey, Summer," Wes Kingston said. "I guess your sister and my brother are both big Taylor Swift fans. Small world, huh?"

Chapter 7

MUSICAL ~~CHAIRS~~ BEDS

"Could you have been any ruder?" Autumn whisper-yelled.

"Under the circumstances, that greeting was tame. Trust me."

"Tame?" Autumn jerked back, releasing herself from Summer's death grip. "You didn't even say hi. You grabbed me by the arm and dragged me into our bedroom. I didn't even get a chance to introduce Randy to Mom and Dad."

"Since when do we bring boys to the family retreat?" Summer hissed.

"Since I found love," Autumn said with a dramatic sigh while spinning around, only to fall gracefully on the bed with her hand pressed to her forehead—nearly missing banging her head on the upper bunk. Summer was surprised an ark full of forest creatures didn't appear to join her in song. "It was so romantic, Summs. There I was watching Tay-Tay live onstage, and our eyes locked over our Bic app. The one that mimics a cigarette lighter, you know? And it was like—*pow*." Autumn made firework fingers. "The most beautiful man I'd ever seen wearing glow-sticks around his neck and singing 'Wildest Dreams.' You'd have loved it. It was the most perfect cute-meet in history."

"You mean meet-cute." And it did sound cute, dang it. But that wasn't breaking news, because Autumn had accumulated a grocery list full of perfect meet-cutes—and not a single one had progressed to more than a month. Her twin had the attention span of a gnat when it came to love. No doubt this was going to be like all the others—with her sister going squirrelly at that four-week-fling expiration date.

God, what Summer would do to experience even one of the situationships her sister fell into. Sadly, her twin didn't even realize how lucky she was.

"I know what you're thinking," Autumn said. "He's different. He's worthy of going in your guide."

Cupid's Guide to Love was a journal full of swoonworthy moments, relationship tropes, and hero archetypes—a real how-to-find-a-partner based on commonality and love language—and it was Summer's.

Summer had collected these tips and tricks from her vast knowledge of 1990s rom-com flicks, classic cinema, and romance novels. It was the difference between finding happily-for-now and finding that one, true happily-ever-after. The difference between Summer living a lonely life as a party of one or a blissful existence with her person.

Her guide was gold—or it would be as soon as Summer nailed that meet-cute. So for Autumn to try to claim part of that felt like all of the other times her sister had outshone her. Not that it was intentional spotlight-stealing, but the result was the same—with Summer feeling like nothing more than the glue holding her sister's extravagant life together.

Summer pressed her fingertips to her forehead and reminded herself to be patient, and that this was just Autumn being Autumn. But she couldn't. Maybe it was that her sister was in "love" and this was the first Summer was hearing about it.

Or maybe, and this was more likely, it was the emergence of that pompous, entitled bag of dicks downstairs who was ruining her life—and her vacation.

"Fine. What makes him worthy?"

"He asked for my number that first night," Autumn began, and Summer had to stop herself from rolling her eyes.

"*Clichéd.*"

"I asked if he was going to call. You know how I act all disinterested and they cling to me like saran wrap?"

Oh, Summer knew all right. Autumn would be dismissive and feign boredom and men ate it up. Maybe that was Summer's problem. She was too eager to find love. Or at least she acted too eager. But she believed deep down that when someone found their other half there was no need for games and tactics.

"Anyway, he said not only was he going to call me, he was going to marry me!"

That *was* romantic. So romantic. Had her sister actually found the elusive love at first sight? Summer believed with all her heart that love at first sight was real—that was how her grandparents had met, and her parents—but Autumn wasn't even looking for love. She'd made that clear. Then again, love was supposed to change everything, right?

"How do you know he's the one?" she asked, genuinely curious. "You've never believed in love at first sight."

"I believe now. The way he looks at me is like right out of one of your romance novels. Swoonworthy. You're right and I'm wrong . . . This should make you happy. You thrive on being right!"

The only thing that brought Summer more joy than

watching the 1999 twist on *Pygmalion*, *She's All That*, with a bowl of pickle-flavored popcorn was being right. So why wasn't she happy?

Autumn looked up at Summer. "Love is the real deal. And Randy is the real deal."

Still not convinced, Summer crossed her arms. "What do you even know about him?"

"Everything I need to know." Autumn's brow folded in on itself and she sat up. "What is your problem?"

"His family is entitled, arrogant, selfish—"

"You forgot *gorgeous*."

No, she'd left that part out on purpose.

"And how do you even know that?" said Autumn. "You met them five minutes ago."

"They own BookLand."

Autumn's mouth slowly unfolded into a guppie pose as Summer watched her process the situation. She knew the moment her twin connected the dots. "That Wes is *your* Wes?"

"He's not my anything except my cross to bear. He's out to ruin my shop and you're inviting him to our family vacation."

"I had no idea."

That was an even bigger problem. "How could you not feel my fury building the moment he got out of the car? You always feel my fury." It was their twin powers at work. But apparently they'd found their kryptonite—love.

"I've just been so caught up with everything, I wasn't paying attention." Autumn took Summer's hand and she felt some of her anger dissipate. "I'm sorry, Summs."

She pulled Summer into a big hug and Summer felt their

heartbeats align like they always did. Recognized the comforting scent of grapefruit mist and hairspray. Her body sank into the embrace as Autumn rocked her back and forth.

"He seems so nice," Autumn whispered.

"That's all a front, don't be fooled. He's a wolf in sheep's clothing."

"Have you considered that maybe, you know, you're doing one of those fast-to-judgment things and being paranoid?"

And there went the warm fuzzies.

Summer jerked back. "Me? You're saying *I'm* the problem?"

"So he sells romance novels? So what. You're the one always going on and on about how romance makes up over half of the books sold in the US. What kind of a bookstore owner would he be to eliminate romance from his offerings?"

When it was put like that, Summer almost sounded like a Karen of a neighbor. Then she remembered the parking issue, having her baby almost towed, and shook her head. "Nope, he's a sneaky, slimy bookstore owner. The store isn't even open yet but he's moved the romance section to the front of his store in the window facing my shop." As if he were flipping her the bird 24-7. "So when my customers pass his window, that's what they see. He's going to undercut me at every turn. And since when do you take a guy's side over me?"

"Never," Autumn said fiercely. "I'm really sorry that I called you paranoid and that the last month has been so hard and I was overseas." Autumn took Summer's hand back and pulled her down next to her on the bed. "Really sorry."

Summer let out a big sigh and rested her head on her twin's shoulder. "That's okay, I get it, you were working too. I'm proud of you for getting this promotion."

"Whatever kind of jerkism Wes subscribes to, he isn't Randy. They weren't even raised in the same country. In fact, they're just now starting to build a relationship. I promise you they're nothing alike."

Summer flopped onto her back and admitted to herself that she was a little bit envious over Autumn's announcement. But that was so petty. She wanted love for her sister, so she needed to be supportive. "And I am so sorry about how I reacted. I was just thrown by Wes showing up." That had to be it. Right? "It sounds like you had the perfect meet-cute and I love that you've found love. You're right, it is definitely *Guide*-worthy."

Autumn rolled her head to the side to look Summer in the eyes. "I am so glad you feel that way, because I wanted to let you know . . ."

A prickle of suspicion poked Summer in the stomach. "What?"

"I'm rooming with Randy."

Summer's eyes went wide with surprise. "But we always room together. That's the point of this trip. Twin Power, remember?"

"It will still be amazing, just different. But in a good way, I promise."

Summer looked around and felt her throat tighten. The familiar yellow-and-white striped wallpaper, the pitched ceilings, and the worn-with-life hardwood floors wrapped around her like a warm blanket. Even though the bed was a bunkbed, Summer and Autumn, unable to even have a mattress between them, always shared the bottom bunk.

So many traditions were already being broken and she hadn't even been in her safe place for a day. It was as if her life and memories were slowly being replaced by bigger, newer, shinier things—and that broke her heart.

"Please don't be mad at me. I love you. And don't let that asshat ruin anything for you. This is still *our* family trip. Everything that is important will stay the same, I promise. And if he makes you sad then I'll kick his ass. Right?"

Summer nodded, but couldn't help noticing the burning behind her eyes.

"Now, are we going to let him win?"

"No."

"Say it with more conviction."

"Hell no!"

"Good, then let's go through my suitcase and pick out something for you that says 'Big Chick Energy coming through.'"

∽

Wes couldn't fault Summer for her reaction. He'd had a holy-shit moment himself at the one-in-a-billion chance of his brother dating Summer's sister.

Her identical twin sister. Which was odd because he could tell who was who immediately, and that was before Summer had realized who he was. Her smile was a bit brighter, her hair shinier, and she had this understated elegance about her. Even though she was in flannel pajamas with a TALK DARCY TO ME T-shirt and bedhead. She'd looked adorable and soft and sexy—until she'd realized who he was. Then she'd looked like Medusa ready to turn his family jewels to granite.

At least he'd had time to prepare. It was clear the moment he'd seen Autumn whose sister she was.

He should leave. He really should. He should climb back in the car and be on his merry little way. In fact, he should leave the country all together and move back to London, where he had a full and very successful life that he'd just walked out on.

After the sudden death of his estranged father, Wes had found himself part-owner of BookLand, a billion-dollar big-box bookstore chain. His father hadn't just left behind a legacy of wealth, he'd left behind a legacy of betrayal and heartache.

Between Randolph Kingston the Second's many mistresses and multiple wives, Wes had learned early on that love and loss went hand in hand. Which was why he was content to keep things casual with the people in his life, especially women.

The second he'd realized Autumn was Summer's twin, he should have canceled. He could still cancel. His things were still in the car so he wouldn't even have to repack. He hadn't met the family yet, so they wouldn't even know that he'd come and gone.

It was clear by the look on her face that she'd been as surprised as he was about the whole situation. But then she'd turned those eyes of fury at him, and instead of apologizing for interrupting her family vacation, he'd puffed out his chest and strengthened his stance, letting her know if she wanted him gone, she'd have to physically remove him from the premises.

Wes rubbed his temples and reminded himself it was a losing battle. If she wanted him gone, he'd go. He'd lived through enough family vacations being unwanted to last a lifetime. Why would he want to willingly expose himself to another go-around?

Yup, leaving was the right thing to do. All he had to do was go inside and get the car keys from his kid brother. But first, he'd kick the wanker's ass, because Randy did not seem the slightest bit surprised at the one-in-a-billion chance meeting.

Wes walked up the steps to the massive wraparound porch, complete with a white swing and bright red door. It was as Great American Dream as a house could get, yet instead of feeling like the door mat said WELCOME, he felt as if he were walking the plank.

A rusty, yet familiar, pounding started behind his rib cage and worked its way up to the sternum. His hands were clammy to the touch, and a bead of sweat slid down his back.

Intent on getting in and out as quickly as possible, he had lifted his hand to knock when the door flew open. On the other side was Randy looking shell-shocked and ready to cry.

"Where have you been? You were supposed to have my back," he said in a rush. "Autumn bailed and her mom dragged me into the kitchen, where her aunt took my palm and read my lifeline and pointed out this little wrinkle here." He held up his hand and pointed to a nearly nonexistent wrinkle of skin. "Do you know what it is? My mojo, bro. It's smaller than the prick of a needle. And don't you dare say anything about my choice in words. So to change the subject, I went to introduce my awesome brother, only when I turned to do the whole Vanna White move there was only air where my big brother should have been."

His brother's pain gave him a perverse sense of joy.

"Where were you, man?" said Randy.

"Having an out-of-body experience because I happened to be invited to a weeklong holiday with my brother's girlfriend's family, and her twin just so happens to be the woman who's cost us thousands of dollars in delays."

"Weird, huh."

Randy and Wes might have grown up estranged but his brother was a terrible liar. He was also a terrible businessman. And a terrible wingman.

"I mean, what are the odds?" Randy chucked nervously.

Wes crossed his arms and shot a death glare Randy's way. "What *are* the odds, you wanker."

Randy nodded and then stomped his foot, throwing his head back like a three-year-old having a tantrum. It wasn't nearly as cute as Summer's tantrum a few weeks back. "God, I didn't figure it out until the other day, and I knew if I told you you'd get all paranoid and say that Autumn is trying to worm her way into our family as some kind of corporate espionage ploy."

Wes hadn't gone that far, but now that his brother mentioned it, it sounded like something Summer would do. What if her surprise act was exactly that—an act—and this was her plan all along?

Randy pointed at him like they were two kids on the playground arguing over who'd dealt it. "See, you're doing it. You're falling down the conspiracy-theory rabbit hole. You really think that she'd be able to guess I'd be at a Tay-Tay concert in Paris? Paris! And I came on to her, not the other way around. Plus, Autumn doesn't even know who we are."

Wes shook his head. "You're saying she has no clue that you're the heir to BookLand?"

"Well, I'm sure she does now, since Summer yanked her aside before I could explain." Realization appeared in Randy's eyes, followed rapidly by panic. He shoved Wes out the door and shut it behind them. "What if Summer told her? What if she dumps me because I didn't tell her first?"

"What did you expect? That Summer and I would act like we didn't know each other?"

"I didn't really think past meeting her parents. I guess I thought I'd say, 'Surprise, our siblings already know each other. Your Best Sister in the World and my Best Older Brother Known to Man are neighbors of sorts!'"

"Jesus, mate. You're in worse shape than I thought. What kind of woman excuses a lie?"

"I didn't lie to her. It was more of an omission."

Wes couldn't really judge the guy. He had an omission of his own, and it involved BookLand and the terms to the estate. Terms Randy knew nothing about.

Wes hadn't been just shocked that his estranged father had left him part of his company, he'd also been irate at the attached conditions—conditions that once again forced Wes into living a life where someone else held the power. He and Randy had just another three months to grow the company or ownership would be passed to the board.

Again, another reason to walk. Honestly, Wes didn't give a piss about his dad's legacy, but Randy did—and Randy was the only family Wes had left. Without help, his trust fund of a half-brother would run the company into the ground in a month, tops, and forfeit his birthright.

Not that Randy was aware of the conditions. That had been another stipulation from dear old dad—that only Wes and the board knew of the one-year clause. So Wes had faced a choice: either walk away from his own life to step in, or watch his brother fail. And Wes knew how that felt so, against his better judgment, he'd relocated, taken the title CEO, and now he was standing in front of the enemy's front door—three things he'd never imagined doing.

"Now you see why I need you here. One little omission turned into a bunch of little omissions and . . . she's going to dump me, isn't she?"

"All you need is your charm and Dad's last name."

Randy got serious. "I told you. She isn't like that, bro."

As far as Wes was concerned, all women were like that. In fact, his ex-fiancée, who'd dumped him after his start-up had failed, had come crawling back the moment his old man croaked and left him a massive legacy. Even Wes's mum had chased all that glittered. It was why she'd gotten pregnant, hoping that Randolph would set them up for life, or maybe even leave his wife for her.

Well, the joke was on Mary. Not only did Randall Kingston the Second had zero intentions of leaving his wife, he also didn't want a bastard son. His wife was trying to get pregnant back in the States with a child who would rightfully take the birthright just because he was born on the right side of the sheets.

"Fine. I'll stay, but no more omissions," Wes said.

Randy flopped into Wes's arm and gave him a big bear hug. Unused to that kind of display of affection, Wes let his arms hang at his sides and endured it.

When Randy finally pulled back, his smile faded. "Wait, are you staying to help me or because you think Summer is somehow behind the best coincidence of my life?"

"Both."

Chapter 8

NO EFFING WAY

Everything will be the same, my ass.

It had been less than an hour since Satan and his leave-it's-mark-on-the-environment, omission-heavy trust-fund-on-wheels had pulled up, and nothing was the same. In fact, nothing had been the same since his business had moved in next door.

The plants in her apartment had died from the lack of sun since she now lived in the shadow of a batholith eyesore. Her gorgeous view of the quaint downtown was now a brick wall. And the royal blue ballbuster dress Autumn had lent her was too snug in the chest because of all Summer's stress-eating.

"God, can anything else go wrong?" she groaned as she pulled off the dress and walked to her closet to see if she'd brought one of her Big Chick Energy outfits.

She snorted. "You don't own a Big Chick Energy outfit."

But this was her turf—literally. They were on the shoreline of the house that had been like a second home to Summer. He was the interloper and she was going to make sure he knew. She wasn't about to let him win a single battle in this war.

"I'm not going to give that asshole even a moment's thought."

"Sounds like I'm in all of your thoughts." The voice came from the doorway followed by an annoying ping of her phone.

Summer didn't squeak or jump; she forced her body to remain unaffected. So he'd caught her talking about him while standing in her undies again. It didn't mean she'd give him the satisfaction of letting him know that he got to her.

Her plan failed when she turned around and watched in horror as he walked over the threshold with a suitcase that probably cost more than her entire jewelry collection, and tossed it on the bottom bunk. Her bunk!

"Um, what are you doing?"

"Unpacking." He looked at her undies. "Am I overdressed for the event?"

She snatched a soft throw off the rocking chair arm and wrapped it around her like a bath towel. "This is my room."

"According to your mum, this is my room for the duration." He unlatched one side of the suitcase, and before she could think she threw herself on it, covering it with her body. In the process she bonked her head on the top bunk.

"You hit your head," he said helpfully.

"You have resting dick face."

He thought about that and then smiled. "Most woman seem to like my face just fine."

"Most woman are easily swayed by a snake charmer. I am not one of those women."

"Good to know, since your blanket parted and is gifting me a view of your knickers. I think it's a thong in Fuck Me Red, so you can see how I'm getting mixed signals."

She jerked her hand behind her to close the opening and found it was, in fact, not open. *Jerk!* "How did you know the color?"

"God-given talent."

"Then let me clear it up for you. We will not, now or ever, have sex."

"Are you declaring your celibacy for me? I'm honored that I inspire such loyalty from you."

"You are so infuriating." She stood chin up as she stretched to her full five foot two. "I meant, with each other."

"Too bad. I'm a five-star shag. I can get you testimonials if you need them."

Gross.

"Women lie." Although she didn't think it was a lie. Wes had this ultra-masculine vibe about him. Big Dick Energy at its finest. Soft-looking lips that could also be punishing. Large, massive hands that could fully splay around her waist. And even through his pressed jeans it was clear that he was massive in other areas.

"Rethinking your stance, love?"

"Not in the slightest, crumpet. So, listen clearly. You're not going to charm your way into my bed."

He crossed his arms and rested a casual shoulder against the ladder that connected the upper and lower bunks. "So you admit you find me charming? Interesting."

"'Interesting' isn't the word that comes to mind." Although what was happening in her belly? All the little flutters were interesting—and concerning. "More like infuriating, irritating, imbecile."

"Imbecile? Do you mean imbecilic? As I don't think a person can find someone imbecile."

Summer caught herself stomping a foot and shouting, "God, I hate you."

"You know what they say, the line between love and hate is a thin one."

"You are mistaking my emotion. This is a love-to-hate situation." Straight out of a rom-com novel and one of her favorite tropes. It went deeper than enemies-to-lovers, so when the couple finally overcame the seemingly unsurmountable obstacles to get past their hate and realize it was love along—what a jolt to the heart. Not that *that* was what this was. This was definitely all hate. So to clarify, she said, "Meaning I love to hate you."

"If you say so," he drawled, sounding almost bored. That is, if one could drawl while sounding like an uptight Brit.

She gripped the latch and reclosed it. "I say so."

He waited until she was done fiddling with the latch and reattached it. "So where do we stand? Are you the big spoon? I'm a great cuddler."

"I don't share."

"Fine. I'll take the bottom bunk." And with that he moved his suitcase to the floor and sprawled out on the bed, even giving it a little test with his hands, before stuffing them behind his head and releasing a sigh. Then the prick actually had the nerve to close his eyes.

"The bottom bunk is mine."

"I'm bigger, therefore I should get the bottom bunk." He gave a little bounce. "Not too firm, with plenty of support. This will do."

"*This will do?*" Fury rose swiftly to boiling point. Where did he get off, thinking he could come in and demand the bottom bunk? *Her* bunk! He wasn't the one on the verge of financial ruin. He wasn't the one who was terrified that he'd have to start letting employees go as soon as his store opened. And he wasn't the one who'd been looking forward to this vacation since last year. "Why are you doing this?"

He ran a hand through his thick, dark hair and frowned. "I don't want to be here either. But my brother asked me to stay and he's never asked me for anything. We're not close and I'm trying to fix that."

She understood that on a core level. A little of her anger sizzled, until it was more of a low rumbling than a rapid boil.

"So you're really staying?"

"I made a promise and I don't go back on my word." He sat and swung his legs over the side of the bed. "Why don't we rock-paper-scissors it? Whoever loses gets the top bunk."

Knowing close quarters would lead to World War III, not to mention the look that would mar her sister's pretty face if Summer had to explain that Wes was leaving because Summer couldn't act like an adult, was too much to take. So she toppled like a stack of dominos.

"To be clear, I am only doing this because of my sister's happiness, not because I gave into your charms," she clarified. "But whoever loses gets the couch."

Resting his elbows on his knees, he held out a fist. "Ready? One." They threw fists. "Two." More aggressive fists. "Three."

Wes presented a rock and Summer presented paper.

"I won!" Oh my god, she'd won. So what if it was just over a stupid bed; she'd taken on Goliath and come out the victor. "I won!" She spun around like she was Julie Andrews standing in the middle of a meadow in the Austrian Alps. "I won! I won!"

"I'm glad you're handling this so maturely."

Summer put her foot on his suitcase and shoved it so that his shoes were used as a bumper. "Don't let the door hit you on the ass—or should it be *arse*—on your way out."

"If you need that cuddle, you know where I'm at."

"Did you forget that I just smothered you to death?"

Wes stopped at the doorway, and with a wicked grin said, "Oh, it's already filed away for future reference, love."

Chapter 9

FAMILY DYNAMICS

After the MMA-style rock-paper-scissors yesterday it shouldn't have come as a surprise to Wes that the Russo family took their competitions seriously. But when he emerged onto the back deck and saw the Olympic-themed decor complete with a big banner stretched out over the end of the dock that read VACATION WARS, he blinked slowly to take it all in.

At the base of the shoreline sat four yellow kayaks, each with a cluster of color-specific helium balloons floating at the head of the boat. Blue, yellow, green, and pink teams, it seemed. Inside each of the boats were two matching neon paddles and a little cooler filled with water. They looked like giant floating bananas.

A warm breeze was coming in off the Atlantic, rippling the waters of the Mystic River. Sailboats tied to personal docks bobbed up and down in the lapping waves. The sun sparkled on the water—and in the distance sat a lighthouse that looked as if it had a hundred years of tales to tell.

"Is it around the buoy or touch the buoy?" Uncle Giuseppe asked, scratching his combover while staring at the rusted buoy about a quarter mile out. It bobbed in the gentle swell, its bell giving a muffled clank as if it had given all it had to give.

Wes could appreciate that state. It seemed to sum up the past three months. He'd been giving without receiving anything in return. From the company, to Randy, to his ex, to his employees. No matter how much he gave, at the end of the day there was still more left to do. Only he was slowly crashing, and he would surely burn if things didn't change. Problem was, he didn't know what needed changing.

"It's around. It's been around for twenty years," Frank said, as if his brother hadn't had a memory slip—something Wes had noticed within the first few minutes at dinner last night. But instead of arguing with him after he'd told the same story three times, his family had sat patiently listening as if they'd never heard it before. Laughing at all the right times, his wife adding little bits here and there about what a brave, funny, honorable—fill in the blank—man he'd been, guiding him when he lost his way.

Most families would have cut the old man off at the second repetitive story. This family? They were different.

They were present and supportive and protective. Wes had never experienced such a fierce bubble of love. Not that he was *in* the bubble, he was merely an observer, but what he had observed touched him as much as it made him lonely.

There had been a moment though, a brief moment, when Giuseppe had told them about his knockout punch in the Golden Gloves fight when Wes had felt like he was a part of it all. It was the second go-around for this particular tale and Wes had felt an energy radiating from the other side of the table. It was Summer looking his way. Her eyes were shimmering with unshed tears and her expression was one of pleading. Pleading with him to go along with the farce. As if she thought he'd embarrass her uncle to needle her.

And that had made him feel like a bloody wanker. Did she really think he was that vindictive—to use her family as a weapon? Then he thought back to all the pranks he'd pulled on her over the past few months and wondered if her assessment was correct. Maybe what he thought of as healthy competition between rival businesses was hitting her on a personal level.

He'd simply nodded, and then at the next pause in conversation he'd asked Giuseppe a question to keep the story going. The gracious smile she'd sent his way cracked something in his chest that had been hardened over for most of his life.

"But I forget how we untie those sailor knots you secure the boats up with. Could you remind an old man?" Frank said.

Pride lit Giuseppe's expression and the two men headed toward the shoreline.

Wes would have offered a hand, except he felt as though it was a brother-bonding moment between the two. And he'd never been all that graceful at navigating conversations that went deeper than F.O.R.M.—a skill he'd learned from one of the many business conferences he'd attended.

When meeting a prospective client, you had to ask about Family, Occupation, Recreation, and then bring home the Message. But there was no message here, there was just love. And that left him dumbfounded.

"You're wrong," someone said, aghast.

Wes looked toward the edge of the dock, where Aunt Cecilia and Summer's mom were standing. Hands dug into hips, shoulders squared, they were in a heated battle. Now, this was what he was used to. Maybe they weren't so perfect after all.

"Yes. A pad of butter makes it smoother," Aunt Cecilia explained.

Cecilia reminded Wes of one of those psychics at the farmers' market who sold incense, dreamcatchers, and spiritual guided voyages into your past lives. Her neck was draped with crystals and she had turquoise bracelets going from wrist to forearm that clanked as she waved her hand dramatically, as if trying to cast a spell. She'd tried to read Wes's hand last night after dinner but, after Randy's mojo prognosis, he'd offered to help with dishes instead—placing his hands firmly under the water and away from her spying eyes.

"It's a pinch of sugar that's the secret ingredient, not butter," Blanche argued. Juxtaposed with Cecilia, Blanche was dressed like a starlet from a 1960s movie. *Mrs. Robinson* to be exact. Slim, regal in stature, in all white linen, with a silk scarf tying her long silver hair back.

"You're not making ketchup. This is marinara. The heart and soul of Italian culture."

"I'm not suggesting that we douse it with simple syrup. Just a pinch to cut through the acidity of the tomatoes."

Wes chuckled, because in this family nuclear war was over whose sauce was better.

"You heard that you can't have two chefs in the kitchen?" Summer said, coming up beside him. He smelled her before he saw her. Like crisp citrus and a warm summer breeze that wrapped around him and made his dick tighten. "Well, that's where that phrase originated from."

A dual ping of AI Cupid's arrows sounded, but they both ignored it this time.

He looked down at her and his breath nearly caught. She was dressed in a simple pink tank top that hugged her curves, and denim shorts—emphasis on *short*—that looked like they'd been jeans in another lifetime. They landed just below her ass cheeks and were frayed at the bottom. Then there were those sexy little cat-eye glasses she always wore, as if contacts were too much of a hassle.

Since the holiday, he'd begun to wonder if her glasses were a barrier between her and the world—like a shield that held people at a distance. Like his expensive suits and ties.

"Is it always like this?" he asked.

She kept her gaze out on the ocean. "I know it can be a lot. But we love as fiercely as we fight." She looked up at him and *pow*—those glasses weren't hiding a thing. Her expression was soft and welcoming and grateful. "I never got to properly thank you for last night and how you handled Uncle Giuseppe. Most people would have let their own uncomfortableness bleed into the conversation."

"Most people are assholes," he said, and a bark of laughter burst from her mouth. "Okay, after crashing your holiday and trying to steal your bunk, I guess I deserve that."

"I didn't handle it much better." Her admission felt like a win in another war that was being waged between them. A war he hadn't known existed until now. "Randy told me that it's just the two of you. That must be hard."

"I wasn't all that close to my dad."

"And your mom?" she asked, her eyes imploring, and even though he knew she was unconsciously using F.O.R.M., it didn't feel like an interview. It felt . . . real.

"She passed a few years ago."

"That must have been hard."

Normally he'd give the standard line about how she was great, his childhood had been great, everything was great, but for some reason he couldn't find the usual lies he clung to. "That was harder. Don't get me wrong, she was intrusive and unreliable and at times difficult. But . . ."

"She's your mom and you loved her." It was said with quiet reverence. There was no way she could relate to his childhood, not with how she was raised, but somehow he felt as if she understood what he was saying. Understood like she'd been burned too.

"Well, this family practically shares the same air. Nothing is off-limits, and no secret will be left unturned," she said.

"Team Swift for the win," Autumn sang, and both Wes and Summer turned at the exact moment. Summer's mouth fell open. Wes couldn't help but snort, which earned him a glare.

Their siblings were dressed in matching white shorts, dock shoes, and pink shirts with a giant photo of the pop artist across the chest. Autumn did a little booty shake and spun around to show off the back, which read TEAM SWIFT: LIVING OUR WILDEST DREAMS.

"Team Swift?" Summer asked. "What the hell is Team Swift?"

"You know, like swift as the river, and of course the goddess who brought me and Randy together. Isn't it perfect?"

"It's perfect, baby," Randy said, swinging his arm around Autumn's shoulders and giving her a long, over-the-top display of PDA. "Isn't she perfect, Summs?"

Every eye went to Summer as if waiting for her answer. As if everyone knew the change of plans except the person who it had affected the most—Summer. To his surprise and disappointment, she retracted those quills normally aimed at him and flashed a too-bright smile. "You've always looked good in pink."

That's when Wes did a double take of Summer's shirt. It too was pink and it too had a team name across the back: TEAM TWINNING: TWINS FOR THE WINS.

Her smile was so big it hurt his heart, but everyone else seemed to be oblivious to the fact that this beautiful spitfire was deflating before his eyes. Except Frank, who gave Autumn a stern glare which she ignored.

Autumn bounced over and took Summer's hands. "Is this okay or is it too much change? I know how you hate change. If it's not okay, then you just need to say so."

Summer looked around for someone to help—anyone—but no one came to her rescue. Wes didn't consider himself to be a knight of any kind, but in that moment he wanted to pull out his shield and protect Summer.

"I thought it was bros to the end?" he said to Randy with a knowing raise of the brow. Like, *get on board, wanker.* Only the wanker shrugged and mouthed, *Family business.*

Before Wes could say any more, Autumn's smile faded and her lower lips puffed out in a practiced pout. "It's okay, right?"

"Of course she's okay with it," Blanche said.

"This is how the guides want it," Cecilia interjected.

They all looked expectantly at Summer, whose smile became impossibly brighter. "Of course it's okay."

"You sure?" Autumn said, as if there were any other acceptable answers.

"I'm sure."

Frank shook his head, like he got what had just transpired

and understood the impossible situation they'd all put Summer in. But then why didn't he say anything?

"She's okay with it," Randy said.

"Of course she is," Cecilia said.

"I mean," Summer added. "It's a game for crying out loud."

Wes leaned down and whispered in her ear, "If you say it one more time maybe I'll believe you."

She blinked slowly up at him as if she were shocked that someone had noticed just how hurt she was by her sister's actions and family's reaction. Then her eyes narrowed. "I don't care if you believe me."

Wes held up his hands as if to say *I come in peace.* "Never implied I did." Then he slung his arm around her shoulders and began to lead them toward the boats. "Do we get matching shirts?"

She elbowed him in the ribs—hard enough that he stumbled. "Over my dead body. Have you kayaked before?"

"I was on the rowing crew at university," he said, puffing out his chest.

"You were probably a beater," she said.

"I prefer company when beating. Are you offering to pick up some of the slack?"

She ignored that. "You'd better be good, or I'm going to partner with Uncle G." They looked at Giuseppe, who was leaning on his wife to make it down the beach.

"Face it, you need me to win. And I know how much you hate to lose."

"Fine. But I'm the captain and you're my skipper. And you know what rhymes with skipper? Zipper." She made a zipper-over-the-mouth gesture. "Capisce?"

Chapter 10

FUN AND GAMES

"You have to paddle *with* me," Summer snapped. "We're going in circles."

They weren't just going in circles—they hadn't even made it out past the break.

Summer was sweating through her shirt as if they'd gone half a mile, but they'd barely moved a yard. And wasn't that a giant metaphor for her life, because it seemed that no matter how hard Summer paddled, the current kept pushing her back. She was a fighter, that's how she was wired, but lately the fight had stolen some of the wind from her sails.

"*You* are paddling in circles," Wes took the liberty to inform her. "*I* am paddling straight ahead."

"*You* are steering us straight into the shoreline! We're aiming for the buoy, not the sand and—" Wes moved slightly, and his calf brushed against her thigh.

Summer had planned on being annoyed by the nearness of his presence, but she never imagined that the sight of a masculine, muscular calf could be so distracting. And with how they were situated in the kayak, with him behind her, his long legs encasing her, they were so close that anytime the boat so much as shifted they made contact—and her belly made butterflies.

But how could that be? They had zero in common.

He's an attractive man, she admitted to herself. Tall and lean, with thick dark brown hair, sea blue eyes, and a jawline so sharp it could slice through steel. So the reaction she was having was totally normal. Right?

Right.

Summer blew out a puff of air to clear the hair from her eyes—and the image of his ass when he was crawling into the kayak from her mind. "Never mind. Just follow my lead."

"Or, how about you let someone with collegiate-level experience take the lead," he said.

"Me captain. You skipper. Remember?"

"I never agreed to that."

"Of course you didn't," she said ironically. "Because why would you do something to make my day a little easier. Why stop the shit-on-Summer's-vacay. Go ahead, have at it, Wes. What else am I doing wrong?" She stopped rowing and rested the paddle on her thighs. "Any more surprises that will inadvertently ruin my favorite week of the year? One week. That's all I asked for. That's all I ever ask for. One perfect week with my family. But, oh no, you and Randy had to come along and ruin it."

Her voice cracked and, *damnit*, she felt emotions bubble up and tighten her throat. Blinking rapidly, she wiped the beginning of what she was horrified to call tears from her eyes on the neckline of her shirt. Her stupid Team Green shirt that matched Wes's. Randy hadn't just stolen her sister, he'd stolen her favorite color, leaving her to battle it out in pea green polyester that made her appear jaundiced.

She felt a hand rest on her shoulder and give it an awkward pat. "You still okay?" he whispered.

No, she was as far from okay as a woman on the verge of a breakdown could get. What was it about him that put her on edge? Sure, Autumn showing up with a boyfriend had put a wrench in her plans, but for some reason she was angrier about Wes. His unexpected appearance, his arrogant smile, his annoyingly sexy accent. All of it made screams of frustration build at the back of her throat to the point where she wanted to bellow in outrage. So she did.

Loud and long and from the deepest depths of her soul. "I! Am! Fine!"

There was a long, thick pause, and Summer was tempted to turn around to see the look on his face. But then he spoke, softly and compassionately. "You're clearly not, love. Do you want to talk about it?"

Well, now she just felt stupid. He'd met her anger with compassion. God, he was infuriating.

"There's no talking on the kayak, remember?" she said.

"Well, there's no more paddling until you tell me what's bothering you."

That's when Summer realized that while she'd put her paddle down, Wes had been paddling and they'd actually made some progress. They hadn't reached the buoy, and the rest of the teams were shore-bound, but they were no longer spinning in circles. But then Wes put his paddle down and they started bobbing in the current.

"I don't want to talk about it."

He laughed loudly in her ear. "You dislike me so much that you'd rather lose a race, which is clearly important to you, than be honest with me?"

"Yes."

"Well, according to the Russo family rules, the losing team has to prepare dinner, which means you'll be stuck in a confined space with me while I show off my cooking prowess." He leaned in and whispered, "You'd be amazed what I can do with a good breast."

She spun a little in his arms and her nipples went hard at the thought of his masculine hands on her breasts. As if they'd launched a homing beacon, his eyes dropped and he grinned. "I see."

She splashed water in his face. "Funny. There's nothing to see."

"If you say so." The way he said it, with the O rolling off his tongue in that British accent, drove her so crazy it was almost like foreplay. At least, that's how her body reacted. All the blood rushed to her face and her heart thrashed wildly at the idea of flirting with the grumpiest man on earth.

"Fine, Crumpet Man, what do you want to hear?" She turned her head to look at him over her shoulder, and when she met his gaze her tummy gave a little flip. "That this is the one week I get my sister all to myself. No distractions. No boys or social media to contend with. The one week when I don't have to pull all the weight of running a small business. The one week a year where I can just be me."

He studied her for a long moment until she felt raw and exposed. She wanted to break eye contact but then he'd win. And she wasn't about to give Weston Kingston another win.

"But are you being *you*?" he asked. "Because the woman I know would never let me get away with what Autumn gets away with."

"She didn't mean to hurt my feelings. She just doesn't like conflict."

"So what? She just expects you to go with it?"

"My family drives me crazy. Someone has to bend, or things can get heated."

"And you have to be the one to bend? Because I haven't seen anyone even sway, let alone offer a compromise. It's just you."

"It's just been a weird day, that's all," she said defensively. "It isn't normally like this. Autumn is, um—she has a big heart and means well, she can just be a little self-centric at times. And my parents just want this week to go well because Autumn has never brought a boy to family vacation."

"Have you? Ever brought a *boy*?"

"No," she said, as if the idea of it were the most ridiculous thing in the world.

"I didn't think so."

"What the hell does that mean?" she snapped. "Are you saying I'm incapable of getting a boy who'd care about me enough to join me on a family vacation? You are such a dick."

Summer had lifted her paddle to smack him when, at the precise moment she turned in her seat, a small current hit their kayak from the side. One minute she was batting at Wes's head and the next she was plunged into the freezing Atlantic water.

Her skin beaded on contact and water shot up her nose. She felt disoriented, not sure which way was up, and panic coursed through her. Then she felt someone grab her arm and tug.

She gasped the second she broke the surface and was sputtering like a fish fountain. A warm hand slid around her waist, fingers splaying around her entire midsection. Her shirt must have ridden up because they were skin to skin and their legs brushed each other as they kicked to stay afloat. It was as if someone had built a bonfire in her stomach, and it was roaring to life at the simple contact.

"Are you okay?" Wes asked, and he did not sound breathless in the slightest. He sounded worried—for her.

She wiped the hair out of her eyes and the moisture from her glasses and took several deep breaths. When the water cleared she saw the prettiest, most intense blue eyes looking at her. Lashes speckled with drops, lips wet from the ocean. His shirt was plastered to his chest, showing off just how muscular he was—something that his usual button-ups and suit vests camouflaged.

He had a swimmer's body, with big shoulders and tight pecs. He was also wearing a smile that was pure cockiness.

"Love?" he asked with an I-caught-ya-ogling tone.

"I'm fine. I've been the Russo family's swimming champion eleven years running, I'll have you know. So I don't need your help." She didn't move though, she noticed. She stayed right up against his body. *For heat of course. Nothing more.*

He bit back a grin. "Then why are you holding onto me for dear life?"

She looked down and realized she was clinging to him like he was catnip. She shoved him away and grabbed onto the capsized boat. It was hard to remain coherent when she was so close to him.

"You put me in a state and that's why we flipped," she said.

His arm rested over the side of the kayak, his big bulging bicep on display. "How serious is this state?"

"Infuriatingly serious."

He reached out to brush her hair out of her face, and there went those damn flutters. "Are you telling me you don't like the state you're in?"

Nope, she absolutely positively despised that he could invoke a reaction from her body. She shoved at him again. "I don't like you."

He was all business when he said, "All you have to do is tell me you don't like it and I'll stop."

"Stop what? Being an ass, flirting with me, coming to my rescue?" She especially hated the last one.

"All of it."

She opened her mouth to say yes she wanted him to stop, but nothing came out except a squeak. His eyes dropped to her lips—which she licked.

His smile extended. "That's what I thought." His legs purposefully wrapped around hers and she shivered—and not from the frigid waters. "When you're tired of boys and ready for a man, just let me know."

And without warning, he flipped the kayak over, sending her plunging back under the water.

Chapter 11

ESTRANGED BROTHERS

Wes hated to lose. So then why had he sabotaged the race? Yup, he'd sabotaged it all right. He knew the second she'd stuck that pert nose in the air as they climbed into the kayak and said, "Try to keep up," that there was no way she was crossing that finish line first. But last? That had been the icing on the cake.

Or maybe the icing had been the way her body had responded to his. The dilated pupils, the shallow breaths, the pert nipples—that hadn't been a side effect of the cold. That had been chemistry, pure and simple. Not that he'd let it go any further than flirting—the woman drove him nuts—but throwing her off her game was entertaining. More entertaining than it should be.

Except she hadn't been the only one whose world had gone a little askew. When their bodies had tangled, and his hand had slid across her soft skin, his dick had raised its mast. The fact that it had happened while in frigid temps was impressive. That it had happened on account of a whimsical, sunny-as-a-summer's-day, diehard romantic was impossible. She had freckles and wore glasses and had this innocence about her that told him life hadn't yet chewed her up and spat her out.

Wes dated sophisticated, slinky ballbusters who wore suits

to work, not T-shirts with ridiculous sayings or frilly sun-dresses. Then again, he had a good eight years and a lifetime of letdowns on her. Not that he had ever been that naive—his childhood hadn't afforded him that luxury. She was the exact wrong kind of woman for him. Or maybe it was more like he was the exact wrong kind of man for her. Where she was soft, he had razor ridges; when she smiled, he flipped the universe the bird; where she believed in true love, he believed it was every person for themselves.

Which raised the question of why he'd been actively pushing her buttons and going as far as to flirt with her. Well, whatever the reason, it needed to stop—now.

Committed to his plan, Wes pulled on dry clothes and walked downstairs. He'd just hit the landing when someone yanked him by the arm and forced him into an empty bedroom.

"You're going to ruin everything," Randy said. Even though he was clearly fresh from the shower, he was flushed and sweating and looked ready to throw up.

"How am I ruining things?" Wes wanted to know. "I'm the one who got stuck with Pollyanna so that you could pair with Playmate Barbie."

With a significant lifting of the brow, Randy said, "They're identical. I mean, I nearly kissed Summer at breakfast. If it hadn't been for the flannel pajama bottoms and TALK BOOKISH TO ME shirt, I would have had a lot of explaining to do."

"Seriously?" Wes's mind reeled with confusion. "You can't tell them apart?"

"Can you?"

"Yes." To Wes it couldn't be more obvious. Summer was softer, more emotionally aware and subtle, carried herself with an understated assuredness that was more than her twenty-four years. Yes, she was naive, but not in a bad way. In an adorable way.

There was nothing understated about Autumn.

Autumn was boisterous, intense, and surface-level. She did have a big heart, but it was often overshadowed by her selfish tendencies. She wasn't a bad person, just someone who'd had life easy and needed to grow up a little. Kind of like Randy.

"Look, I'm trying to win over the family, and I can't do that when you're pissing her sister off."

Wes snorted. "I think you have that backwards. She's the instigator."

"What is this? Middle school?"

"I don't know, are you going to pass Autumn a note that says 'check yes or no'?"

Randy's face went serious, like it had when their father died. All it took was five or so months for Randy to go rogue and take off on a spontaneous trip to follow Taylor Swift. A bad feeling settled in Wes's stomach.

His brother peeked his head out the door then silently closed it.

"What's with the 007 behavior?" said Wes.

"I don't want Aunt Cecilia to feel my energy and blow everything." Randy stretched out the neckline of his polo. "I'm going to ask Autumn to be my wife."

"Then why do you look like you're going to vomit?"

"Because this is the real deal, bro. She's the one, my person. You know, the whole "you complete me," boom box over my head, pulling up in the white limo with red roses while I stand out of the sunroof."

A knot formed in Wes's stomach immediately. The last thing they needed when trying to grow the company was Randy to be even more distracted than usual. He's like a dog with a butterfly in his periphery—easily distracted.

"This is bad timing. We've got the new location, the board breathing down our backs, and a grand opening timeline that is near impossible. And you know how you can become absorbed with a shiny new project."

"So we postpone the opening. The board will get it."

"Whoa, you said *proposal*. Now you're talking wedding?"

"When it's right, why wait?"

Jesus! "How soon are you thinking?"

"In the next month. That's if she says yes." Randy's eyes went wild with desperation. "She'll say yes, won't she?"

"You should be thinking about the board and this opening, not some wedding and garter toss. The board would jump at the chance to catch us with our pants down."

Randy looked confused. "The board has always had our backs. This will be no different, you'll see. They'll understand."

"No, they won't." They'd be thrilled, because that would mean that they'd gain control of the company. Not that he could tell Randy that.

"Business comes and goes. Love only comes around once."

A bite of anger tightened painfully between Wes's shoulder blades. "Not in a business like ours. You're the vice president of operations, you can't just decide to take a few weeks off when we're in the middle of the make-it-or-break-it moment. Especially not after your disappearing act. Your job is to literally run the daily operations of the company. Be on the ground floor of new openings."

This was why Wes should have never involved himself in his father's business. It wasn't that Randy wasn't teachable, the kid just didn't have any interest in learning. He thought that because he'd grown up with his father running an empire and had an MBA from a fancy Ivy League that he knew everything he needed to know to run a successful company.

"You're the CEO *and* president, I think you can manage for a few weeks without me."

"I'm the interim CEO, and is this about my title? I didn't pick it, Randy. Your dad made that choice. Without consulting me. So don't pull this rank-and-title crap. It's bollocks."

Randy's face fell, and all that anger morphed into embarrassment. "I know. It just hurt, you know? He'd always told me that he was training me to take over, then he hands the golden key to you."

"You can still run things. I'm only here until the company stabilizes, then we can hire a new president together and you can take over as CEO."

"I know." Randy ran a hand down his face. "That makes it even worse. I don't want your hand-me-downs. I wanted Dad to want me for the position."

"Is that what this is? You and Autumn? Is this a distraction, or some way to get back at dear old Dad?"

Randy held up a hand. "No. I swear. I love her."

"You've known her, what? A month?"

"Sometimes it happens in the blink of an eye."

Randy was a go-with-the-flow kind of guy. Wes was not. Not only was he suspicious of any woman claiming love months after Randy had come into a fortune, he was suspicious of marriage in general. Why jump in with both feet when there was no guarantee it would last? Just look at his own life.

"I only want to make sure you think this through."

"This isn't a business deal, Wes. It's my life."

"Exactly."

"And this is how I want to live it."

Once Randy set his mind to one of his stupid plans, he wouldn't back off until he did it. So if Wes wanted Randy to see the light, he was going to have to go about it in a careful way. Randy needed to think he'd come the conclusion that this was too much too soon on his own.

"I'll try harder. As long as you promise me you'll really think about it."

Randy clapped Wes on the shoulder. "Already thought it through, bro. I'm ready to get hitched."

Summer had been waiting for this vacation all year. The big bonfire, toasting s'mores, playing catch with Buttercup on the beach, sitting around showing off the Russo Vacation Olympics trophy, which was really just a piece of carved driftwood that was supposed to look like an arrow but looked like a penis. Yet it was the downtime, the lack of a schedule, and the spontaneous family moments that sparked her fondest memories. The right balance of relaxation and family fun. But right now she wasn't having fun.

Her vacation had been hijacked. By a brute of a Brit who didn't seem to give a rat's ass about her current state of distress. Which was why, instead of being in the kitchen, swinging

her hips to ABBA, cooking her "loser dinner," she was pleading with her auntie for a Wes-depravation stroll along the
beach with Buttercup.

"It's linguine alle vongole, Auntie. You're the master of
linguine."

Cecilia looked thrilled by the compliment. "Would you
like to go on the record with that?"

If it got her out of spending an hour in the kitchen with
Wes, she was almost willing to take the heat. But her mom
would never forgive her. She might even disown her.

"Well, it's better than mine. Last time you said my linguini
had the texture of spaghetti squash."

Cecilia shivered. "It wasn't your best showing. But I have
faith in you."

"Since when?"

"Since you'd rather welch on a bet than cook. I raised you
better than that. Unless there's a particular reason why you
look like an all-around plague has soured your face."

"I just wanted you to use your gift to sniff out any potential problems with the Kingston brothers," she said, knowing
Cecilia loved a chance to show off her gift.

"Besides Randy's little mojo problem . . ." Cecilia let her
finger deflate down like a shrinking penis. "I see no other signs
of anything but love."

"What about Wes?" Summer asked, and wished she'd just
kept her mouth shut because Cecilia was like a dog with a
bone and she'd just sink her canines into this Wes situation.

"Are you asking about his love line?"

"What? No!" she said, too vehemently. "I just meant, think
of it as a way to get to know Randy through his brother. Isn't

it an auntie's duty to vet the guy her niece brings home? You could use your sight to see if Wes is a good guy. Birds of a feather and all that. You can tell a lot by the company people keep, the way they dress, and the way they were raised."

"We let you prance around naked until you were six. I don't see you streaking down Main Street." Cecilia took inventory of Summer in her boy-cut shorts and baggy top and *tsk*-ed. "Such a shame. If I had your boobs, I'd be naked all the time. #FreeTheNip would be my daily motto." Suddenly Cecilia gasped and clutched her turquoise necklace. She began to hum and stare off into the distance. "Your grandmother is here with a message."

Summer looked around the kitchen even though she knew she'd not see a trace of a ghost. But it was fun to play into the magic of it all. "What is she showing you?"

Cecilia held back a smile, loving that her niece was playing along. "She's showing me water, and a white knight, and, oh my, you're naked."

"You're seeing me naked?" Summer asked, her face heating with the memory of earlier, when she and Wes nearly had a naked moment in the water when the only thing between them was wet, paper-thin cotton.

"Don't sound so horrified—I changed your diapers, missy. And it's better than those grannie panties you wear."

"I don't wear . . ." Then she trailed off because it was too late. Cecilia's hand tightened around her necklace and she began to sway and hum louder. "I see Cupid himself and his little bare bottom coming to poke you with his arrow."

"Now there's a naked cherub who wants to assault me with his arrow? Such a man thing to do."

Cecilia blinked and her expression was back to of-this-world. "Say what you want, but your guides have spoken. And they're making it clear that boring old Summer isn't going to snag her man."

"I'm not boring." In fact, her life was a giant fireball of chaos. Just look at her shop's books. And her wardrobe. Summer had ninety-nine pieces of clothing and a boring ain't one.

"That's what a boring person would say. Now, get out there and break out of your bubble. Set yourself free and let that spontaneous and bold side run the show." Cecilia patted Summer on the behind and sent her on her way. "And go and get started on that linguini. I'm famished."

Summer trotted toward the kitchen, her chest tightening like she was taking her final walk down a concrete corridor. "Dead man walking" came to mind.

She hadn't seen Wes since the kayak fiasco, when they'd got caught up like seaweed in the riptide. When they'd actually spoken to each other like they didn't want to rip off the other's head. He'd been almost sweet with his concern and laser-focused attention. And she'd been, well, turned on.

"It was the adrenaline," she assured herself. "Nothing more."

Then why was she staring at herself in the hallway mirror, wishing she'd put on something more attractive than an outfit fit to clean out the garage? She ran her fingers through her frizzy hair, trying to tame it, then puffed her lips out like Autumn often did.

Nope, just looked like roadkill who'd sucked on a lemon.

"What was nothing, love?" a voice asked, and it took everything Summer had not to jump out of her skin.

"Jesus, we need to put a bell on you," she said.

As if on cue, their phones pinged in unison, RoChance in full swing.

"You were saying?" he asked, and she tried hard to appear unaffected in his presence.

A hard feat, since Wes was leaning against the wall as if he were holding it up with his sculpted shoulders. He was in slacks that hugged him to perfection and a gray button-down that made his eyes look even more intense. And then, just like out of a novel, a curl of hair fell over his forehead.

"Oh, the talk with my auntie?"

"The one where she implied you wear granny panties? I can vouch for you that your choice of underwear is not boring. On the record, of course."

"What do you know about my panties?"

"More than Dog Boy."

"Gah!" She marched past him and into the kitchen, stopping shy at the threshold, surprise and gratitude forming a knot in her throat.

The rustic antique table was set, with a bouquet of flowers in the middle. All the ingredients were on the counter, chopped and placed in organized glass bowls, like this was some British baking show. And in a strainer in the sink were dozens of fresh clams.

"You went to the market?" She picked up a clam and examined it thoroughly. It was a perfect specimen of what a clam should look like. "And the Crusty Clam?"

And what had she done? Read on the deck, sucked down a cold glass of Pinot, and thrown on some ratty clothes.

"The market, yes. And the Crusty Clam only to rent some clamming gear."

"You know how to clam? I don't believe you." She picked up the clams and swirled them around in the water, changing it out as sand escaped from the tightly shut shells.

"There is a thing called Google," he said, but Summer knew he was full of shit. These were clams from an expert clammer. So he was either lying and had bought them off Benny at the Crusty Clam or he'd done this before.

She wanted to bet on the lying part, but her gut said that he knew his way around a clam shovel and a kitchen.

"Did you clam in your loafers and tie?"

He smirked. "Wouldn't you like to know?"

Yes. Yes she did. Because when he'd shown up for the race earlier that day and had been wearing cargo shorts that hung low on his hips and a faded Oxford tee, her mouth had watered. Before that she'd never seen him in anything but starch and stick-up-his-assery—like he was now.

"By the way," he said. "You owe me a hundred dollars."

"You spent a hundred bucks on groceries?" she choked. She could have bought all those ingredients and three bouquets of flowers for half that. But instead of doing what she was supposed to be doing, she'd gotten lost in a book. "Let me grab my phone and I can Venmo you my half." Which was her grocery budget for two whole weeks.

"No, I am a respectable man and settle my bets. I lost. I pay for dinner," he said. "But my time is valuable. So while you were primping—"

"I wasn't primping."

He ignored this. "I was in here waiting. You were ten minutes late."

She pulled up her calculator app on her phone, did some

quick math and choked. "You make six hundred dollars an hour?"

"Closer to seven, but I was giving you the friends and family discount."

How was that possible? They did the same thing, worked in the same industry and she was living in an nine-hundred-square-foot apartment above her shop with her sister and he was living in the lap of luxury.

She made a few swipes on her phone and his immediately pinged.

He pulled it out of his back pocket and lifted a brow. "Are you sending me an arrow on your dating app? You know you can just come out from behind the screen and ask me out."

She snorted. "There is RoChance I'd ever date you. Plus it's just pinged because we're in the vicinity of each other. And an algorithm never lies."

She ignored the ping of the app as he grabbed an open bottle of chilled Pinot Grigio and poured them each a glass. He handed one to her and lifted his in toast. "I don't know. This feels kind of date-like. You, me, wine, cooking, flowers. Screams romance."

He'd bought the flowers for her? She didn't know how she felt about that—or about the way her heart melted a little.

"If you check your phone, it was your money arriving for your part of the groceries, not an arrow. I guess there is something to bulk pricing, but I'd rather be broke than sling Big Box–priced books that hurt the author's bottom line to the masses."

Her barb didn't even phase him. "Give yourself a raise."

She choked on a laugh. "With what money?"

This gave him pause. "You have nonstop customer flow. How is that possible?"

Her hackles rose and she felt a defensive prickle at the base of her neck. Along with some embarrassment. She wasn't the best businesswoman, but she was the best woman to run her grandmother's bookshop.

"Some of them are regulars," she admitted, pulling out the pasta board. "I encourage them to come in for the coffee and a read."

He turned off the water which he was using to fill up the pasta pot. "Hold up, love, you're saying that you let them sample your products for free?"

She floured the cutting board and started separating the yolks from the whites. "It's called community."

She looked up and he was helping. They were actually working in tandem. Then he broke the moment when he said, "It's called bad business. Here, scoot over." He bumped her with his hip and took over kneading the pasta.

"You think you can make a better linguini than me?"

"My last name might be Kingston, but my mum is Italian and my nonna taught me my way around a kitchen. And Jesus, how did you manage to get flour all over the counter? You haven't even started cooking."

Her cheeks heated with embarrassment, but her tone was all sass. "Cooking is an art. It's about going with your gut."

"Cooking is a science. It's about following the instructions."

"Instructions are for amateurs." She picked up a glass bowl filled with chopped parsley and took a pinch to inspect. "Oh my god, it's all the same exact size. Even your cooking skills are starched."

"At least my result doesn't resemble a flour bomb exploding in the kitchen. I keep it nice and tidy."

Maybe it was the pompous look on his face, or that he would choose to wear slacks and loafers on a family vacation. Or maybe it was because she'd had a lifetime of her family calling her Pig Pen for the little messes that she left in her wake, but something in her snapped.

"Flour this," she said and picked up a palm full of flour then blew as hard as she could.

A white cloud the size of the Dust Bowl exploded into the sky, and when the air cleared Wes looked like a ghost with flour all over his dark hair. His shirt was dusted and his face was puckered. He looked like a pissed-off Pillsbury Doughboy.

Then the most miraculous thing happened: he threw his head back and barked out a laugh. A laugh that came straight from the belly. A laugh she'd never heard from him before. A laugh that was contagious, because no matter how hard she tried to hold onto that anger she couldn't help but laugh back until they were both clutching their sides.

Their eyes caught, and something freeing and bright passed between them, and she wanted to capture it and hold onto it for a rainy day. Or the next time he did something to piss her to high heaven.

"I'm sorry," she said, still chuckling. "I went a bit far."

"You think?" He stuck out his hand. "Truce?"

She took it. "Truce."

Before she knew what was happening, she was being yanked forward and into his arms. She struggled half-heartedly to escape but he snaked his arm around her waist and pulled her into a big bear hug, every inch of her connecting with every inch of him as he rubbed himself back and forth, transferring the flour from his clothes to hers.

They were both laughing so hard that neither of them noticed just how many body parts were touching until she felt a little zing from her belly to her toes. Wes must have noticed as well, because his embrace turned from friendly to more intimate, his hands splaying over her hips. And when their eyes locked her next laugh died on her lips—which he was staring at.

They both stilled and she took stock of just how intimate their embrace had become. Her palms were on his pecs, leaving behind two flour marks in the shape of handprints, and his hands were on her ass—likely doing the same.

And for the second time that day, tension coiled between them like a loaded spring. Neither spoke, but when she looked into his annoyingly perfect eyes a whole conversation passed between them.

Want.

Lust.

Desire.

Danger.

"What are you doing?" she whispered.

"Helping you cook dinner."

"No, you were about to mansplain how to do something I mastered before I could reach the counter."

"So you used to make pasta naked," he said, which told her he'd heard her and her auntie's entire convo. "If it's tradition, we can both strip down."

Her nipples tightened. "I already lost once today, I'd hate to be disappointed again."

Before she knew what was happening, he was pressing her against the counter. She could feel his heat surrounding her, his biceps brushing her arms as he leaned in to whisper, "I assure you, I'm an aim-to-please kind of man. One test drive and I'll ruin you for other men."

She swallowed hard. "In your dreams."

He moved even closer and her body trembled. His lips grazed the curve of her ear and he said, "Are you denying I've never starred in any of *your* dreams?"

She turned in his arms and looked him straight in the eyes, which meant craning her neck back to look all the way up his six-foot-three frame. "Never."

He cracked a knowing smile. "Then what's the harm in a little kiss to test my theory that you and I would crack the sheetrock."

Oh. My. God. Did her lady parts just moan?

"We can't even make pasta without arguing."

"I think, for us, that's foreplay, love," he said, sounding as surprised as her over his epiphany.

Horror shot through her. It couldn't be. But what if he was right? What if all of this was one big game of cat and mouse? Which lead to the most important question. Did she want to be caught?

No. absolutely not, she told herself. She'd rather burn her entire library of Judy Garwood novels than sleep with the man who was trying to put her out of business. Her attraction to him was merely from sex deprivation. She could admit he was handsome in that polished way Wall Street men were—he had masculine hands, and a magnetism about him that could con a bunch of unsuspecting small business owners into welcoming his big business with open arms.

"It's loathing."

"Then how about we make a wager of our own. A pasta-off. If I win, I get that kiss."

"A kiss?" she croaked, the color of her cheeks deepening. "Why would you want to kiss me?"

"To prove there's something here that can't be ignored."

She didn't need a test to prove that. Her body was practically putty and they were both fully clothed. "There's nothing between us," she lied.

"Then there won't be any harm in a little kiss," he challenged—and oh, that superior tone of his pushed her buttons.

"Okay, fine. But no tongue."

"Since when does the loser get to set the terms of the spoils?"

"Since they're my lips." And since she could already imagine his mouth on hers, assured and demanding. Feel his hands on her waist—and other places—moving with confident intent.

Abort. Abort. That would be the smart thing to do, but she couldn't resist a dare. Especially one thrown out there by a man who had bested her at every turn. A man who drove her to the brink of insanity. A man who needed to go.

"And when I win, you have to go back to Ridgefield first thing tomorrow," she said.

That charming smile drooped at the corners in a vulnerable way that had her regretting her words. She'd hit a sore spot, and for the first time this imposing, impenetrable man seemed a little more human. A little softer, and less like he could carry the entirety of Great Britain on his shoulders without breaking a sweat.

"Is that what you really want?"

"Yes." That was a big fat lie, but for the first time in her life her poker face must have held because he didn't call her on it.

"Agreed then. I win, I get a kiss to prove that there is something between us. And if you win, I'll be on my merry way, and you can enjoy the rest of your holiday experiencing life through the pages of one of your love books."

"They're called romance novels."

His charm immediately reappeared. "How do you say it? Tomato-tomoto?"

She rolled her eyes. "We say it, *bring it on.*"

Chapter 12

THE CHASE

She wanted him gone.

Wes didn't know why he should be so surprised or hurt, but there it was, that same ache that came with being unwanted. It was a rusty but familiar feeling that stemmed from summers spent at his father's, where his stepmother had gone out of her way to let him know she was counting down the days until his departure. That was why, when he'd been old enough to make his own decisions, he'd told his mum he didn't want to go to the States anymore. He'd been twelve. And his father hadn't tried to convince him otherwise.

Wes had promised himself that he'd never allow someone to make him feel unwanted again. Yet, here he was, sitting around the dinner table with a family who could make Attila the Hun feel welcome—except the woman next to him, who would rather gut herself from throat to belly than be in his company. And, as fate would have it, the only available seat was next to Summer. Even though she was sitting on the edge of the cushion, as far away from him as possible without falling off, he could still smell her airy scent, see the faint hint of freckles on her nose, feel the heat her body was radiating.

"What?" she whispered.

He blinked. "What?"

"You're staring at me. Did you spit in my serving?"

"No, I'm just waiting for you to take the first bite so that I can see the exact moment you realize that I've won."

"You drenched your pasta water with olive oil. What kind of Italian does that?"

"I merely added a dollop to the boiling water so that the noodles wouldn't stick and become gummy."

"Well, if you use the precise amount of flour, it won't stick or become gummy."

"Then why did I see you cutting off the ends of two noodles that were stuck together?" he asked, and saw the anger simmering in her expressive eyes. If looks could kill, he'd be six feet under.

"Do you mind? I'm trying to enjoy my meal in peace." She swatted at him like he was an annoying hornet, although she was the one with the stinger out.

"Enjoy away."

The rest of the family were already halfway through their meal and Summer hadn't touched hers. She'd been too busy scrutinizing her relatives as they compared the two dishes, analyzing every nuance and twitch.

Wes's dish was on the right and he was proud of the plating. It was the perfect helping of pasta, twisted into a volcano-esque mound, sprinkled with fresh-cut Italian parsley and coarse ground pepper. It was sophisticated and could rival any five-star establishment in the city.

Summer had gone for everyday dishware, with her linguini piled high in the pasta bowl, giving it a homestyle feel. It reminded him of dinners spent with his nonna when his mother was working late or pulling a double shift. It was rustic, real, and not pretending to be anything other than what it was—a homecooked family meal. It awoke a yearning inside of him that he'd suppressed ever since his grandmother's passing.

He watched Summer pick up her fork and twist up a giant helping of his pasta that filled the entire utensil, and his palms began to sweat. He didn't know why he cared what she thought about his cooking, and he couldn't remember the last time he'd gone out of his way to impress a woman, but he wanted to impress the hell out of her—and her family.

Suddenly, it was about more than just winning a bet. It was about proving to Summer that he wasn't this monster she'd made him out to be. And he needed time to do that. Time to turn her opinion of him in his favor.

They were going to be working next door to each other—at least until he moved on to the next project, which would be Los Angeles. It would be nice to live in harmony. Even better would be to take the feud between the sheets and argue it out in bed. He'd meant what he'd said, they'd shatter the sheetrock. He was sure of it.

But while he knew she wanted him, he was pretty sure she still hated him. Which meant he needed a plan. And a good one. He only had a week to prove to her that they'd be great together—physically. Emotionally, they were like oil and vinegar. But if he could just occupy her mouth for two minutes, he knew he could get into her bed.

"Go on, love. Take a bite," he encouraged.

She took a sniff and then crinkled her nose at him. His stomach dropped. Then those lush lips of hers parted and put she the fork in, and he knew the minute she realized that he wasn't bullshitting about his cooking prowess. Her extra-ordinary eyes went wide with genuine surprise and then something resembling panic flickered there. This wasn't going to be the sweep she'd expected.

"So?" he asked. "Too much olive oil?"

"It isn't terrible. A little overcooked, but not terrible," she said quietly, and he laughed. "I'd give it an eight out of ten."

"It's a winner and you know it."

"We'll have to see what the judges say," she said primly. "But don't get your hopes up, you still haven't tasted mine."

"Then let's rectify that." He picked up his fork and spoon and twisted up a small bite of noodles, twirling it against his spoon so that it didn't splatter everywhere. He took a sniff and examined the noodles.

"For God's sake, this isn't a wine tasting. Just eat the damn pasta," she whispered, exasperation in her tone.

"Nervous?"

"Irritated."

"Turned on?"

"You wish. Now take a bite."

He catalogued the nerves tugging at her lower lip. Interesting.

To put her out of her misery, Wes took a bite, and *bam*, it was like a food-induced orgasm. Perfectly cooked, the right firmness, and the exact right ratio of flour to egg yolks. Perfection.

He took his time chewing, really dragging it out to piss her off. She sighed and sat back in her chair, crossing her arms over her chest with impatience. He licked his lips.

"So?" she asked when he was done with the big display.

He took the cloth napkin and dabbed the corners of his mouth. "In one word?"

He leaned in until their thighs were brushing and he could smell the faint scent of jasmine, sea air, and parsley on her skin. He ran his nose down the shell of her ear and whispered, "Orgasmic."

He could hear her breath catch and see the pulse at the base of her neck race. She slowly turned to look at him and her eyes dilated with desire. They fell to his lips and slowly tracked back up, and when their gazes locked again he could have sworn she moaned.

Yup, she felt it. He wasn't in this craziness alone.

"What are you two talking about over there?" Autumn said, with brows raised and suspicion in her words.

"Noodles," Summer said casually, but her voice was pitched.

"From here it looked like the topic was closer to *ca*-noodling."

Summer shot Autumn a murderous look and Autumn just smiled. The rest of the family exchanged looks of their own, as if having a conversation about him and Summer without including him and Summer—and he didn't think he'd like what they were saying. It was one thing for him to shag her, it was another for her family to play Cupid.

"Now that you mention it," Blanche said, "they are sitting quite close together."

Summer moved so fast to the other side of her chair that she nearly fell off. Wes reached over to steady her with a hand on her thigh and she nearly jumped out of her skin.

Cecilia pressed a palm to her chest. "Oh my."

That was it, just "oh my," but Summer reacted as if she'd just announced that her nonna had arisen from the dead.

"Yeah, oh my," Randy said, in a WTF tone directed at Wes.

"What is your heritage, dear?" Cecilia asked Wes.

"Half Scottish and half Italian."

"Italian, you say. Isn't that interesting, Summer?"

"Very interesting," Autumn chimed in.

Summer looked as if she wanted to curl up and die, and Wes felt a protectiveness wash over him. He didn't mind putting her on the spot, pushing her buttons, but he didn't like it when other people did. Even if they were her family.

He needed to erase that discomfort from her face—immediately. So he moved his leg so that it bumped her thigh. Instead of pulling away, she actually swayed closer to him, and then to his utter surprise she took his hand under the table.

"What's interesting is that nearly everyone finished their plates," Wes said. "I think it's time for a vote. Push forward the plate you think is superior."

Everyone glanced at the others while Summer nervously squeezed his hand—hard. Clearly, there was more to this than just besting him. Coming out the winner went deeper than a bet for her. Summer was a people-pleaser to her core, and wanted desperately to have her family on her side. Wes almost said that they should call off the bet, but then Frank made the first move, pushing his daughter's dish forward. Wes was surprised when Cecilia pushed his forward.

One by one they went around the table until it was three to three, then Summer pushed her plate forward and glared at him.

"A tie? This can't end on a tie," she said. "There has to be a winner."

"Why, dear?" Blanche asked. "Does the loser do the dishes?"

"Oh, my senses are telling me there's more at stake than a dirty kitchen," Cecilia said.

"I don't know," Giuseppe said. "We all know what the kitchen looks like after Summer's been in there."

"Pig Pen," her family said in unison, and there it flashed again. That same look she'd given him earlier in the kitchen when he'd poked fun at her cooking style.

She went from smiling to shutters closed in no time flat. Being called out for her free-spirited nature clearly upset her. But it was as if everyone else in the room was too busy laughing at the inside joke to realize that it was leaving Summer on the outside.

Before someone could say anything else to upset her, he said, "Actually, we have a winner."

Every expression in the room went wide with surprise when he cast his vote and pushed Summer's bowl forward.

"You're voting for me?"

"It is the superior dish," he said quietly. "I might hate to lose but not as much as I hate to lie. Congratulations."

He wasn't sure what he expected. For her to burst into song and dance at his early departure? But it sure as hell wasn't a frown. "You don't have to do this."

"Yes." He wiped his lips with his napkin and stood. "Yes, I do. As for our deal—"

"Forget the bet. Let's just call it a tie."

"A bet is a bet, love."

"Speaking of love," Randy interrupted. "I have an announcement. Well, more of a gift."

Wes's stomach bottomed out. Less than a few hours ago

his brother had promised to take things slow and now he was presenting a small jewelry-shaped box like it was the Crown Jewels. Jesus, this couldn't be happening. Summer was right—their siblings were losing their minds.

"It's not a ring," he said, and thank Jesus. "But it's a promise of sorts."

Autumn squealed with delight as she took the gift like a lady who was used to getting jewelry-shaped boxes. It was hard to give her the benefit of the doubt when she was so easily accepting of what probably amounted to a fifty-thousand-dollar gift a month into a relationship. It just proved love had a price.

Autumn's smile was as wide as Summer's frown. It was like Pooh Bear with a pot of honey versus Eeyore with a prickly thistle.

After some fanfare, Autumn opened the box and gave a dramatic gasp. "Is this what I think it is?"

Jesus, what was it? She held the box to her chest so that no one could see what was in there. But her face said it would set the family back more than fifty grand.

"It is, babe."

"The one on the Upper West Side?"

"It is."

"It's too much."

"My woman deserves the best."

"Would you two like to fill us in?" Summer said, and although the rest of the family couldn't see, her hands were in her lap wrung so tightly they were white.

Autumn flipped the box around and his stomach didn't just bottom out—it felt like a wrecking ball went right through his middle. Because attached to some gaudy key-chain was a set of house keys.

"Randy bought us our dream house," Autumn said, and the ladies at the table swooned in harmony. All except Summer, who looked confused.

"You hate that part of town," Summer said.

"Not the Upper West Side in Ridgefield, silly. Manhattan," Autumn said, and Wes watched the color drain from Summer's face and quickly catalogued the devastation bracketing her mouth.

"Manhattan?" Blanche asked. "You've always dreamed of living there."

"What a wonderful place to start your new life," Cecilia said.

Frank said nothing, but quietly reached under the table to take Summer's hand. She gripped it like it was the one thing holding her together.

Autumn looked at Randy all cow-eyed. "That's what we said when we saw it. Summs, you'll die when you come visit. It's this cute brownstone with brick steps and an iron rail, just like *You've Got Mail*. And, Dad, there's an actual yard, which is so hard to come by in that neighborhood. I'm going to have the best garden."

"You hate getting your hands dirty," Summer pointed out.

"Oh, we'd hire someone," Randy said.

Of course he would. I mean, what's an extra five hundred bucks a month when you blow a cool three mill on a "starter house."

"You bought a house for my sister without consulting her?" Summer asked.

Randy looked uncertain. "It's romantic, right?"

"It's selfish. You're assuming she wants to leave the state, leave her family."

"It's a sign of maturity to stop wasting money on rent and invest in a home," Randy countered softly.

"It isn't if half the partnership can't afford the mortgage," Wes said under his breath.

"Oh, I never expected her to pay for it. I'm doing this for her. It's a surprise and a gift."

"What the actual fuck?" Wes said. "What happened to taking it slow? And how are you going to run the Ridgefield location from New York? We still have to get it running and profitable. Then there's the LA location."

"We'll work it out."

"No, you mean *I'll* make it work."

"Don't ruin this moment for me, man. I've been waiting to do this in front of her family for weeks. Hell, since I met the girl."

Funny—Wes had been trying to get him to just come back to the country for weeks without much success. Now he knew why. Wes was trying to avoid a board takeover while Randy was busy playing house with a gold digger.

There were a ton of questions from around the table about square footage—two thousand and eighteen to be exact—was it close to restaurants—only the best for his baby. Summer, on the other hand, had gone uncharacteristically quiet. Sitting stock still in her chair, devastation written in every inch of her posture, her lips working really hard not to quiver.

"So you're leaving Ridgefield?" Summer asked in a hushed whisper, and the table went silent.

"I know what you're thinking, Summs, and I promise you

nothing will change. Ridgefield is only a couple hours by train. We'll see each other all the time."

"When did you even have time to look at houses?"

Autumn and Randy shared a guilty look. "We actually came back to the States a few days ago and spent the weekend in New York, and thought it would be fun to go house hunting on a whim."

"When were you going to tell me you were thinking of moving out?"

"I didn't know it would be this soon. I mean, why get everyone all excited if it didn't work out. Plus, you know I've always dreamed of living there."

"I know," Summer said with the saddest fucking smile Wes had ever seen. "I'm happy for you. But it's just a big change all at once. I mean, your job is here, your friends are here." *I'm here* hung in the air, but Autumn wasn't reading the room.

"Those things come and go, and you can't move forward when you're stuck in the same place."

Summer winced at her sister's statement, because she was stuck. Her business was in Ridgefield, she couldn't just pack up at a moment's notice and move based on some whim. Another reason why they could never work.

"You're happy about this, right?" Autumn asked, once again playing on Summer's loyalty to her family and selflessness.

"Why not? I mean, people come and go."

"She just learned about this, maybe we should let the happy couple work it out," Wes said.

Randy looked flustered. "I really thought I was doing a sweet thing. This is sweet, right, babe?"

Autumn took his hand and smiled. "It is. You are the most romantic person on the planet."

"Eventually, my work will be stationed in New York, and I don't want what happened between Wes and his ex-fiancée to happen to us. Distance is brutal on a relationship and he had to walk away from love."

Summer's eyes met his, and he felt the full weight of her judgment. "You gave up love for a job?"

"Not all of us have your choices."

"Yes, you do. And you should choose love, every time. No question."

And that was when he was reminded of the true romantic and naive girl who believed love ruled the world. She was a dreamer and he was a doer. Not that she didn't work hard, but her dream was wrapped up in a thousand square feet of romance novels. His was one billion-dollar project after another. Another reason to not get involved—he'd already left a woman once for a job.

Randy raised his hand as if to speak. Frank, who seemed about excited by the news as Summer and Wes, gave him the floor. "I want to do this right."

Summer gasped. "So the right thing is she gives up her life for yours? How 1950s of you."

Her dad put a hand on Summer's arm. "I think what Summer is trying to say is that she and Autumn are very close and being away from each other will be hard."

"But Wes and I did it. We flew back and forth for years."

"But we're not you and Wes. It's not apples to apples. My sister and I mean everything to each other," Summer said, her misery so acute it physically pained him.

Autumn straightened. "If I meant everything to you, you would be happy for me right now. No one has ever done anything this sweet for me. Ever."

"I just feel like you're giving up yourself to make someone else happy.

"Isn't that the definition of love?"

"Not if you're the only one sacrificing," Summer said. "Can't you two see that this is moving too fast?"

"You are such a hypocrite. You were willing to give up huge parts of yourself to make it work with Ken. I mean, you're even considering going to his wedding to prove to, well, who knows, that you're still friends."

"We are still friends."

This was news to Wes and he didn't like it—not one bit. Sure it was one thing to retain a friendship with an ex, but go to his wedding because she had something to prove surely meant that she wasn't over him—and where did that leave Wes?

"In what dream world? He left you for a stupid entry-level job. And you're upset that a man who loves me and wants to be with me took a step toward being in a serious relationship? Oh, I forgot, you don't know about those."

"Low blow, Autumn," Summer whispered. "Am I the only one seeing red flags here?" she asked the room. "This isn't like Autumn."

"Maybe it's Autumn in love," Blanche said.

"And didn't you just say that you should choose love every time," Randy said, and those misty eyes went pissy. They were hot with anger.

"Thanks for that helpful reminder," she said as she stood.

She set her napkin on her chair and left. Wes was torn between going after her and killing Randy. But Summer purposefully didn't meet anyone's gaze, a clear fuck-off to the room, and Randy was filling everyone else in on the house's history and multiple patios.

Wes hadn't felt as helpless as he did right then since he'd been the unwanted kid on the outside who didn't fit into either world in front of him.

Chapter 13

MEET-UGLY

Breathe in.
  Breath out.
  Repeat.

That's what Summer kept telling herself as she scrambled out the back door, down the patio and onto the dock, her bare feet pounding the wooden planks, still warm from the day's sun. She didn't stop until she reached the very end, her toes hanging off the edge. She punched her hands down by her sides and dropped her head back as far as it would go. Then she let out a shout loud enough to carry across the river.

"Motherfucker!"

This was a nightmare. The whole thing. And she didn't see a way out of it. But the first step was getting her emotions under control. Hard to do when she was so riled that she was sure steam was coming out of her ears.

"Breathe in. Breathe out. Repeat," she said, closing her eyes. "Breathe in. Breathe out. Repeat." Slowly, her heart rate went from near-stroke to stressed-out, but the anger hung on.

Sitting down on the dock like she used to when she was younger, she dangled her legs over the edge, the water crisp and refreshing on her bare feet. She looked out over the crystal blue waters and down the row of docks and Queen Anne houses that lined the river.

God it was pretty. Most of the neighbors had turned in so their lights didn't wash out the millions of stars overhead. The gentle lap of the tide was noticeable beneath her, swaying the dock and licking the shoreline, creating a familiar cadence that helped calm some of her nerves. But not the confusion.

Firstly, Wes had just bested her in pasta. Bested her! She knew for a fact that her dad had only voted for her because he would always have her back. Autumn had voted for her because that's what twins did. And Randy had voted the same as Autumn because—well they did everything together it seemed. The only reason she'd won was because Wes had made a valiant gesture—which still made no sense to her.

Winning was in his blood. He'd rather jump into the river in one of his thousand-dollar suits than lose—especially to her. So then why?

Secondly, why had her heart sunk when she realized she'd won? She was getting exactly what she'd wanted—Wes gone. Yet she felt as if she were losing something important.

Was he really going to leave? Of course he was. Wes might be a lot of things, but he wasn't a welsher. Which meant that in twelve hours their house would be minus one.

What had she done? Autumn was going to kill her. Absolutely kill her if she ever found out. She was supposed to be playing nice, not evicting her twin's possible future brother-in-law.

Lastly, Autumn was leaving her behind. Packing up and moving a train ride away. No heads-up, no forewarning, no time to prep. Summer hadn't even known that they were house-shopping. Heck, she didn't even know Autumn had a boyfriend to go house-hunting with.

With her auntie and uncle and her parents in Florida, Autumn was all she had left. Or whatever parts of Autumn were left over after Randy. And now she was losing her too.

The anger simmering now felt more like desperation. Paralyzing desperation.

It reminded her of the summer when Autumn had dared her to streak through the neighbor's yard and do a cannonball off their dock. To be funny, Autumn had grabbed Summer's bikini bottoms and taken off, leaving Summer nearly naked in the river.

That was when Summer had experienced her very first meet-cute. She had been sixteen and never kissed and used to have nightmares that she'd die a kissing-virgin. But Daryl Sanderson, her long-time unrequited crush, had happened upon her and brought her a towel, which had been Autumn's plan all along. Only, Daryl's plan had been to land a date with Autumn, turning Summer's first meet-cute into a never-ending string of meet-uglies. He'd laughed when she'd got her wires crossed and gone in to kiss him. Then he'd told everyone in town about it the next day. She'd been humiliated, and that day had shaped the way she'd interacted with men ever since.

"Screw you, Daryl Sanderson," she mumbled to herself now.

Maybe her auntie was right and she needed to take some risks. Mr. MBA had told her that she lived her life though the characters in her books. Well, she did that because it was safer than putting herself out there. Just look at Dr. Daniel. She'd put herself out there and wound up with dog snot on her leg.

"Screw you, Dr. Daniel. Screw you, Daryl Sanderson. And

screw you, Weston Kingston!" This time she said it with more conviction. And damn it felt good.

"Screw you, Daryl Sanderson," she said, yanking her T-shirt over her head and setting her glasses on the dock. "And screw you, Weston Kingston." She shed her pants, and in nothing but her thong she ran off the edge of the deck and cannon-balled into the water.

The chilly jetty was like a slap to the face, clearing her head and shocking her into the moment. Bubbles erupted all around her, and she sank deeper and deeper until she was in complete darkness and the white noise of the world was silenced. Her heart rate slowed and suddenly everything became clear.

She was tired of things happening *to* her. Tired of being an emotional doormat for every Tom, Daniel, and Daryl Sanderson who crossed her path. From this moment forward she was going to be the one making the choices on the direction her life would take. She was no longer going to sit back and wait for life to happen—she was going to be the happen in her life.

She waited until her lungs stung from the lack of oxygen and then resurfaced. When she did there was a blurry shadow standing on the edge of the dock. A six-foot-three frame with broad shoulders and blue eyes. Even in the inky night the piercing blue cut through.

Just the thought of him catching her while she was naked made her nipples celebrate by blowing their party poppers. What was wrong with her that she was unable to stop reacting to a man she loathed? A man who, for months, had been insufferable.

She wrapped her arms around her chest like that would hide the fact that she'd just dived practically naked into the river. "How long have you been standing there?"

"I was about to announce my presence when you dropped your trousers."

"And how were you going to announce yourself? Weston Kingston the Third, hailing from London and bookstore royalty?"

"For your information, the only third in the family is Randy."

"But you're the oldest." By a few years, as she surmised. Randy was her age, twenty-four-ish and Wes was in his early thirties.

"I'm—what do they call it—the bastard of the family. I'm surprised my father even wanted me to carry his last name."

The rage she was clutching so tightly loosened. How could it not? There was a hint of emotion in his voice as he shared with her what was a horrible part of his childhood. That alone told her just how deeply it affected him.

Like her interaction with Daryl Sanderson, it had probably shaped all his relationships moving forward.

"You father sounds horrible," she said quietly, while bobbing in the water.

"Who is this Daryl Sanderson chap, and what did he do to deserve the honor of being on a list with me?"

"It's a love-to-hate kind of list."

Wes toed off his loafers and socks, then tugged his pant legs up to his knees before taking a seat on the edge of the dock. It was a boyish, casual action that had her heart rolling over a smidge. "Those are some pretty strong emotions for someone you're desperate to kick out of your house."

And the rest of that rage morphed into embarrassment.

He lifted a brow, and that's when she noticed his usually coifed hair looking as if his fingers had run through it dozens of times. His shirt, which he'd changed before dinner, was no longer flour-covered, but was untucked and wrinkled. It tugged at a soft spot deep in her chest.

"I'm sorry about my behavior in the kitchen and then at dinner. You just seem to rile me up, and then with Autumn's news . . ." She shrugged. "It was a lot to take in, and I took it out on you."

"Are you saying you want me to stay, love?"

"I'm not sure what I'm saying."

"Then how about you tell me about Daryl Sanderson while you ponder the pros and cons of me sticking around."

Lord help me. Daryl was the last person she wanted to talk about, but he'd shared something personal and it was only fair to return the favor. "He was my first meet-ugly."

He laughed. "Meet-what?"

"You know, the opposite of a meet-cute, where you experience this amazingly romantic encounter with a stranger and you think, this is it, only it's a one-sided feeling or fate decides to pull the rug out from under you—sometimes literally. You know what I mean?"

"Yes, love, I do."

"An example would be meeting someone at the dog park and thinking it was a date, when in reality he just wanted you to dog-sit."

"Ahh." His voice was threadbare. "So what did Daryl do to join this list?"

"I was sixteen and Autumn dared me to cannonball off

Daryl's dock naked." She pointed to the dock in question. "Then she stole my clothes, and before I could formulate an escape plan Daryl happened upon me. It was like the perfect meet-cute. A damsel in distress, the guy I'd had an unrequited crush on for years coming to my aid with a towel."

"That sounds noble."

"We sat on the edge of his dock talking for hours, his hand touching my knee whenever a difficult topic arose." It had been, up to that point, the most riveting conversation of her young life. It was the perfect meet-cute. "Suddenly he went shy and said he had something to ask me," she continued. "I assumed it was to kiss me."

"Summer," Daryl had said in this hushed and intimate tone. "There's been something I've been dying to do all week."

"Really?"

"Yeah," he said, leaning in closer.

This was it. This was going to be where she lost her lip-virginity. And she couldn't have asked for a more perfect background. The moon was full, the sky crystal clear, and the boy was Daryl Sanderson.

Daryl freaking Sanderson!

"I know it's a big ask." He reached out and ran his thumb down her jawline. "And it probably seems like it's coming out of nowhere since we've never really talked much."

"We've talked," she said dreamily. Well, she'd had millions of conversations with him—only they'd been directed to her pillow. But tonight, he'd shared—he'd really opened up to her.

"I feel like I know you," she assured him, closing her eyes and puckering her lips. She leaned in and—

"He asked if I could put in a good word with Autumn and

maybe even give him her number. He said he could barely speak when he was around her, then had the gall to ask me if I understood."

Oh, Summer had understood. It was the same tongue-tied syndrome that had afflicted her everything when she was within breathing distance of Daryl. He had the same affliction it seemed—just for her identical twin sister.

"Did you give it to him?"

She felt her cheeks heat like a beacon in the dark night. "That's the sad thing, I did. I even told Autumn she should go for him."

Wes reached out with his feet and wrapped them around Summer's waist, drawing her closer. She rested her arms on his calves and held on for support. Her heart nearly exploded in her chest from the building emotions. "Do you mind if I ask—why?"

Normally she would mind. It wasn't fun replaying one of the humiliating times of her life, but for some reason she shook her head. "It's like I'm hardwired to please. I'd rather take one on the chin than make a situation more uncomfortable."

"Is that why you didn't really say what was on your mind at dinner?"

She looked away. "What do you mean?"

"Randy's impulsive and idiotic decision to buy a house."

"You think it's dumb too?" she asked, a giddy feeling zinging through her body at not being the only one to see reason.

"I think it's ludicrous. They've known each other a month—maybe. Randy and I have just taken over our father's business and we have a deadline to meet or we lose—"

He stopped short, as if he'd said something he regretted.

"Or you'll lose what?"

He ran a hand down his face and worried his fingers through his hair. "I can't believe I'm going to tell you this. I signed a fucking NDA, and telling you, my competitor, could cost me everything."

"Not only am I a good listener, I am also like a vault with information. And I'd never use something told in confidence to sink your business. That's not who I am."

"That's hard for me to understand, because I'd use any means necessary to make the company successful. But for some reason I believe you."

What a sad life he must have to be so afraid to trust. "I don't want to make you do anything you'd regret."

He seemed relieved for letting him off the hook even though her insides were screaming at her because she wanted to know what was weighing this Adonis down.

"Let's just say that we have a deadline to reach as per my father's demand, and Randy is acting like we're kids again playing Monopoly. Not that he knows the real stakes, again as per my father's demands."

She used his feet to scooch closer and his ankles relocked around her ribs. Her very naked ribs. "That sounds lonely and stressful."

All this time she'd only been thinking about her business needs. Never once had she considered that he might be in a similar situation, to save his family's company. Or that her antics were making his life impossible. From holding a town hall meeting to stop construction of his shop, to supergluing his front door to his building shut, she'd pulled out all the stops. In comparison, his retaliation had been warranted.

Whoa, wait! How had he gone from villain to valiant in a single conversation? While she wanted to understand where he was coming from, really get to know him on a deeper level, that would be a bad decision. She was already softening on him, and she didn't need positive feelings floating between them.

"Don't you worry about me, love. There isn't much I can't handle."

But why should he be forced to handle it alone? She couldn't imagine navigating life without the support of her family. She shouldn't be moved by this confession; it pulled her into dangerous waters. But the intimate setting of them, all alone, the night surrounding them, creating a safe and private exchange of secrets for only the two of them to witness. It made everything feel real.

No longer were they stuck in the tit-for-tat war that was safe and familiar, a protective wall between them and their attraction for each other. His confession had broken down that wall, at least low enough for her to see over it to the man he hid from the world. A sad and lonely man who didn't have it in him to trust or love. Something she needed to remember if she were to keep her heart safe. Which was the only reason she could come up with for what she did next.

She raised her hand out of the water. "Can you help me out?"

His eyes heated because he knew that she was almost naked under the surface. "As you wish."

The moment they grabbed each other's hand, Summer tugged—hard. Caught off guard, Wes went splashing into the water headfirst, leaving a ginormous wave in his path that engulfed Summer right along with him. She swam to the surface, but something—or someone—grabbed her leg and yanked her to the side. She tried to swim away but it was no use, he was bigger and stronger. When she finally crested the surface she was laughing and choking.

"You think you're funny?" he asked with a big and beautiful smile on his face.

"I know I'm funny." She cupped her hands and forced a giant splash in his direction, plastering his hair to his head and causing him to cough up water. He returned the favor by grabbing her waist and pulling her toward him and then back under.

She put her feet on his egg-crate abs and launched herself off like he was the pool wall. She made it less than an arm's length before he caught her ankle and pulled her back to him. He was so strong that she crashed into his body, chest to chest, thigh to thigh, their legs tangling as they struggled to stay afloat.

Then they just stopped kicking and began to float under the water. She opened her eyes and found him staring at her so intensely that some air bubbles escaped from her lips.

Neither moved as they sank deeper, interwoven like a pile of fishing lines. His hand went possessive around her waist and pulled her into his body, then he rested his forehead to hers.

They remained like that, arms around each other, bodies pressed together, foreheads touching, eyes locked. Even though they were both running short on air, neither of them made for the top—instead sinking until they touched the river bottom. The sand slid through her toes, his hand slid further around her waist. Intimate but not crossing that threshold. She wrapped her legs around him as he sat on the river bottom, with her straddling him.

Then it happened. The one thing she'd promised herself she wouldn't do—she kissed him. It was gentle, almost asking for permission. Then he was kissing her like he'd known this would happen and he'd just been waiting.

His lips cradled hers over, slow and thorough. He tasted salty and dangerous. He felt even better. His body was hard and muscular. And speaking of hard, his erection pressed from the V between her legs all the way to her belly button. His hands, oh his magical hands, were rubbing ever so slowly down her spine, his thumbs pressing deep into the tissue as he went.

She wasn't sure where he was going to stop, but he moved purposefully over the slope of her lower back and down her ass, his thumbs traveling under the lace of her thong, tracing the crease of her backside.

She moaned into his mouth as he palmed a cheek in each hand and yanked her against his hard-on. She locked her ankles behind his back to keep the delicious friction between them.

One minute in his arms and she was reaching orgasmic levels.

That's how she sat until the oxygen ran out and her lungs were burning for release—and that wasn't the only part of her burning for release. She was so lost in him that she didn't realize he'd pushed off the ground until they breached the surface like a submarine after months of being kept in the dark.

Instinctively, they both gasped for air.

"What was that?" she asked, her voice sex-hazed.

"You kissing me."

"You kissed me back," she argued.

He cupped her cheek. "I was giving you the perfect meet-cute."

"So that was a pity kiss?" Her tone was sharp.

"Pity kiss?" he asked on a laugh. "Love, I've been thinking about you nonstop for months. What you'd feel like, taste like. How it would be to have you moan into my mouth. That was no fucking pity kiss. That was months of built-up sexual tension."

"It's building by the moment," she whispered, locking her arms behind his neck. "I'm sorry about your suit."

He chuckled. "No, you're not."

"No, I'm not," she agreed. "It's nice to see you rumpled and human-like."

His eyes implored her to understand. Really hear what he was saying. "I am human, love. I might come across indestructible, but beneath the walls is a guy who is scared to death to see what the right person can uncover."

He said it as if she were the right person. Like she made him vulnerable in a way that others had not. But hadn't he been engaged?

"That goes both ways," she admitted.

"Good to know." He kissed her nose and disentangled them and started swimming to the ladder. He hoisted himself up and was on the dock in one fluid masculine move.

"Then where are you going?" she asked, wanting him to come back and finish what he'd started. "Don't you want to finish?"

"Love, ten minutes ago you wanted me out of your house. Now you want me inside of your body. You're sending off mixed signals. Plus, I don't argue well when my dick is this hard. So before we go there, I'm going to catalog what happened for later tonight, then be on my merry way."

"You're just going to leave me like this." Hot. Pent-up desire coursing through her and making her lightheaded.

"I'm leaving before I somehow turn this meet-cute into a meet-ugly."

Her body cooled faster than a cryogenics tank and she was back to boiling mad. "So this was a game to you?"

"You're the one demanding there be winners and losers at every turn. That sounds like a game to me."

"Well, don't worry, this particular game will never be played again."

He shook his head, and drops of water showered the wooden planks, and she couldn't help but appreciate the way his clothes clung to his body, showing off a massive tent in his slacks.

He laughed. "That's what I thought."

And before she could get in the last word, he was strolling up the dock and into the darkness, and for some stupid reason she found herself smiling.

Chapter 14

THE WISE OLD MAN

Wes had managed to sneak into the house undetected, showered, and now he was lying on a lumpy couch that was a few inches too narrow and two feet too short for him. It was well after midnight and he was still wide awake. So was his dick.

The memory of Summer's tits pressed up against his chest while her tongue was down his throat was fresh in his mind. That kiss had made him feel more alive than he'd felt in years—more confused as well. This destructive attraction could only lead to disaster. Yet, instead of heading home to strategize his grand opening, which was the smart thing to do, he was lying on an uncomfortable couch strategizing ways to stay. Not just stay, but be asked to stay. Which made no sense.

He had an entire empire depending on him and all he could think about was Summer and the way she'd opened up to him earlier. The way she'd looked when she'd been laughing. How free he'd felt when she kissed him. It had taken everything he'd had to walk away, but he didn't want to be another Daryl or Dog Boy—another failed meet-cute. He'd rather wonder for the rest of his life what sex with Summer would be like than be another disappointment. And he knew deep down that if he'd stayed even a second longer they'd have had sex. Just like he knew that if they did she'd regret it, and he refused to be another regret to another person—especially her.

He wasn't looking for a relationship, but he was looking for more than a hormone-charged quickie. Wes didn't mind being a pain in her ass, but he refused to be just a distraction from what had become a shitty day for her.

More importantly, he wanted to change her mind about him. He wanted a second chance to make a first impression. Bottom line, he wanted her.

Wes punched the pillow and turned over, nearly falling off the couch. He was just getting settled when the hall light clicked on. He squinted and saw a shadow emerge and something akin to giddiness bubbled up in his stomach. Was she actually coming to him? Was she there to open up, talk about earlier, and admit she liked him as much as he liked her? His dick sure hoped so, since it happened to be his copilot whenever she was around.

"Summer?" he whispered.

"Sorry to disappoint," a distinctively male voice said. "It's just me."

"Me" turned out to be Summer's father. Frank was dressed in flannel pajamas. His white hair was sticking up like a Q-tip and he had a knitting bag under his arm, complete with knitting needles and yarn sticking out the top.

Behind him was a potato with legs, snorting with every step she took.

Wes sat up and rubbed his eyes to be sure he was seeing what he was seeing, but no matter how many times he blinked, Frank was still there. The older man took a seat in the recliner and pulled out his knitting. Buttercup collapsed like she'd run a marathon, then farted.

Maybe he hadn't been as stealthy as he'd assumed and this

was the whole "What are your intentions with my daughter" speech. Or maybe Frank knew about the bet and was there to ask Wes to leave in the morning as per the terms.

"Did I wake you?" Wes asked.

"No, I did this to myself," Frank said. "I forgot my CPAP machine at home, and my snoring woke Blanche so I'm couch-bound for the rest of the week. What's your excuse?"

"I got kicked out too, but for being an ass."

Frank chuckled and pushed back in the recliner. "We've all been there, son. At least you're self-aware enough at your age to admit when you're in the wrong. It took me forty years to admit that."

Wes wasn't admitting he was in the wrong, he was just admitting that there was a better way to handle the situation than poke the bear. But damn she was sexy when they went toe to toe. No one, and he meant no one, ever took him on. His life was full of "yes sir" people, and it was refreshing, and infuriating, to have someone call him on his shit.

"You could go back in and apologize," Frank suggested. And without blinking he pulled out what appeared to be a doll from his Mary Poppins bag.

"No, we rock-paper-scissored, and I lost."

"Guess no one warned you that Summer is the row-sham-bow champ of the family. Girl has this intuitive nature about her."

Wes didn't have to be told twice. He had already surmised that. "Normally I'm the champ."

Frank picked up the needles and started weaving in and out like a knitting champion. "Sometimes winning can be really lonely."

Didn't he know it. When it came to business, Wes put winning above everything. He didn't understand the inner workings of relationships, but he knew how to win. So that's what he did. Put everything on the line for the bottom line.

"In my world, winning is the only acceptable outcome."

"I used to think that until my need to win hurt the people closest to me." *Just like you're hurting my daughter* hung unspoken in the air.

Wes ran a hand through his hair. "I'm not doing anything to your daughter. I'm just doing what needs to be done to make my dad's business a success."

Frank went quiet, as if formulating his response. The longer the silence stretched on, the more anxious Wes became.

Finally, he said, "I know men like your father. They're very difficult to please."

Wes snorted. "Difficult is an understatement."

"Then why are you doing this?"

He was leery of responding and preferred to keep everything close to the vest. But there was something about this guy, like Summer, that made him want to open up. And here Summer was afraid that Randy was a bad influence on her sister. It was Summer who was a bad influence on Wes.

He'd wanted that kiss and he'd gotten it. Only after he'd told her damning things about himself that could be used against him.

"I'm doing it for Randy."

"Family is a good reason."

Wes was surprised by how affected he was by the old man's approval. He'd stopped seeking approval from people a long time ago. But to be handed it without seeking it released a complicated knot of emotions in his gut. Wes didn't have a lot of experience with father-son relationships, but if he had, he'd imagine this was what a good one would feel like.

"But is it the only reason?" Frank asked.

"Does it matter?"

Wes was the only one in the company who could pull off this opening, who had the skills to do it, and so he did what needed to be done. There was no way he'd admit the real reasons—not to himself or anyone.

"Reasons always matter."

Summer was right and he didn't know jack shit about relationships. He was all business, but that clearly wasn't translating well into his personal connections. But Frank seemed to be able to balance both.

"You appear to be at a crossroads. I've been told that I'm a very good listener," Frank said.

And for the second time that night Wes found himself saying things he shouldn't be saying. Breaking an NDA to seek advice from a man who probably made less in a year than Wes made in a week.

"What Randy doesn't know is that there's a stipulation to the will. If we don't grow the business within the fiscal year and open the Ridgefield location on time, then the board takes over. We only have a few months left. I don't give two shits about my dad's approval, but Randy still does and I don't want him to come to the realization that our old man cared more for his company than his sons."

"In my personal experience, I have found that the line between business and family is a tricky one."

"You seem to have it figured out."

Frank chuckled and put the knitting down. "Son, I put my family through hell. Two bankruptcies, and even lost the family home."

Wes didn't know what to say. His fiancée hadn't even managed a long-distance relationship with him, while Blanche had stuck it out through two bankruptcies and they were still madly in love.

"What happened?" Wes asked.

"I was a mom-and-pop minnow who got gobbled up by the big sharks. All it took was a chain store opening in my county and we were out of business in under a year."

Is that how Summer viewed him? As the shark waiting for a vulnerable moment to attack? It wouldn't be surprising, since that was how he'd acted from the first time they'd met.

"I should have tightened the belt, but instead I tried to compete and doubled down on equipment and lost," Frank went on. "I imagine that Summer feels like she's going to relive that moment again. She's so afraid to fail financially."

"She knows how to put on a brave face and put up a good fight."

A knowing smile crossed Frank's face, and Wes wanted to ask him what he was seeing that Wes was clearly missing. "Summer is usually the peacemaker. Funny that."

Yeah, funny that.

"Well, she has it in for me," he said with a smile of his own.

"Then maybe you should ask her why. You might be surprised at what she says." Frank's voice lowered. "Did she tell you that her shop once belonged to her grandmother, then Blanche, and now it's Summer's?"

"I think I learned that somewhere along the way."

"That's three generations of devotion. Three generations of determination. And three generations of pressure to make it a success."

Wes could relate to that. But he had a billion-dollar net to catch him if he fell. Financially, Summer had herself.

"If the shop closes, she wouldn't look at it like a learning experience, she'd look at it like she'd failed her grandmother and her mother. There's a lot going on in her mind and her life—hardships that she rarely shares. It might be nice for her to get some of it off her chest with someone she isn't afraid to piss off."

"Are you suggesting that I offer to become her verbal punching bag?" The thought of that wasn't as unappealing as it should be.

"Maybe start with being her friend," Frank said.

"I imagine I'm the last person Summer would want to be friends with." Although earlier that evening they'd been friendly. More than friendly. And he wasn't just talking about that kiss. They'd exchanged secrets that felt more intimate than sex.

God, sex. Instead of sleeping on the couch he could have been making love to Summer in her bed. Only he'd walked away. More like ran, because he'd been scared of the emotions she'd stirred up inside him.

And why was he thinking about sex with Summer when he was sitting three feet from her father? Because she made him lose all common sense.

"May I ask you something?"

"Shoot," Wes said. After years of raising capital, running

companies, and being interviewed, there weren't many questions that could stump him.

"How do you feel about my daughter?"

His pulse thundered because he was, indeed, stumped. How did he feel about Summer? When they were arguing she drove him nuts, but when they were still, sharing space and stories, she evoked feelings he hadn't felt since his grandmother was alive.

He didn't mind going toe to toe with her, but got angry when other people did. She was bad for business, but he couldn't imagine her anywhere else than behind the counter at her bookstore.

"My honest answer is that it's complicated."

"Well, before you go any further, you might want to figure it out, because Summer is exactly what she seems—a hopeless romantic who believes in true love and sees the good in people. She loves with all her heart and isn't afraid to be vulnerable. But she's had the rug pulled out from under her so many times that I fear once more and she'll lose that part of herself."

"Just because I might have feelings for your daughter doesn't mean I'm pursuing her," Wes said, and they both knew it was a lie. "I believe love can be a weakness, and most people are in it for themselves. I am the last person she'd want to be in a relationship with."

That didn't mean that there wasn't this pull between them that was getting harder to ignore.

"I saw the way you looked at her at dinner. You tipped the bet in her favor and took the loss because you could see how upset she was that she hadn't impressed her family."

"It was a silly competition."

"To Summer, it was a way to honor her family's love of food."

"Then why did they vote for me knowing that it would hurt her?"

"Our family always listen to one another, but some of us have a hard time actually hearing what the others are saying. And when you have someone like Summer, who keeps everything close to her chest, it's easy to forget just how sensitive she is. She feels things differently than the rest of us. Deeper and more intense. Her ability to love is greater than anyone I've ever met."

"Which can be used against her."

"Strange, I see it as a strength. And maybe if you open yourself up you'd start to see it that way too."

"How do you suggest I do that?"

"With the women in this family, it's one button at a time," Frank said. "Now, we going to row-sham-bow for the couch or what?"

Chapter 15

I WANT YOU BUT
I CAN'T HAVE YOU

Wes wasn't going to make a senior citizen sleep in a chair, which left two options: sleep on the hard floor or bunk with Summer. Neither choice was optimal, and one had the possibility to cause more trouble than the other, but the decision was easy.

I must be a masochist, he thought, as he walked up the steps. Then again last night he'd achieved zero sleep on the too-short, too-lumpy couch.

The lights were off but there was a soft glow from a phone coming from the bottom bunk. The faint shine illuminated her face, which was scrunched up in complete concentration. He didn't think she even knew he was there.

Without moving an inch, her eyes shot up and narrowed directly in on him. "What are you doing?"

"Seems your dad is in the doghouse too."

"That sounds like a you problem."

"Now it's an us problem, because your family has some kind of weird talent for rock-paper-scissors."

He walked in and kicked the door shut behind him. Knowing it would piss her off no end, he tossed his pillow and blanket on the bottom bunk—her bunk.

Fast as lightning she wadded it up and threw it in his face.

"Is this your way of saying you want a pillow fight?" he asked. "PJs or not? I'm open to either."

"You wish. And this"—she pointed between them—"is not happening."

"Strong words from someone who almost 'happened' just a few hours ago."

"It was the wine," she lied. "I wasn't clear-headed."

"You hadn't drunk since before dinner."

"Maybe I had some down on the dock," she challenged.

"Did you?" He flashed his trademark smile that had a ninety-nine percent chance of her panties hitting the floor. She appeared completely unaffected.

"No," she begrudgingly said. "And that . . ."—she pointed to his smile—"doesn't work on me, so you might want to save yourself the time and give up now."

He took a few steps closer, and both of their phones chimed. She rolled her eyes.

"Someone thinks we're a perfect match?"

"A stupid algorithm says that. And my mother told me to never trust an algorithm with sketchy intentions. They'll always disappoint in the end."

"I don't disappoint, love. I can give you a list of references if you'd like." She ignored this and went back to studying her phone. "You might think that it's a stupid algorithm, but I noticed you have yet to delete the app."

"Neither have you."

"I just like to see the way your face scrunches every time it goes off. But if it offends you so much, here."

He reached for her phone and she clutched it to her chest.

Whatever was on her screen, she didn't want him to see. Which made it all the more interesting. "What's wrong, love? Were you looking at my profile?"

She scoffed.

"Then what?" He reached for it again, and again she dodged. "Stalking me online?" This time when he reached for it, he snatched it. They struggled for a moment, then he wrestled it from her hands.

He looked at the screen and froze. What the actual fuck? She was cyber-stalking someone. Just not him. "Why do you have Randy's Instagram page up?"

"None of your business." She snatched it back and then sat on it.

Like hell it wasn't his business. They'd just played tonsil hockey earlier that night. Had she been thinking about his brother? "Why are you scrolling through Randy's stuff?"

"Not that I owe you any explanation, but I can see where your mind if going and it's a hard no. I'm stalking him for Autumn."

"Why would Autumn ask you to look into my brother?" he asked and her cheeks went red. She didn't answer. "Summer?"

"I was trying to find out what kind of man buys a house for someone they've known for a month."

Wes had been thinking the same thing all night, but he didn't want her to know that. "Maybe a man in love?"

"Or a serial proposer. That's who. Did you know your brother has been engaged before?"

"Yes."

"Twice?"

"Well, it seems like Autumn might be in it because he's

also the kind of guy who buys a woman a house a month after knowing her. So if anyone should hire a PI, it should be me."

"My sister would never marry for money!"

He laughed. Summer lived with her head in a book and thought the best of everyone. Except, of course, if their surname was Kingston. "Everyone has their price."

"So the second fiancée was a gold digger too? How convenient to blame the women when the common dominator is a man."

Wes didn't know what to say because he'd never known there was another fiancée. What did that say about him? That he didn't even know his kid brother had been a breath away from marriage *twice*. With an ocean between them, and only summers and DNA connecting them, they'd never been all that close, but he'd thought their relationship had been worthy of a call about something as important as marriage. That the engagement hadn't lasted wasn't the point. He'd been left out of a huge moment. He wasn't sure why he was so surprised—that pretty much summed up his childhood—but a rusty and forgotten pinch started in his chest.

He tried to bury his disappointment but, intuitive as ever, Summer picked up on his emotions.

"You didn't know?" she said softly.

"Like I said before, Randy and I are getting to know each other properly. We've been in touch over the years. Birthday calls and such, but not close. It wasn't a possibility when my father was alive but with him out of the picture . . ." He lifted a shoulder and let it fall. "Who knows?"

"So you really want to stay for him?"

"Yes." That was part of the reason. The other part was looking at him with tangled bedhead, glasses perched on her nose, and so much compassion on her face it was hard to maintain eye contact.

"Then I won't let our personal issues get in the way. As long as you promise me something."

"Anything" popped out before he could stop it.

"If you discover Randy has even an inkling of cold feet, you tell me." Disappointment flooded him that the favor had nothing to do with him. "I don't want her to give up her home, her job—heck, her life—and move to New York only to be left with nothing."

"As long as you promise to give my family a fair chance."

"Deal," she said, and he grinned because Wes was part of the Kingston family, which meant she was willing to give him a chance too. At what? He didn't know. But he was giddy all the same.

"Now, scoot over."

"I said I would give you a chance, not that we'd sleep together."

"It's the only free bed in the house. You wouldn't expect me to sleep on the floor next to your dad and his snoring, would you?"

She grimaced and he saw the first crack form. "Sleep in the recliner."

He lifted a brow. "Love, I'm six foot three. That would look like a preschool seat with me in it."

She snickered, as if she'd like to see that sometime.

"And your aunt and uncle don't strike me as the throuple type, which leaves here."

"Fine, but you get the top bunk."

"Again, six-foot-three."

He tossed his pillow and blanket on the other side of her and started to crawl over.

"What are you doing?" She was batting at his head, his shoulders, his jaw, anywhere her hands could swat.

He rolled over her completely and made a big show of getting comfortable before lying down.

"Nope. Not happening." She shoved him but he didn't budge. "You are not sleeping there."

"Okay."

He rolled back over her making sure all their good parts lined up, and held still for a moment until her breath caught, then he shoved her into the depths of the bed, with him on the outside, stretched out and taking up most the mattress.

"What are you doing?"

"Making myself comfortable."

She shoved at him and again he didn't budge. She growled. "This isn't even your room. Look at the nameplate."

In the moonlight he could see, hung on the door was a chalkboard, with SUMMER & AUTUMN scribbled in bubble lettered chalk. He climbed out of bed, walked casually over to the sign, then simply erased AUTUMN and wrote ASSHOLE.

It was barely there, but he saw it. The slightest ghost of a smile tilted her lips. Which amused him.

"My dad made it really clear no boys in the bedroom after dark."

"Funny, because your dad told me to come stand my ground."

She leaned back against the headboard and crossed her

arms, which told him that she was a) pissed, b) not wearing a bra, and c) closer to caving than kicking him in the nuts.

"This is the hill you want to die on?"

"No, but this is the bed I'm going to sleep on, and since I'm a big guy there's no way I'll fit up top."

"Well, the floor looks nice."

"Scooch." He shoved her by the shoulders and she rolled over. He took the now-empty space and sprawled back out. "Be sure to keep your hands to yourself."

"It won't be a problem. Trust me."

"You do realize you're on the inside, which makes you the small spoon."

"I don't spoon."

"But do you fork?"

~

Summer woke up all tingly. From her fingertips to her toes and everywhere in between. It didn't take long to figure out why. She was wrapped around a hard, delicious, jerk of a man. He was fast asleep on his back and she had one thigh thrown over his, and her right hand was a scant inch from what appeared to be a massive top-of-the-morning-to-you.

His breathing was deep and steady, the breath of a sleeping man—thank god! If he saw the way she was full on *groping* him, he'd never let her live it down. It would erase any advantage she had in this bookstore war of theirs.

Remember, he's going to put you out of business.

But he is so freaking hot!

Hot-headed is more like it.

And entitled.

And prideful.

And sweet when he's vulnerable.

Irritating when he was breathing in your space.

But right now, they were sharing the same breath of space and she wasn't irritated. She was—ohmygod! She was turned on. Like tingles and flutters and little vibrations in her southern region. It felt exactly how she imagined one of the heroines in a romance book feeling.

She chanced a quick glance that turned into a string of inappropriate sneak peeks. Who could blame her? Even through his T-shirt she could see the ropes of sinew and muscle. His long lashes fell on his cheek and his lips were full and kissable. And the stubble that defined his already defined jawline made her fingers itch to run their way through it.

Then there was the way he smelled. Spicy and adventurous, like buttery leather and the *Kama Sutra*. Without moving much, Summer nuzzled her nose against his chest and sniffed him. And those flutters flitted awfully close to foreplay. Just one more sniff, then she'd sneak out of bed and take a cold shower. Or maybe a hot one, and think about him while she found some much-needed release.

First, she had to find a way to detangle herself, then crawl over him, and slip out of bed without waking him. She took in one last sniff and closed her eyes, because he also smelled like every woman's walking sex fantasy.

She removed her leg first and he didn't budge. His breathing was still so rhythmic and reliable she nearly jumped out of her skin when he said, "Did you just smell me?"

"No!"

"Then what were you doing?"

"Welcoming the morning with a yawn. You just happened to be there."

He chuckled in a raspy, sleep-rough voice that made her panties wet. "And your hand? Is that headed to my kind of good morning? I mean, another inch and you're at the promised land."

"It's not my fault you pulled me on top of you in the middle of the night."

"Love, your hands are cupping me like you own me and mine are tucked respectfully behind my head."

How horrifying. He was right! In fact, he wasn't touching her at all. She was the one instigating the cuddle. She jerked her hands back and sat up so fast she banged her head against the underside of the top bunk.

"Ow." She cradled her head.

Eyes closed, chin to her chest, she held her injured head in her palms.

"You okay?"—his tone one of genuine concern. "That sounded bad."

Her pride had taken the biggest hit. Summer had a hard head. But then she felt his fingers slip into her hair, and she really played up the bonk. With a sigh she let her head fall back onto his strong shoulder.

"There we go. Isn't that better?"

It was his voice, that I-am-a-sex-god-and-you-want-me tone that drove her nuts. She turned around and batted him. "Get your hands off me."

"You're the one clinging to me a like I'm a stripper pole. Plus you were the one who had the sex dream about us."

"I did not." But she totally had. And the heated cheeks were proof for all to see.

"You said my name," he pointed out.

"Because I was smothering you with a pillow."

"But you moaned."

"In your dreams."

"That was your dream, love. But I'm game for swapping our dream stories. Mine starts with you in those sexy librarian glasses, those mile-high heels you always wear, and nothing else."

"You're wrong about all of this."

"Your nipples seem to disagree. And what did we say about lying?"

She smacked him. "Get out of my bed."

"Ladies first."

She realized she was in nothing but a short T-shirt and a thong. "A gentleman would let the lady choose."

"You did choose. You chose to go pants-less to bed. Plus, it's more than I saw you wearing when you were changing. Hell, or at the shop. Is this becoming *our* thing?"

Refusing to let him make her uncomfortable in her own room, she threw back the covers. "Get over yourself!"

She rolled over him and he gave her butt a little pat, which sent a zing of unwanted interest up her spine. She crawled out of bed so fast she nearly fell, then she stormed off to the bathroom acutely aware of the weight of his stare. She closed the door and sank against it, equal parts pissed off and turned on because she'd caught a silly glimpse of his not-so-silly, impressive morning glory.

She knew he felt something toward her, but she wasn't

sure what that was anymore or what side of the hate-to-love equation his feelings fell. Even worse, her treacherous hormones seemed to be switching sides with each encounter.

Chapter 16

ENEMIES TO
FRENEMIES

Overtly aware of Wes in bed—*her* bed—on the other side of the door, she opted for a cold shower, which did nothing to ease her problem. With a quick rinse and dry, she pulled her hair in a high ponytail, threw on her running outfit, and released a sigh of relief when she opened the door of the bathroom to find the room empty.

Grabbing her running shoes, she went into the kitchen, where the family was gathered around the table. Upon her entrance the room went silent, and every eyeball turned her way.

As the silence grew, dual chimes from the RoChance app on their phones signaled that there was a soulmate in the surrounding area. She felt Wes's grin zero in on her.

"Good morning," she said with the sunniest smile, meeting everyone's gaze except for one. "How did everyone sleep?"

"Like a baby," Wes said. "Dreamt all night and straight through the morning. Care to know what I dreamt about?"

She ignored this. "Anyone else? Mom?"

"Lonely," Blanche said with a dramatic pout in Frank's direction. He took his wife's hand and brushed a kiss across her knuckles.

"I'm sorry about the CPAP machine."

"You've already apologized. But maybe tonight you can cuddle me while I fall asleep."

Frank smiled the smile of a man deeply in love. "It's a cuddle date."

"Speaking of cuddle dates . . ." Wes said, and Summer narrowed her gaze at him.

"Auntie?" she said while walking to the espresso machine. "How did you sleep?"

"The real question is how did you sleep?" Cecilia asked with an accusatory grin.

There were other grins. All around the table. Amused and aimed at her. "Look, I don't know what he told you, but we only slept together—"

"He didn't tell us a thing, but this is juicy news," Blanche said. "Did you use protection? You know that there is always a box of *condoms*," she whispered the last word as if the whole table couldn't hear, "in the medicine cabinet for just such a situation."

"Good to know," Wes mumbled.

"We did not use a condom!"

Frank's expression was one of scolding dad. "Do we need to have the talk again?"

"God no!" Summer took a seat and felt her cheeks turn to flames. "The first time was traumatizing enough. What I meant was we just slept together. *In the same bed.* Nothing happened."

"Well, there was the cuddling," Wes said, ever so helpful.

"Which was an accident. You take up nearly all the bed."

"Like I said, I'm a big guy." He winked.

"It sounds like a happy accident," Blanche said, and Summer could tell she was already picking out their ship-name.

Wummer? No, that rhymed with "Hummer."

Sesley? That was even worse. Sesley rhymed with "What a messily."

Another reason they were incompatible. Their ship-name options were terrible—or accurate. Because this was a messily. In her vulnerable and natural state of mind, instead of repelling him she'd cuddled him. Waking up in his arms wasn't as abominable as she'd imagined. Which was a different problem all together because, if she were being honest with herself, she had imagined how it would feel to wake up next to him. More than once.

It was that stupid, ill-timed, mistake of a kiss. He'd caught her at a vulnerable moment when she'd been thinking of all her past dating mistakes and there he'd been, looking at her like he wanted to devour her.

Well, it wouldn't happen again.

"It was no accident," Auntie Cecilia said. "And Mr. Gentleman over here didn't say a thing. He didn't have to, I already knew." She turned to Wes, pride in her posture. "My guides came through strong this morning. It was no mistake."

Summer dropped her head into her hands. "Can we talk about something else, anything else, before I have at least one cup of coffee in me?"

"Then we can discuss the cuddling?" Wes asked.

A throb started behind her right eye.

Cecilia turned to Wes and became very serious. Third-eye serious. "About your plumbing, dear."

Wes spit out his coffee. "My plumbing?"

"Yes, I need to warn you. You have a, uh, *plumbing problem*," Auntie whispered the last two words, "that will make things difficult. If you know what I mean."

Wes looked at Summer for help, but she left his ass hanging in the wind. Even snorted out loud.

"My plumbing is just fine. I assure you," Wes said, sounding ever so the head of a billion-dollar company.

Cecilia stared off into the distance and began to hum. Her gaze went hazy and then, just like that, she was back to earth. "My guides say differently. But plumbing isn't really breakfast talk, now, is it?"

Summer reached for a doughnut and found a single maple-glazed—her favorite—left on the plate. She went to take a big bite, turning to rub it in Autumn's face, and that's when she noticed her twin was mysteriously absent—on doughnut morning!

"Where's Autumn?" she asked, setting the doughnut down.

There was a silent exchange of glances at the table that made her belly hollow out. "What?"

"She took Buttercup for a walk when she heard you come down the steps," Randy said.

"Family business," Wes whispered to his brother.

"I am family," Randy argued, and the ladies cooed their reassurance. "See, bro."

Summer wasn't sure what Wes's expression meant, but she felt a sudden pinch in her heart. Was he upset that Randy would have a whole new family, a welcoming family that absorbed him into their fold, just as he was reconnecting with his brother?

You okay? she mouthed to Wes.

His response was a barely visible nod, which likely meant he was far from okay. Her first instinct was to reach across the table and take his hand. Reassure him that he wasn't on the outside. That he wouldn't lose his brother. That a heart had the capacity to love many people at once. Then she remembered, *Hummer*. And yes, what a mess indeed.

Then he mouthed, *Are you okay?*

She could have nodded—should have nodded. But she found herself sharing with him another vulnerable moment and shook her head.

Can I help?

Immediately she remembered the steady beat of his heart, the safe vibes that had come off them that morning when they'd snuggled. Strike that: when she'd snuggled. Had he snuggled her back at some point during the night, or had he merely endured the raw affection?

It looked as if he were about to stand, so Summer stretched out her foot so that their toes touched, and she gave him a tap that she was okay. She wasn't sure what surprised her more, that she'd initiated contact again, or that he received it and gave a tap back.

She smiled to let him know he was part of the group and that his concern meant something. His eyes shot to hers and gratefulness flickered in the soft blue depths. He tapped back his thanks. And they sat there for a moment, just like that, with their feet touching and a million words silently passing between them.

"I'm sure Buttercup just needed to use the restroom," her dad said, breaking the hold Wes had on her.

She turned to Frank. "You don't have to lie. I know she's mad at me."

Summer hadn't taken the news well and had ruined her sister's moment. Still, she was taken aback. Her sister had left the room on doughnut morning to avoid seeing her. This hadn't happened since they were kids and they'd had an argument over who was the biggest Shawn Mendes fan. For the record, it was Summer.

"Maybe you should go talk with her," her mother said. "She was pretty upset last night."

"You both were," Wes whispered, and her heart tripped over itself at the verbal support.

"He's right," her dad said, always having her back. "But I think it's time to talk this through."

She thought back to what she'd promised Wes last night— that she'd give his family a chance.

"You're right." Summer grabbed the doughnut and headed out the kitchen door.

It didn't take long to find her sister. Autumn was sitting in their favorite spot, the porch swing, with Buttercup at her feet, panting. The dog couldn't be bothered to lift her head for a hello, but she did wag her tail in greeting.

"Can I sit?" she asked Autumn, who was still in her PJs, which she noticed matched Randy's. "I come bearing gifts." She held out the plate as proof.

"There's a bite taken out of it," Autumn pointed out.

"I got hungry between the kitchen and here," she said, taking a seat and handing over the maple-glazed olive branch. "I saved the rest for you." Her sister didn't budge. "It's the last maple one, you know, and instead of fighting you for it, I'm offering it to you. That's love."

"I guess we can split it," Autumn said. "Since we both said

some hurtful things last night." Autumn put up a hand to her ear, like *I'm ready to hear what you have to say*.

Not getting caught up on why *she* had to go first, Summer took a deep, cleansing breath. "I'm sorry."

"And?"

"And maybe I'm a little jealous because everything comes to you so easy."

"And?" Autumn prodded, but her expression softened slightly.

"Maybe I judged Randy too harshly." Man, that one was hard to say. Especially after she'd found out he was a serial proposer. But now wasn't the time to say anything.

"And?"

"And it is kind of romantic, if you're into grand gestures like that." Summer sighed. "I was wrong to jump to conclusions. I'm really, really sorry. I just don't want to lose you too. First Auntie and Uncle moved to Florida, then Mom and Dad followed, and these past few months you seem to be slipping away too. And now you're moving."

"Possibly moving."

Hope flickered. "What do you mean *possibly?*"

"If you'd given me two seconds to speak for myself, you'd know the answer, but you were so busy trying to be right that you didn't give me a chance to respond. Or use our twinning powers to sus out how I was feeling in that moment."

"I haven't felt twinning this entire trip," Summer admitted quietly.

"Because you're too focused on getting under Wes's skin."

"He gets under my skin, not the other way around."

Autumn lifted a questioning brow. "Why does everything

happen *to* you? You accused me of not making my own decisions, but it seems that life is running you too."

Summer's wrist itched. "What does that mean?"

"No one is asking you to work yourself to death. Between the bookstore and helping Mom and Dad and going on all these meet-cutes that you know will lead nowhere. Where in all that is you standing your ground?"

It reminded her of when Wes had said that he was all logic and she was all emotion. Maybe there could be somewhere in the middle.

"I came here to apologize. How did this get on the topic of Wes?"

"Alright, subject change. What's going on with you and Wes?" Autumn said around a mouthful of doughnut.

"The only thing going on between Wes and me is a war." *And cuddling and kissing.*

"You looked more allies than enemies kayaking, when you were pressed against his sculpted, muscular, wet body."

"I was trying to keep him from drowning."

"And when you announced to the room that you'd slept together you went bright red."

"You weren't even in the room!"

"I heard you out here. As for the blushing, I'm your twin, remember? I feel what you feel, know you better than anyone. I mean, I had to visit RandyLand after that intense interaction last night."

Summer put her fingers in her ears. "RandyLand? Seriously? I can't unhear that."

"So you're saying there is absolutely, positively nothing going on between you two?"

No, she wasn't saying that, because it would be a lie and she didn't lie to her sister. But admitting that they'd kissed *and* snuggled would turn her sister into Autumn the Match Maker. Between her mom, Cleo, and the app, she had enough matchmakers in her life.

"It's complicated. Is he hot? I'd be a liar to say no. But we are mortal enemies. This whole ceasefire thing is temporary."

Autumn waggled a brow. "Temporary could be a lot of fun. And from the confident swagger, I bet he's a fun master."

"Need I remind you that, if things go how you want them to go, he's going to be your brother-in-law."

"Need I remind you that you haven't had any *fun* since Ken. So what if he's your enemy? Angry fun is freaking hot." Autumn gave Summer's shoulder a gentle bump. "And isn't that what this week is all about? Leaving our regular lives behind and having some fun."

Could she do that? Could she be enemies with bennies and then go back to the real world, where one of them would likely lose their dream in order for the other to capture theirs? She wasn't sure.

And the lack of clarity scared her.

Chapter 17

QUIET MOMENTS

Fact. She wasn't wearing a bra.

All she had on beneath the [BOOK-TRO-VERT] * NOUN: A PERSON WHO PREFERS FICTIONAL CHARACTERS TO REAL PEOPLE T-shirt, which hung down to her thighs, was possibly a thong. Possibly.

Since he couldn't prove it one way or the other, he'd go with *completely naked* beneath the soft cotton.

Her hair was in a towel, her face was fresh from makeup, and those silky legs were on delicious display. Then there was the way her breasts moved slightly back and forth seductively, attracting his gaze, as she made her way into the bedroom.

She hadn't spotted him yet. So he allowed himself to really look at her in this unguarded moment, and what he saw took his breath away. How could he be so damn drawn to the woman who picked a fight with him every step of the way?

She didn't pick a fight this morning, he reminded himself. When Randy had so easily identified himself as part of the Russo family, it had been an unexpected hit to the gut. The emotion caused by the sucker punch had been part a sense of loss and part jealousy. He understood the loss. Here he was trying to solidify a relationship with his brother and Randy was already jumping ship. But the jealousy?

Once upon a time, Wes had craved a family. He'd squashed that desire years ago. Then why was he envious of the idea of Randy spending holidays, birthdays, and summer vacations at the beach house with the Russos? Sure, Wes might get an invite here or there, but it would always be as Randy's plus-one. And that gave him heartburn.

Jesus. He ran a hand down his face. One kiss. One talk with her dad. A few days of summer fun. And here he was wishing for things he couldn't have. When this week came to an end, and they went back to their regularly scheduled lives, he wouldn't even be a blip on their family radar. Unless he could change Summer's mind, he'd also go back to being her enemy.

But there had been a shift between them this morning. A gentle coming-together when they were both hurting that had felt surprisingly good. As a rule, Wes didn't rely on the comfort of others because he never knew when it was going to be yanked out from under him. But Summer somehow had this effect on him that he couldn't explain. It wasn't weakness so much as a rightness. He knew she felt it too.

Hell, she'd initiated it. He'd nearly sighed aloud when her toe had nudged his. Then she'd rested her foot side by side with his, showing him support. Validating his feelings without him even understanding what he was feeling.

Like right now, he didn't know what he was feeling. Lust? Like? Both? Certainly not indifferent. Which was why when she took her towel off her head and went to bend over to retie it, he made his presence known.

"Once again I am overdressed," he said amusedly, and she squeaked. "Or is it that you can't keep your clothes on around me?"

Her hands went straight to her bum, and she tugged the hem of her shirt down to her knees. Which only made her tits stand out more.

"What are you doing here?"

"It's bedtime." He patted the mattress next to him and she rolled her eyes. "Just waiting for you to finish up in the loo."

"You could have announced yourself. What kind of knight in shining armor are you?"

"Of course you believe in knights in shining armor. Why am I even surprised. What is it called in that love guide of yours?" He grinned at the idea that she'd call it a guide. As if finding love were as easy as following a few simple steps. "An imperfectly perfect meet-cute?"

"It's not enough for you that I'm physically vulnerable, you have to make me emotionally vulnerable? And this is not a meet-cute. This is the opposite. This is a meet-ugly."

He looked around the room and then back to her. "I don't know. The moon is full, the night alive with the sound of water gently rushing over river rock, and we've just had a chance encounter where the hero finds the heroine fresh from the shower, in nothing but an old shirt. Sounds like a meet-cute to me."

"What do you even know about meet-cutes?"

"According to the *Cupid's Guide to Love*, we've shared several meet-cutes."

"You've read my guide? That's personal!"

"Then you might not want to leave it open on the bedside table."

"I would say a gentleman wouldn't snoop, but then again a gentleman also wouldn't steal a woman's bed."

"I'm not stealing. You have a whole half to yourself." He gave it another pat.

"Nope, tonight I'm sleeping on the top bunk."

She angrily flicked off the light, which only made it more intimate. The moonlight shining through the slit in the blinds illuminated her form—every curve and athletic inch. The way the light caught her eyes, it made them look like tumblers of whisky.

He watched as she strode across the room. She paused at the bed as if deciding what to do, and his heart stopped dead in his chest. He was thrown by how much he wanted her in his arms again. Because she didn't know it, but he'd held her all night and it had been amazing. Her body had nuzzled against his, relaxed and missing the usual tension she carried from all the stress she took on for herself and her family. He no longer liked being a part of that stress.

"I'll sleep up top," he offered, standing.

"No, you're right. You're too big for the top bunk."

"I don't mind sharing. Unless you're afraid you'll move from spooning to forking?"

He expected her to snort and blow it off; instead she looked thoughtful for a moment and said, "Yes. And can we leave it at that?"

His voice was rough when he said, "Yes." Although the last thing he wanted was to stop talking now that she was opening up. She'd done her best to avoid him today by going on walks with Buttercup and reading down at the beach, but he'd been hyper-aware of her since their game of footsie.

He watched her shadow gracefully walk up the ladder and heard the mattress sink as she lay down. Breathed deeply as the scent of her shampoo drifted between the mattresses, and strained his ears, waiting for her to speak. But she didn't.

An intense silence blanketed the room, where all they could hear was each other's breathing. The longer it went on the harder his breathing became, until his lungs just gave up. Right when he was about to crack, to ask her about her day, she whispered, "Name one."

He rolled onto his back and stared at the piece of wood that separated them. "One what?"

"A meet-cute."

"Well, when you had my guys' cars ticketed and then I tried to have your car towed. That would be an enemies-to-lovers meet-cute. There was the coincidence of the dating app. And we can't forget the time we both showed up to find the other on their vacation—that would be a serendipitous meet-cute. Then there's the one bed."

"There's two beds, you're just stubborn."

"Fine. The sharing the bed—forced proximity."

"We're not sharing a bed," she said, so quietly he nearly missed it.

"Love, you might be on a different mattress but you know damn well we're sharing a bed."

To his surprise she didn't argue. "Name another one."

"We've got the opposites-attract thing going, and now, this."

Even though he wasn't sure what this was, he was enjoying it. When they bantered her eyes lit up, and her smile was damn beautiful. It didn't hurt that she was in nothing but a T-shirt, but his attraction to her in that moment went way behind the physical.

"You mean the hate-to-love trope?"

He chuckled. "Love, you don't hate me. In fact, I think you might even like me."

"You're dreaming again."

He closed his eyes and smiled. "Maybe I am."

Her answer was silence. Which he gave her. He let her have the space he needed to digest what was happening between them. Another foundation in a romance novel—sharing secrets. He had a secret to share and didn't want to miss the opportunity.

"I want to apologize."

"For what?" she asked.

"I promised to make things easier on you and I've been pushing your buttons."

"You like to push them." The sound of her voice said she wasn't as opposed to his pushing as she was letting on.

"Not when it hurts. When I'm uncomfortable I like to banter but I think you see it as me picking on you. But it's the exact opposite, and I'd never want to hurt you."

"I make you uncomfortable?"

If he was wrong about that then what else was he wrong about. "Love, you scramble my brain."

He could hear her shift onto her side, and scooch to the edge of the mattress so that she was as close to him as she could get without falling off the bed.

"I apologized to Autumn today," she admitted.

"I wanted to ask you how it went but I didn't want to pry."

"She accepted my apology but didn't really apologize back."

"That must have hurt." He knew that kind of hurt. Never once, after all the rejection and neglect, had his father ever

apologized. Wes had overcome it, but Summer was so emotionally in tune with the world around her, such a
people-pleaser—even at the risk of her own heart—he
imagined it must have stung. "Is that normal?"

"Yes, but it never really bothered me until today," she said.
"I realized it's a pattern between us that I don't like. But I
don't know how to fix it. I mean, was I wrong last night?
Shouldn't a couple include the other when doing something
as important as buying a house together? Or at least give
their partner a heads-up before announcing the news at
family breakfast."

"I'd would want my partner with me, but Randy and I are
very different. He's the grand gesture, I'm the steady day-to-
day kind of guy."

"There's nothing wrong with steady."

He took in her words and let them settle. His past girlfriends had complained that he was so stable and steady that
there was no room for impulsiveness. He imagined that after
a while Summer would come to the same conclusion.

"You and Autumn seem to be different in a lot of ways too."

"That's becoming more and more apparent every day. I
just don't want to get lost in the shuffle."

Feeling as if she needed human contact at that moment,
he held his arm up and was surprised when she took his hand.
"I know what that feels like. When Randy was born my dad
lost interest in me. Why dote on a bastard kid when you have
the real thing?"

"I'm not sure how to even respond to that," she admitted,
giving his hand a squeeze. "My dad gave me all the love and
support I needed, and I can't imagine how it would feel to be

robbed of that. It makes me mad that you didn't have the same opportunity to experience love."

He held onto her like she was his lifeline, a deep sense of understanding arching between them through the simple contact of holding hands.

He gave her hand a squeeze. "Did we just go from frenemies to confidants?"

"I don't know. Maybe."

"Isn't that another foundation of a meet-cute: sharing secrets? Who knows? Next you might find yourself kissing me in the river."

"You kissed me," she argued, but her grip on his hand seemed to tighten. "But it doesn't matter who kissed who and who kissed who back, it isn't going to happen again, Wes. We have four days left of this trip, and then we go back to being enemies."

"It doesn't have to be that way."

"Doesn't it?" she whispered. "Right now, it's easy to forget what's waiting for us back home. It's easy to pretend that the kiss wasn't a mistake. But when we get back, I'll still be in the shadows of your behemoth bookstore, and one bad month from closing my doors forever."

"The kiss might not have been planned, but it wasn't a mistake," he said, hoping to god she recanted her statement. That kiss had been one of the best moments of his year. He'd felt more alive, more passionate, more adamant that he was headed in the right direction than at any time since he'd received the call that his father had passed—when he'd been, for the first time, the chosen one, only he hadn't wanted to be chosen. Now, when it came to Summer, deep down in the depths of his soul that he didn't like to acknowledge much, he wanted to be chosen by her.

"Summer, you can't avoid this topic forever. At some point you're going to have to be honest with me. And if I truly was a regret on your part, then I'm sorry. But I don't think that's the truth. And I don't want to talk about it until you can give me the truth."

"Good night, Wes," she said, avoiding the question, but he noticed she didn't let go of his hand straight away.

Chapter 18

FUN AND GAMES

"Do I need a safe word?" Wes asked as Summer zip-tied their wrists together. She wasn't holding his hand, just letting her wrist fall limp. But they were tied together for the next few hours, which meant she couldn't escape a real conversation about that kiss and what it meant.

Like all the Russo women, she was dressed in a thrift-store wedding dress, complete with a train, tiara, and veil. Her shoes were red Converse, her hair in a ponytail that was invented for a man to grab and tug. His hands tingled just looking at the way it exposed the length of her neck. It was shocking how something as simple as a glimpse of a part of her that was usually covered could be a turn-on.

She had her contacts in today, and even though he liked the unobstructed view of her beautiful chocolate eyes, he missed the way her glasses were always perched on her nose, highlighting the smattering of freckles that had grown darker in the sun.

"I don't know, maybe," Summer said, side-eying her sister, who was grinning from ear to ear. "Never in the history of the infamous Russo Selfie Scavenger Hunt have we ever been tied together." She looked pleadingly at her mom. "Is this necessary?"

"Last year, you two won in less than fifteen minutes. We

figured it was time to up the challenge," Blanche said, looking oh-so-innocent.

"Twinning!" Autumn shouted, giving a fist bump to outer space.

"Well, there will be no twinning this year," Summer replied, but Autumn was already engaged in a PG-13 display of affection with her boyfriend. "Just winning, and we're going to kick your butts."

Autumn immediately broke off the game of tonsil hockey and stared Summer down. Her hands went to her waist, which jerked Randy into her. "How do you figure? I always carried you."

Summer's smile faltered a bit, and Wes tilted his head so that his lips were resting near her ear and whispered, "Don't let her fool you. Every win you've ever accomplished has been because you are determined, passionate, and damn impressive. You're one hell of a special woman. You don't need a knight or your sister to fight your battles. You have yourself and you're enough."

She turned her head slowly until their mouths were practically lined up, and met his gaze. Her breath hitched. "You believe that?" she asked, as if none of the other men in her past had bothered to tell her what an amazing woman she was. It made him want to punch her ex in the nuts—Daryl Sanderson too.

"With all my heart."

Her eyes were wide with gratitude and something akin to warmth. "Thank you," she whispered, her gaze dropping to his lips briefly.

"You've got me cuffed, you're in a wedding gown, and

you're staring at me like you want me to kiss you but you can't even hold my hand. I'm getting mixed signals here," he said, quietly so that only she could hear.

"My brain must be misfiring."

Her blush told a different story. "Are you ready to say it yet?"

"I don't know."

"Well, let me know when you are."

"What are you two whispering about?" Autumn teased.

Summer turned to her sister and took a few confrontational steps forward, dragging Wes behind her. "About how we're going to kick your backside! A billion-dollar algorithm says that Wes and I are the perfect match."

"I thought you didn't believe in algorithms?" Wes asked.

"Today I do." She gifted him a smile that lit a fire in his chest. Then she twisted her hands to go palm to palm with his and linked their fingers before pumping their arms in the air. "Bring it, sis."

As if on cue, both of their phones pinged letting them know there was a verified match within the vicinity. Letting them know *they* were a verified match.

Wes was starting to like this app. He also liked the fact that she hadn't deleted hers. Because if she had, she wouldn't have been able to snoop around his profile, which she definitely had. The app told him every part of his profile she'd clicked on. Which had been all of it.

They'd breached a wall last night. Not a physical one, but an emotional one, and he wanted to keep exploring. Oh, he wanted to keep kissing, but that would come in due time.

"All right," Uncle Giuseppe said excitedly. Because he

wrote the clues, he and Cecilia were sitting this one out and acting as referees. "I have your first clue. When you get there, another clue will be waiting. Line up at the start line, and when I finish reading the clue the race will begin. The first team to snap all the pictures will win."

"Ready?" Summer asked, her eyes flickering with a joy and anticipation so contagious that he couldn't help but smile back. He also couldn't help but fall into them for a long moment, and when he surfaced something had shifted in his rib cage.

"Ready," he said back, but somehow his gut told him he wasn't just talking about the race. He was talking about something deeply more important.

Giuseppe cleared his throat and in a booming voice announced, "The first clue is: *Go to the first place you saw the angels and strike a pose.*"

It was as if a shot had rung out. Screaming and giggles erupted from the group, causing passersby to stare. Not that people weren't already staring at the two generations of women in wedding gowns, their skirts pulled up to their shins and running shoes on, in the middle of old-town Mystic.

"A church?" Wes guessed.

"Shhh, and no, the old cinema downtown," she whispered in his ear as if it were a matter of national security. "My dad took us all to see the *Charlie's Angels* movie one summer. Let's go!"

"The new one or the original?"

"You're such a Brit. The original was a show, the movie was with Drew Barrymore and Lucy Liu." She looked at the competition, who was disappearing around the corner, their veils flying like kites behind them.

"No time to jabber. We're not going to lose this time."

She took three steps, then came to a halt because he hadn't moved.

"What are you doing? We're going to lose!" she snapped. He could see the fierce competitiveness in her eyes, flickering like a bonfire with gasoline.

"You want to win? Then admit you kissed me first."

"Are you serious?"

"Deadly." He held his ground. It was bugging him that she was hot then cold. He didn't want to be the mistake. That one word summed up his entire life. First with his dad and being the result of an affair. Then his ex, who'd said that their whole relationship was a mistake. He'd loved her enough to have proposed but everything he'd experienced was clearly one-sided.

She looked at the empty start line and sighed. "Fine. I got swept up in the moment."

"You mean our meet-cute."

"Yes, our meet-cute. And I kissed you. Happy now?"

He took a casual stroll forward. "After you."

She lifted her hand to show the zip ties. "Really?"

He took one big step, which forced her to take two, and said mockingly, "Hurry up or we're going to lose."

It took them a minute or two to find their groove. With the height difference it made for a comical display of her tripping and him hunching down so as not to yank on her arm.

"Why do you have to be so tall?" she grumbled, going in the opposite direction to her family.

"Women usually call me tall, dark and handsome."

"I'm not like other women."

Didn't he know it. And that was part of the problem.

"Do you even know where we're going? You're walking in the wrong direction."

"I'm not the nine-time reigning champion for no reason. I know a shortcut. I know this town inside out," she said with that smile that was as bright as a summer's day.

And that's when Wes realized they were still holding hands, running at a full-on sprint down the Main Street in Mystic. Racing by the brick-faced shops and streetside cafés with brightly colored awnings and hand-painted windows while laughing. Seagull cries mixed with the crashing of waves sounded in the background, and the salt in the air was so thick he could taste it. A cool ocean breeze came in off the water, and excitement pumped through his body in anticipation of what was to come next.

He hadn't felt this free in years, and nor had he had so much fun. The last time he'd felt this connected to a group was when he'd played rugby at university. Since then it had been him and him alone. Even with his ex, he'd felt alone at times. And he'd never noticed until now just how isolating that experience had been. Even if she didn't realize it, Summer was giving him a gift. The gift of companionship. And it felt good.

"In here," she said, pushing open the door of Funky Book Junction. The bell on the door echoed throughout the store as she burst in, dragging him behind her. The scent of aging paper and incense greeted them, reminding him of the used bookstore back home where he'd spent every free hour perusing and reading when the clerk wasn't looking. When he found a special one, he'd save up his money that he'd earn by mowing lawns and splurge. He still had his collection of Harry Potter books. They sat on a shelf behind his desk at his apartment.

"Summer Russo," someone said in a scolding tone. "What have I told you about running through the store? The books aren't going to get up and walk away."

"Sorry, Ms. Louise." Summer slowed to a brisk walk. "It's the annual Russo Selfie Scavenger Hunt, and I'm in it to win it."

"And you have a new partner I see." Two eyes and a gray bun peeked over the counter. "A real-life Prince Humperdinck, it appears."

"More like a Joe Fox," Summer corrected. "An algorithm put us together," she explained, as if that was a normal response.

Ms. Louise came out from behind the counter. She was about as tall as a middle-schooler, built like a fire hydrant, and had apple cheeks. Her muumuu was a shade of green that Wes needed sunglasses to look at, and she had on bright white orthopedic shoes. But that didn't slow her down. She was by their side in a blink, jogging with them into the belly of the shotgun-style shop.

"Where can I get my hands on this algorithm?"

"It's called RoChance, and it connects with matches in your vicinity. Supposedly perfect matches. But they're still working out the glitches." She side-eyed Wes.

"I am not a glitch," he said defensively.

"If you don't want him, I'd be happy to have a fun little glitch after I get off work," Ms. Louise said, looking Wes up and down. "But I'm not looking for strings. Just thought I'd put that out there."

"I'll drop him off after we win the scavenger hunt," Summer said, not slowing down.

"We can trade. I've got something you might be interested in. I found a signed first edition of *Outlander*."

He felt Summer stop in her tracks. "What happened to keeping the pace?" Wes said.

"It's a first edition," she said, sounding conflicted. She looked at Ms. Louise and then at Wes. "What do I do?"

"Are you really going to risk losing for a book?"

"I've been looking for this book since I was sixteen."

"Signed book," Louise said. "And it will walk off the shelves by afternoon. I guarantee it. The Cool Hookers Book Club meets here at three."

"Tick-tock tick-tock," Wes said, tapping his watch.

"Any dog-ears?" Summer asked.

"Not a one."

She looked up at Wes with a helpless and lost expression, and he wanted to be that knight in shining armor. "I'll buy the book. Here's my watch, it's worth a hundred of that book. We'll be back."

"I'll pay you back," she promised, and this time it was him that stopped in his tracks.

Women always accepted gifts from him. Even expected them. But this woman didn't want him for his money or what he could get her. She was holding his hand just because. So she'd called him a glitch, and maybe he was. But around her he felt as if someone had troubleshooted all the bullshit out of his life.

"Let's just get that picture," he said, taking a large step forward and opening the back door for her.

"We'll be back," she said to Ms. Louise. "Don't you dare sell that book!"

The second they cleared the exit she took off like a rocket. "There it is, and Autumn and Randy are already there! Move faster."

"Winning!" Autumn screamed as she snapped the selfie and took off eastbound, down Destiny Boulevard.

By the time they made it to the historic theatre, which had the original vertical CINEMA sign lit up like it was 1961 and *Breakfast at Tiffany's* had just been released, they were both winded and laughing.

"Okay, strike a pose," she said, and they both did their best Charlie's Angels impersonation as he snapped the photo.

"A pretty great meet-cute if you ask me," Wes said when she pocketed her phone. "Boy and girl racing around town, zip-tied together, in a wedding dress and suit, to win a plastic trophy."

"I've read better," she said primly.

He slid his arms around her waist, and damn she felt good there. He was going to have to thank Autumn for the heads-up. He loved seeing Summer off balance, and this zip-tie stunt had definitely thrown Summer off her game.

She was flustered being this close to him, and that brought him a perverse happiness. She was cute when she was flustered. It was as if her body was telling him what her words were not.

She shivered.

"You want to retract that statement?"

"No time, we're off to the next stop. For all we know your false start put us in last. And we are not going to lose to Autumn."

He realized just how important this was for her, and more than ever he wanted to be that guy for her. The guy who crossed the finish line with her. Who held her hand while she found her independence. "We aren't going to lose, love."

That earned him a big smile, so bright and affectionate it warmed him from the inside out. In fact, this whole thing reminded him of earlier times with his nonna, when she'd bring out the board games. They were too broke to go to the movies or other outings. Instead they did board games, puzzles, cards. And he couldn't remember the last time he'd had this kind of fun with someone. Actually, it was the day before he'd left for private school on scholarship. The day he'd walked away from his childhood to become a man his mom could rely on, and break the cycle of poverty.

"Now, the next clue. We have to find it."

"Look up," Wes said, pointing to the marquee. He read, "*See a penny pick it up, and all day long you'll have good luck.*"

She took both of his hands and squealed. "The wishing well! It's just around the corner."

"Well then, we better get going," he said.

With Summer as his tour guide, it took them less than three minutes to locate the fountain. And that was with her pointing out every nook and cranny that she'd spent time at as a kid. He could almost picture her in her pigtails, riding a bike and smiling at every person she passed.

It made Wes wonder what that kind of childhood must have felt like. If the one week they spent here every summer had made up for the hours Frank worked, the bankruptcies, the loss of security. Although the Russos were one of the closest families he'd ever met, he saw the scars in Summer. The ones she tried to keep hidden from her loved ones.

The ones he and his bookstore were bringing back to the surface.

"It's said that when you make an offering to the deities and make a wish with a pure heart, then kiss the penny, that your wish will come true," she explained as they approached the fountain, which was overflowing with pennies.

People's dreams, he realized.

When was the last time he'd allowed himself to dream of something that didn't involve stock options or spreadsheets? It had been so long he wasn't even sure what to wish for. Then he looked down at Summer and knew what he'd wish for.

Another kiss.

He reached into his pockets and came up empty. How ironic was that. He ran a billion-dollar company, drove a car worth more than some people's houses, but when it came to something as simple as a penny for a wishing well he didn't have what was required.

"I don't have a penny," he heard himself say.

"I've got this." She pulled out a handful of pennies from a special coin purse in her fanny pack and he chuckled.

"You come armed with wishes?" Of course she did. She believed in fate and meet-cutes and the kind of love that most people didn't have the capacity to provide. People like him.

"A true romantic is always armed with wish-making powers," she said, as if it were fact. And maybe in her life it was a fact. But not in his.

She placed a penny in his palm, and he wasn't sure what to say. She was slowing down the race to make a wish with him.

"Now kiss it and throw it into the fountain. And don't forget to make a wish."

He did as he was told, even closing his eyes like she had. Then he threw it into the water and watched it disappear into the mosaic of copper and silver. And as if by some magic, his penny landed directly on top of hers.

"Wow," she said. "What are the odds?"

"What are the odds?" he repeated. "What did you wish for?"

She gasped. "That's not how wishes work."

"I'll go first. I wished for my brother and I—"

She pressed her hand over his mouth. "Don't. You'll jinx it. But it's sweet that it's about your brother."

"Did you just call me sweet?" he mumbled against her hand.

"Maybe."

He took another penny, locked eyes with her, and kissed it and tossed it in. She visually swallowed. "What did you wish for?" she asked, breathless.

"That's not how wishes work. And I don't want to jinx this one."

"Now you want to go all quiet on me?"

He cupped her hips and stepped closer, and then raised her hand to his mouth and kissed her fingers. "Sometimes you can speak without saying a single word. The question is, are you listening?"

"Oh my god!" Autumn said, breaking the moment. "How did you get ahead of us? Randy, they're ahead of us! I knew we didn't have time to go to RandyLand."

"There's always time for RandyLand."

Wes grabbed her by the hand. "We're ahead of you because we're going to win. Come on, love. Where to next?"

"Where else but the wedding chapel. It is tradition to end there." She looked down at her dress and smiled. "It's always ends at the place where two generations of love were cemented. Now say cheese!"

⌒

Summer handed Wes a bow tie that was tacked to the wall.

"Let me put this on so we can take the final picture," she said, reaching up and securing the silk around his neck, while his own hand dangled from the zip tie. It brought her so close her scent enveloped him like the salty air, and damn she smelled good. Like hot summer nights and the romance section of a library.

Between fundraisers and formal corporate events, he knew how to tie a bow tie with one hand restrained behind his back, but he would rather pretend not to know so he could get her fingers on him. Interesting, since he never liked to admit that he couldn't do something. But he couldn't seem to get close enough.

"Your hand is in the way," she said, trying to swat it away but finding it difficult since they were tied together.

"What do you suggest? Cutting off my wrist?"

"If it would help, then yes." She looked up at him with a teasing smile. And thrift-store dress or not, she looked beautiful.

"I bet this isn't how you imagined your wedding," Wes

said, looking around the cozy seaside church. Stained-glass windows portraying stories from the Bible spanned twenty feet up the wall from the wainscoting to the ceiling. The pews were few, but made of hand-crafted mahogany. And the A-frame roof made this neighborhood church feel warm and welcoming.

"Why do you say that?" Her hands moved with speed as she looped the silk around itself.

"Well, it's so small. I imagined you'd want a big event, hundreds of people, to pay witness to Cupid's big moment."

"Actually, I want to get married here, where my parents and grandparents did. And I'd want a small beachside reception at the beach house with my family and closest friends."

She was a never-ending surprise. Every woman he'd ever dated looked at weddings like a trophy in order to outdo their friend with the biggest event. On the other hand, this woman wanted to win a dollar-store trophy.

"What about you? I imagine you'd want the fanfare," she said. "A loafer-required event."

He chuckled and her delicate fingers brushed his Adam's apple, which sent a jolt of electricity straight to his groin. "I never got close enough to plan the actual wedding, but my ex wanted the whole shebang."

Still focused on the task, her gaze was on his tie, but he could sense her awareness of their proximity. "To me, love is the whole shebang. I don't need to prove it to anyone except my partner."

"And how would you prove it?" He wanted to know because he'd never had a role model for what healthy love looked like.

"Romance is the everyday nurturing of love."

That made sense, since she was a born nurturer. Not that he was a guy who needed to be nurtured. In fact, he'd built his life around being self-sufficient, created a world where he needed no one. But coming from her, it sounded nice.

"How about you? You and your ex were engaged?"

"We were." But then his company had been struggling, and then his dad had died and he'd been needed in the US, and his fiancée's love apparently didn't allow for being broke or different time zones.

And if that wasn't a bucket of cold water on this situation. Wes was leaving. Maybe not next month, but the plan had always been to open the store in Ridgefield and Los Angeles and then go home and run the company from London. He had no business pursuing anything with this woman who'd already been burned before. He didn't want to be the wash-and-repeat for her.

He'd already caused her enough problems. Problems that could tank her company. Problems that a week ago he didn't give a shit about. But he did now that he knew more about the woman behind the bookstore war.

He was so lost in thought, in the reality of what his business could cost her, he didn't realize that she was done with the tie and staring at him with concern. She gently tugged his hand. "Are you okay?"

He bent at the knees to get her in line of sight. "Actually, no. I wanted to say sorry."

Confusion furrowed her brow. "For what?"

"For all the stress that's waiting for you back home. I know that most of it comes from the fact that I decided to open up my bookstore next to yours," he said quietly.

She took both of his hands. "You didn't know."

That shift behind his rib cage became more prominent.

"We should probably snap the picture," she said, but neither of them moved. They were both too caught up in the moment of youthful freedom and warm summer days. The longer they stood there, the hotter the air between them grew.

She scooted closer and so did he. His thumb was rubbing the inside of her wrist, and she lifted their attached hands and opened her hand so that they were palm to palm and then she laced her fingers between his.

"But I did," he went on, hoping that what he was about to admit didn't ruin all the ground they'd covered in the past few days. "I knew there was a bookshop on the block. I just didn't care."

Instead of anger, her face went soft with uncertainty. "Do you care now?"

"Very much. But I don't know how to fix it."

"That you care is all that matters to me."

He lowered his voice, which came out rough like gravel. "I care."

His eyes flashed to her lips, which was fine because hers were doing the same. But it was the dreamy look in her gaze that stirred up something old and painful in his gut.

He was leaving. Period. And she was staying. Period. And as much as he wanted this to happen, needed it to happen, there was no way this could work. Yet, here they were, dressed like a happily wedded couple, about to seal the deal with a kiss.

He looked at her looking up at him and he could see the warmth in her eyes, and the longing for something real. And if there was one thing Wes wasn't it was the real deal. Not when it came to relationships. His past confirmed that over and over.

"Wes," she whispered, placing a hand on his chest.

"What happened to this being a bad idea?"

"You happened. You've shown me parts of you that I didn't know existed. Parts I connect to."

He placed his hand over hers. "You were right the first time around. This is a bad idea."

Hurt and confusion filled her eyes and he felt like shit. He wanted to say it was him and not her, but just then the doors to the church burst open.

He took a step back.

"Isn't that sweet," Blanche said from the doorway to the church.

"I bet we can be sweeter," Frank said, with so much love in his voice Wes felt like he was watching a moment made for just the two of them. He looked back to Summer, who was looking everywhere but at him.

Frank held out his arm and Blanche took it, and they slowly made their way down the aisle, walking as if they were at their wedding. All that was missing was a priest and the organist.

Summer narrowed her eyes. "It's a ruse!"

"What?"

"They're being sneaky and trying to blind us with their love. Hurry up and pose."

Wes looked back at the perfect couple and he couldn't believe his eyes—they started running toward the altar.

"They're going to win!" Summer said.

"Not on my watch."

Wes didn't even hesitate. He flung Summer over his shoulder in a fireman's hold, his zip-tied hand clamping down on her ass, and sprinted. Around the pews, up the aisle, and sliding across the altar.

Then he grabbed Summer's phone and aimed. And that's how he ended up carrying his bride over the altar and snapping a picture of him cupping her bridal-ed ass.

Chapter 19

BEST FRIEND ADVICE

"I'm not talking to you," Cleo said, her judgmental frown big as ever coming through the computer's screen. Her cropped pink and brown hair was in little space buns on either side of her head, and she had stripper red lipstick on her lips, which were tilted down in a frown.

"That will make our weekly business meeting challenging," Summer said.

She was sitting outside on the edge of the dock with her laptop, trying to get a rundown on the shop's weekly numbers. She wore cutoffs and a bikini top, her bare feet dangling in the cool water. Man, could she use another of week of this kind of solitude.

She could use another week of other things too, but she wasn't going there. Because he'd made it clear that he wasn't going there. Ever since their almost-kiss at the chapel—and it had been an almost-kiss—she couldn't stop thinking about Wes and how quickly he'd retreated. Or how much he'd laughed throughout the day. Sure they'd already had full-on lipsing sessions, but not in a place where I-do's were exchanged.

Summer didn't think Wes had much to laugh about in his life. He was too busy trying to survive or save the world. But yesterday they'd laughed until they hadn't. Then they'd shared part of their souls with each other. Then he'd friend-zoned her. Her mortal enemy had conned her into being friends, made her believe that he wanted her as much as she now wanted him, then he'd bailed.

Not only had he gone out of his way after to make sure they were always with the group, he'd headed into the den the moment they'd arrived home, claiming he had business calls to make. Well, she had a call to make as well, which was why she'd come out to the dock with her laptop, because she needed a sounding board. And with Autumn and Randy out for a walk on the beach, she'd phoned Cleo.

"What's challenging is accepting that my best friend didn't invite me to her wedding."

Summer rolled her eyes. "It wasn't a wedding. It was the Selfie Scavenger Hunt, and you know it always ends at the chapel."

"Yeah, but you've never ended it with 007 as your groom. And he was smiling." Cleo thought for a moment, then shrugged with indifference. "I guess if I had my hands all over that cute little ass of yours, I'd be smiling too."

Summer's heart leapt. She hadn't wanted to look at the photo. It would make earlier real. Make the connections they'd made real. And the way he'd recoiled real. But her curiosity won out. "He was smiling?"

"Like an idiot. I couldn't tell if it was because he was constipated or actually happy. I barely recognized him without the resting frump face. But he looked less like a mouth-breather and more . . . human. And the zip tie gave off a dom vibe. I mean, a hott with two Ts."

"The zip ties were meant to mess with me. So was pairing me up with Wes. Autumn has been nonstop Randy-fixated. I haven't had more than a few minutes of her to myself. And when I do, we're arguing."

"You never argue."

"I know. But she's so caught up in this relationship she isn't thinking straight."

"So what's new? Your sister doesn't have a responsible bone in her body. If something is exciting and new, she's all about it. Once it loses its shine, she's looking for the next big thing, without any thought to the carnage in her wake," Cleo said, and Summer's immediate thought was to defend her twin. But she wanted to hear her friend out, because Cleo had never voiced anything negative about Autumn, and Summer wanted to know if she was missing something important that would give her insight into the person she believed she knew best in the world.

"Give me an example?"

"In the past five years she's had seven jobs, more boyfriends than I have fingers and toes, has covered her half of the rent only on a quarterly basis. Shall I go on?" Cloe asked, even though the question was rhetorical.

Summer knew that was how other people saw Autumn, but she also knew her sister. Knew what made her tick and what made her happy and what made her scared. And losing your home at seven was scary. Even scarier was overhearing their parents talk about how close they had come to being homeless. Watching their dad and uncle load up a U-Haul with all their belongings and moving them into the apartment above the shop with Cecilia and Giuseppe, where none of the things around them were familiar, was traumatizing. It had left scars. Deep scars that never really went away.

That's why Autumn was the way she was. It was easier to break things off before they were pulled out from under you. Whereas Summer chased connection, her twin ran from it. Which was what made Summer so nervous about the Randy situation. Autumn was making permanent decisions without taking the time to see if she was going feel cornered and run. Or maybe she was attracted to the stability of someone who would never lose their home.

Not that Autumn would ever date someone for their money. But Summer could see the appeal of having that kind of financial net to catch you when things became bleak.

"You know what our childhood was like. Tons of love, not a lot of stability."

"But you aren't kids anymore. Autumn is a woman, so any leniency she got when she was younger is used up," Cleo said. "Has she paid you back?"

"No. But she promised she would."

"Has she even brought it up?"

"Like I said, we haven't had much time to talk with Randy butting in. But tomorrow is Twin Day, and you know how important that is."

"Great. It'll just be the two of you, so at some point tomorrow you can bring up her loan, because payroll is due again on Friday, and once that goes out we're going to be stretched thin to make the mortgage."

Summer's palms began to sweat, and her heart began to pound painfully. "That bad?"

"It's just a slow month. Which is why I decided to charge an entry fee to your live podcast."

Insecurity hit her like a hammer on a nail, causing her

to expel all the breath in her lungs.

"No one will come! Who would pay to see me chatter on about books and cake recipes?"

"Not true. The fee for the podcast is a purchase of the book, and they've been selling like crazy. It's nearly a full house already."

"A full house?" She gulped. "I don't even know if Autumn will be around to help me."

"Which is why you and I are taking on the town's smut coalition."

"You and I?" Cleo had never participated in the podcast. She had always sat on the sidelines cheering Summer on. She'd said it was too mainstream for all her opinions.

"Girl, you didn't think that I was going to let you take on your biggest podcast alone, did you? You need a cohost, and I need an audience. Plus, people love me."

"Um, you're more of an acquired taste," Summer laughed.

"It's called originality. You're reliable and I'm controversial. And every great show needs some controversy."

"I'm not sure that *Jane Eyre* needs the oppression and imprisonment of women as a topic."

"Of course it does, but that's for another discussion. This one will be based on the love story, that your listeners will eat up," Cleo said. "That doesn't mean that I didn't direct women to *The Wide Sargasso Sea* so they can understand Bertha's origin story."

"Of course you did."

"There has been such an interest, I was thinking that one of your podcasts can be on parallel books, where we read a classic and then a modern story, movie or book that used the original work as the inspiration for theirs, like *Emma* and *Clueless*, *Sabrina* and *The Summer I Turned Pretty*, and then compare them. There are so many to choose from."

For the first time since the call started, Summer felt a beam of hope. "That's a great idea."

"I also think we should come up with questions for the guests."

"Guests?"

"Yes, like guest authors or romance gurus. You can even bring on a matchmaker. Then we can come up with thought-provoking questions that really get the audience engaged and view romance in a new light."

"You've put a lot of thought into this," Summer said, with so much apprehension in her voice it cracked.

"And I'm not going to let you shoot down another one of my ideas. Stop being a wuss and live a little."

Was that how people saw her? As a wuss?

"Thank you so much for that insight."

"Anytime," Cleo said. "And to pay me back, you can start by getting your sister to pay you back."

"She said she'd do it from her quarterly bonus." That had been the deal, and in Russo tradition Autumn always stuck to her deals. Look at her and Wes. She'd promised to give his family a fair shot and she had. And what had come of that change of heart had been as nice as it had been confusing.

"Did she give you an actual date? What quarter she was even talking about?"

"She'll pay me back," Summer defended. "Autumn never breaks a promise over something so important. She knows it came from my wedding fund, and she knows how important that fund is to me. But if we're short, I can always temporarily borrow from what's left."

"But you shouldn't have to," Cleo said, and Summer could tell her friend was exasperated. She'd never been all that pro-Autumn even if she'd never said anything overtly negative about her twin, but she didn't know Autumn like Summer did.

"She'll pay."

"Well, I hope it's soon, because things here are looking grim." Cleo paused so long that Summer knew there was more to the story. "Did 007 tell you that BookLand has upped their opening date by a month?"

"What? Where did you hear that?" Because this was news to her.

Cleo turned her phone to the side window and aimed the screen toward a big banner that hung above the front entrance of the building next door. It read: GRAND OPENING, JULY 1ST.

"That's less than a month away. How are they going to pull that off. Before I left for Mystic, they were still putting in the shelves. Except for the window displays, there wasn't a single book out."

"They've hired another night crew. They've started pulling double shifts around the clock," Cleo said, then her face came back into frame. "He didn't tell you?"

"We don't really talk about business," she said. "We try to keep conversations on topics that won't start World War III." But she was still cut. His silence on something so important hurt her in places it shouldn't.

"We need to come up with a retaliation," Cleo added. "Something to piggyback on the crowd he'll draw."

"Like a big author signing?"

"Exactly that. Sloan Chase has a new book coming out in a few weeks. What if we booked her as a special guest and had a book signing following the podcast?"

"I'm sure she's already got all her publicity lined up. Besides, Sloan Chase sold more copies than the Bible last year. I think she might be a little out of our league."

"She wasn't before she got famous. Who knows, maybe the nostalgia of coming back to where her first book signing happened will be enough for her to say yes. She's a local girl. Do you still have her contact info?"

"Yes." A bubble of excitement tickled her belly like champagne on her tongue.

"Then what's the harm in asking?"

"Nothing," she said with more conviction. "I'll tell her my mom, who gave her her first big break, will be there. That we can discuss where she started and where she is now." It was a brilliant idea. But on the same day as Wes's opening?

"Why do I feel like there's a but?"

"Because I don't want to sabotage Wes's opening."

There was a long, pregnant pause where Cleo's mouth gaped open like she was a fish out of water. "You've slept with him!"

Summer didn't want to lie but she also didn't want Cleo's wrath. "We have shared a bed, where there may have been a cuddle."

"And?"

"I might have kissed him." Summer closed her eyes. "In the river. While I was nearly naked."

Cleo was silent again. She reached up and fiddled with

one her of space buns. Her expression was one of *I'm considering slashing your tires.* "You went skinny-dipping with him?"

"I just told you I kissed him and you're concerned with the state of my dress?"

"Skinny-dipping. Kissing. A faux-wedding. Deep and meaningful conversations. Are you feeling him?"

The real question was, was he feeling her?

Summer exhaled a deep breath. "I'm in trouble, aren't I?"

⁓

"What do you mean your boss didn't approve the time off?" Summer asked Autumn, who was sitting looking guilty as hell in her pajamas. "I thought it was a work trip."

"It was," Autumn explained. "Just not how you think." Autumn puffed her chest out and put her shoulders back. The expression on her face was one Summer knew well. She was about to drop a bomb—one that would derail Summer's life.

"Explain," she demanded, but she almost didn't want to know the answer. She'd been so excited about this new podcast idea that she didn't want to ruin her mood. But she needed to know that she'd be able to pay the mortgage this month.

"I'm going to become an influencer," Autumn said proudly.

"Do you know how many fashion and makeup influencers there are out there?"

"Not just fashion—I'm going to become the face of 'Dress for Sex-cess: How to snag a man in thirty days by manifesting sex-scess.' Sure, there will be hair, makeup, and fashion tips, but it's more about building the inner goddess. How to find that right guy and reel them in," she said, as if all she had to do was put up a few pics and videos and she would become social-media famous. "I mean, look at me and Randy! I was dressed for sex-cess when I met him. I had put in the hard work upfront so that when he appeared I was ready. All the guys and steps before led me to the one."

"You know that I am the first person to be pro-love, and I will always support you in following your dreams, but quitting your job? That's a little premature, don't you think?"

"I didn't quit. I got fired," Autumn said, without a hint of remorse or fear of the uncertain. "You took out a loan and gambled your savings on a bookstore—what's the difference?"

The differences were numerous. "I had Mom and Auntie to help. They let me slowly buy them out, supported me through the transition, and I made sure I had the money to pay for a year of payroll, mortgage payments, inventory, and utilities. I didn't get fired, then decide to start a business and pray for it to rain Benjamins."

"That's why I need your support," Autumn said, and her confident tone turned saccharine-sweet. There was a big ask coming. "The money I borrowed, I have a few thousand dollars left, and I wanted to know if I could hold onto it for another few months."

Anxiety soured Summer's stomach. "What about your end-of-quarter bonus?"

"Turns out when you get fired there is no bonus."

That sour feeling became an all-encompassing panic that lit her body from the inside out. Betrayal and disappointment only fueled the already-raging inferno. Cleo had been right.

Her sister hadn't just broken her promise. Between her immaturity and selfishness, she'd screwed Summer in the process.

Even worse, she'd kept this all from her. Just like Wes and the new grand opening date, she'd lied by omission. The old Summer would have let things slide, but the new Summer, who was tired of being a doormat that just lay there and took it, was done playing nice to keep the peace.

"I need that money, Autumn. I don't care how you come up with it, but you will pay me back by quarter's end."

Autumn's brows disappeared into her hairline at Summer's tone, but Summer didn't care. That money was her safety net, in case anything happened to her store. And it looked like she'd need that safety net sooner rather than later, when her neighbor opened his doors.

"Can't you just pull from your wedding fund?" Autumn asked quietly.

"I already did. For you."

"And I am so thankful. I'm not saying I won't pay you back, I just need a little more time. And I need your support."

Summer didn't know what to say. By supporting her sister's dreams she would have to put her own dreams in jeopardy.

Old insecurities that she thought she'd dealt with rose up and hit her like a sledgehammer to her chest. She'd always supported Autumn, no matter how rash and outrageous the ask. But Cleo was right, it was time to put herself first.

"Why don't you ask Randy?"

"And have him think I'm a gold digger? No way. Plus, I don't want him to know just how bad my credit is and that I'm practically broke."

"Aren't those things people talk about when they're going to move in together?"

"People with money don't talk about money. They just assume that everyone else has it."

Summer had assumed the same thing about Wes. But the more she'd gotten to know him, the more she'd realized that his quest for success had become more about taking care of his brother than a money grab.

"But you don't have money."

"But I will." Autumn grabbed Summer's hands. "I promise you I'm going to make this a success, just like your shop."

Summer wanted to laugh. She was one grand opening away from going under. Not that she wanted her family to know that. And now she had a plan of action, which hopefully meant she wouldn't have to tell them ever.

God this was a mess. An Autumn-made mess. Or had Summer played an unknowing role in it? She never should have lent her sister the money with expectations of getting it back in the allotted time. She'd known in her gut it was a risk, but she'd taken that risk because love trumped everything. Her mom and aunt had loved Summer enough to give her a shot at her dreams. What kind of hypocrite would she be to deny her sister another few weeks?

"If you promise to tell Randy the truth, I'll think about giving you a short extension on the loan."

Autumn pulled Summer into her arms and rocked her excitedly back and forth. "You're the best sister ever!"

Yeah, the best.

Chapter 20

FRIENDZONED

Summer was romantically challenged. She had taken it from a perfect meet-cute to the friend zone. And by her frenemy, of all people. She was cursed.

That was a lie—not the cursed part, that was as true as the day was long, but about them being frenemies. Because for a moment there yesterday, something had changed between them. Then he'd recoiled so fast he'd nearly fallen over.

Summer snuck out of bed early to avoid him because he'd been avoiding her. He hadn't even come to bed last night, opting to sleep on the family room floor rather than be in her presence.

Well, she wasn't going to let him ruin her day, because today was Twin Day and that meant laughter, fun, and freedom from all the bullshit that was going on in her life.

She put on her pink #TWINNING crop top, cutoff jean shorts, and pink cowgirl boots, just like she did every year. But today felt more imperative than years past. Today there would be no talk of Randy or borrowed money or brownstones in New York. Or cold-footed fiancées.

Today would be a day to recapture all the memories they'd created over the years. Today was the day they'd become twins again.

And Summer needed that. Needed to get back to being sisters and remind Autumn of their unbreakable bond.

Parting her hair down the middle and putting it into two French braids, part of their dress-alike tradition, Summer was practically bouncing on her toes as she applied her lip gloss. She even used a touch of mascara—because, why not?

Today was also important because she needed to get out of this house and away from Wes. Sneaking down the stairs, she tiptoed through the hallway and into the kitchen, and froze.

Because there he stood, the man she was trying to avoid, shirtless, sweaty, sipping a glass of water like he owned the place. His was such a large presence she could barely breathe. Especially when she caught a glimpse of his glistening abs. Suddenly, the kitchen felt too small and intimate.

He pushed off the counter to leave and she held out her hands. "Don't leave on my account. I was just heading out."

He took in her outfit and his lip curled up. "Where to? A hoedown?"

"Not that it's any of your business, but Autumn and I are going to the boardwalk for Twin Day. Are you auditioning for *Thunder Down Under?*"

"I'm British, not Australian, and I just came back from my morning run. See anything you like?"

She remained mum on the topic.

"What is this Twin Day?" he asked, leaning back against the counter.

"It's a yearly trip where we eat too much candy and pizza and funnel cake, then we ride the Gravitron. Whoever pukes first must wear the Cone of Shame. Which is a bright orange traffic cone with LOSER written across it. And before you ask, you aren't invited. It's a no-boys-allowed kind of affair."

"Good thing I'm a man."

That he was. A tall, dark, dangerously attractive man, who wasn't her prince. Not that she wanted him to be, but a tiny piece of her had begun to believe that he could be. That in the right setting with the right timing they could build on that connection that had started to bloom. But he'd doused that in gasoline then put a blowtorch to it.

"Men are worse than boys. They know how to disappoint like it's a god-given talent."

His expression went soft and serious. He set his glass down and walked toward her until they were toe to toe. She could smell the sea air and clean sweat on his skin.

He cupped her face. "I never meant to disappoint you, love. That's why I stopped things before they could even start. I thought that would be for the best."

"But it already started. We were having a fun time until you made it weird. You didn't have to friend-zone me—we were already there." A flash of hurt sliced through her. "Unless you don't want to be friends."

She saw the look of regret on his face. "We are friends. I just didn't want to cross a line we can't uncross."

"You're the one who said I was giving mixed signals. You were forcing me to say I meant the kiss, then you wrote me off. Was this some kind of game?"

"God no. I would never do that. I would never hurt you."

"But you have. You tried to have my car towed, you make fun of my shop, you didn't tell me that concrete was going to be poured and would block the driveway. I should have seen this coming."

"You're right. I should have told you about the concrete and that was a shit move on my part."

"That's it? That's your big apology? That it was a shit move? Be still my heart. God, you're such a guy! It's no wonder you moved up the grand opening and didn't have the balls to tell me."

"Wait. What are you talking about?"

"The big banner hanging across all of downtown announcing your new grand opening on July first." He just stared at her as if she'd grown a third nostril. "Don't pretend that you weren't trying to mess with my head. We have fun here, become friends, then we get home and you're like, 'Oh, by the way, surprise! You're going-out-of-business date is closer than you thought.'"

He was in the middle of pulling out his phone and punching in numbers when he said, "I don't have a fucking clue what you're talking about. But I'm going to get to the bottom of this."

His tone was dialed somewhere between *what the fuck* and *someone is going to fucking die.* The shock was so genuine she believed him, and guilt about her delivery rushed through her like a tidal wave.

"I thought you knew."

He held up a finger for silence and said to the other person on the line, "What the fuck, Harper? Did you think I wouldn't find out?"

Before she could say another word, he was stalking out the back door and talking in a tone that made her think that if she were Mr. Harper she'd be peeing her pants. The funny, easy-going guy from yesterday who'd laughed and smiled at her had vanished, and back was the Boardroom Barracuda who was rock-hard, singularly focused, and intimidating.

Her heart told her to follow him, give him support, but her brain reminded her that he didn't want help. Wes was a lone wolf and liked it that way. There was no way to change that in a matter of a week. To think so would be stupid.

Then again, she'd thought that before he'd opened up about his past. The Wes he'd shown her in the last several days would accept the support. Maybe even appreciate having someone to help him work through whatever was going on at his company. To stay or to go, that was the question.

One she didn't get to answer, because Autumn came bouncing in with her pink boots and braids. "We look hot, sis."

"That we do," she said, trying to force a smile.

"Hot doesn't even cover it," Randy said, walking in behind Autumn and wrapping his arms around her from the back. "This is every guy's dream, to go on a date with twins."

Autumn playfully elbowed him in the gut and he gave a dramatic gasp. That's when Summer noticed it. The T-shirts. Autumn's said I'LL BE YOUR BONNIE to Randy's I'LL BE YOUR CLYDE, with arrows pointing to the other.

"Where's your TWINNING shirt?" Summer asked as her heart sank, because she knew that just like Autumn's shirt, this day was about to end in a shootout. "It's Twin Day."

"I know. I know. But—"

"Don't blame her," Randy said. "The first night we met she told me about this day and I just wanted to be a part of it. Is that okay?"

"The whole point of Twin Day is for Autumn and I to have alone time. Our parents don't even come."

"Well, we're a package deal now, right, baby?" Randy asked.

Autumn kissed his chin. "Right."

Randy kissed her nose. "It's not a big deal, right?"

How was she supposed to answer that honestly? It was a gigantic freaking deal. Being alone with the Swifties would be uncomfortable as hell. But she'd promised to give him a fair chance, and sharing the day with him might give her insight into who this man who had stolen her sister's common sense was. So she let herself sit in the uncomfortableness for a moment and decided that it would be easier to endure the awkwardness than start another fight.

"You know what?" she said. "If you want him to come, then he can come. Far be it for me to stand in the way of true love."

Autumn yanked Summer into bear hug and Summer could feel their hearts beating out of sync. "This is going to be fun, I promise."

Summer couldn't think of a single circumstance where being a third wheel would be fun, but she'd promised to give Randy a chance. She was turning over a new leaf when it came to Wes and treating him like she treated everyone else—with respect, acceptance, and a genuine smile on her face.

"Bring on the fun."

∞

Summer was trying, she really was, but she was struggling to get into fun mode. Ice cream had been shared, pizza consumed, and candy had been inhaled, but she'd felt like an interloper the entire time.

Randy had made an effort to include her, but between the PDA and the sexy talk she felt like an outsider.

They were standing in line for the Gravitron, and instead of holding Autumn's hand like always she was standing behind them trying to hold onto her cookies. They hadn't even reached the top of the line, and already Summer was getting cold feet. Not that she'd let anyone notice. There was no way she was going to wear that LOSER cone for the rest of the day.

So far she'd smiled when she was supposed to smile, laughed when Randy made a dad joke, listened when he went on and on about how he was the new VP at the company and how much his car cost. Unfortunately, the only thing they had in common was their love for her sister. And by the time they made it to lunch it was even more clear that he was enamored with Autumn. So Summer decided to play on that.

Autumn was a beautiful soul, even when she was acting a little self-centered. Not many people saw that deep into her twin's soul and got the gift of Autumn's immense capacity for love. But Randy had seemed to uncover that in her, and that was something to celebrate.

Summer had opened her mouth to say something along those lines, but instead she blurted out, "Are you going to fuck over my sister?"

"Summer!" Autumn scolded. "Take that back."

"It's a fair question," Randy said, slinging his arm around Autumn's shoulders. "And no, I would never hurt Autumn."

"What happened to 'love can conquer all'?" Autumn said. "You're supposed to be my ally here. You're always my ally."

"And I am being that now. Do you know about his past two fiancées, who he left after they'd uprooted their lives for him?"

"Yes, as a matter of fact I do. I know the whole story. I've even DMed with one of them and they spoke highly of Randy—told me how he'd helped them transition back into single life after the breakup." Autumn crossed her arms. "The question is, how do *you* know?"

Summer's face went beet red. "I may have looked him up on Insta."

"You promised me that after the Stanly fiasco you'd never do that again. You promised!"

The betrayal in Autumn's expression made Summer feel guilty and embarrassed, and like she'd broken sis-code. How would Summer handle it if someone had done the same to her? Not well. Stalking someone's socials was wrong, which meant Wes had been right. And that irked her.

"I know, and I'm sorry. I was just worried that you hadn't talked about the important stuff"—she gave Autumn a scolding look—"before you jumped into things. I mean, this seems like a whirlwind."

"We've talked about what matters," Randy said, as they took a step closer to the entrance of the ride. "There isn't anything that would change the way I feel."

Summer glared at Autumn, and Autumn glared back in defiance. So she still hadn't told Randy about her financial woes. This was bad. Very bad. He might say things like that now, but thinking you know how you'd react and actually reacting were two separate things.

Summer had been so engrossed in the conversation that she didn't notice they were next to go until the employee asked them how many. Autumn said, "Two," and that was the end of that. Decision made: Summer was left to go by herself.

And that was how Summer ended up on the waiting dock for the Gravitron next to the employee with more piercings than fingers to tell her she could board the ride.

A wave of nerves washed over her, causing an obnoxious souring of the belly. She was going to have to go it alone. A place in life she'd need to start getting used to. When her sister moved to New York, Summer would be left all alone. Sure, she'd have Cleo and her loyal customers, but no family.

Summer watched as her sister and Randy held hands as the bottom of the ride dropped out, leaving only the velocity to keep them upright and plastered to the wall. Autumn looked as put together as ever, but Randy was a chartreuse shade of green, gripping onto Autumn's hand as if he were in labor.

To her dismay, neither threw up on the ride, but that didn't mean they were in the clear. Twin Day 2021 had taken two hours, but Autumn had blown chunks on the Tilt-A-Whirl in a spectacular way and been sentenced to a full twenty-four hours in the Cone of Shame. It had been amazing. But now Summer felt like she was the one at the disadvantage.

She'd had the confusing run-in with Wes this morning, drunk three cups of coffee, then eaten her weight in saltwater taffy and funnel cake. Then there was the fun fact that Autumn clearly didn't want her to go with them on the ride, officially making Summer the third wheel. If that wasn't bad enough, she was going to have to hold her own hand on the ride, since she was watching Autumn and Randy go around by themselves.

The ride slowly came to a stop, and Randy gave her a big wave as they exited through the back gate. Mr. Piercings opened the entrance and asked her, "How many in your party?"

Summer had just opened her mouth to tell him "one," when her RoChance app chimed, letting her know a potential soulmate was within range, and someone said, "A party of two, please."

She turned to find Wes resting his palms on either rail, leaning on them enough that his biceps bulged to the point of stretching out his T-shirt. A shirt that had #WINNING WITH HER and an arrow pointing to the left in glittery pink puffy paint across the chest. It was clearly homemade and the sweetest thing anyone had ever done for her.

"What are you doing here?"

"I heard you were in need of someone to fill out your party of two." He tapped the bill of her hat. "Plus, I couldn't pass up seeing you in the Cone of Shame."

"Oh, you're going to be the one wearing the cone. Mark my words. I have a stomach of steel."

Chapter 21

FRIENDS WITH BENNIES

"How do you feel?" Wes asked, crouching down so he could meet her gaze beneath the rim of the neon orange parking cone. The poor thing looked miserable.

The second the ride's bottom had dropped out, Summer's stomach had also bottomed out. She'd puked all over his shoes, which was why he was walking around in trout-shaped flip-flops he'd bought at a tourist trap for way too much money. What a pair they made.

As for the other pair, they were standing in front of them in line for the Ferris wheel, making out. It was PG and he expected Summer to say something very librarian-like—"No kissing in the stacks" or "Keep your tongue to yourself"—but she was just staring up at the Ferris wheel looking like she was going to throw up again.

She wobbled a bit to the right.

"Whoa, stay with me," Wes said, steadying her by the arm. It was clammy and shaking. "You're going to be okay," he whispered.

"No," she clarified. "We're going to die."

"We don't have to do this." He pointed at the exit, the one near the front of the line where chickens *bok-bok*ed their way out.

She eyed that exit for a long while, as if weighing her

options. "I am tired of being a wuss. So of course we have to do this. It's Randy's choice to pick his favorite ride. It just so happens to be a death trap. But I'm turning over a new leaf, sitting in the uncomfortableness of it, and giving your family another chance."

He didn't like that she considered herself a wuss, since she was the bravest woman he knew. But he liked the last part about giving him yet another chance. He'd blown it yesterday at the chapel, then again this morning when he'd phoned the chairman of the board in the middle of a conversation, so he'd come to apologize for pulling back and to explain his reasoning.

She was correct, he was sending mixed messages, and it was his responsibility to explain to her why he'd been acting that way. She deserved at least that.

"So you don't like heights? So what? Everyone has their fears. Plus, remember, together we're winning!" He pointed to the puffy paint on his shirt and smiled.

Summer pushed the cone back on her head so she could see his eyes. "What's your fear?"

His gaze locked with hers. "That I'll end up like my dad and hurt the people closest to me."

She took a small step forward. "You don't talk about him much."

"There's not much to say. I didn't know him really well. I grew up in England and only saw once him a year."

"How did he hurt you?"

"He made it clear that I was the least important person in his life."

Her cheeks went red with rage. "He was wrong, and shame on him for making anyone, especially his son, feel like that."

"Are you getting mad on my behalf, love?"

"Yes. Yes, I am."

He liked it when she got spicy. Especially on his behalf. "That was a long time ago."

"Maybe up here." She pointed to his head, then his heart. "But not in here."

Randy took that moment to stand on the railing right next to the DO NOT STAND ON THE HAND RAILING sign and shout, "I love this woman." Then he hopped down and kissed Autumn. A crowd formed around them and cheered them on.

Summer looked from Randy to Wes. "What if Randy's never ready to step up at the company?"

Wes had been asking himself that question for months now. He loved his brother, but it was as if Randy was living in an alternate reality where having the last name Kingston meant he could sit in an office practicing his golf swing and still make things happen.

"Then I'll do whatever it takes to find him a job he'd be good at," he said. "Well, look at this, we're next," he said with a smile.

"Oh god." She clasped his hand hard enough that he winced.

"I can take the blame and say I'm afraid of heights," he offered.

She snorted. "I know you're just saying that to make me feel better. But it's not like anyone would believe that you're afraid of heights."

"I'm afraid of plenty."

"Like what, apart from turning into your dad?" She said the last part with compassion.

He could lie to her and come up with something comical, like spiders or the white tops of candy corn, but they were about to get loaded on to the Ferris wheel and he needed to distract her. Plus, a part of him wanted to tell her the truth.

He climbed into the swinging seat and tugged her to him and said, "You, love. I'm scared of you."

She was so thrown off by his admission that she plopped down in the seat next to him. The gate locked in front of them. It wasn't until they started to move that she seemed to realize what was going on, and she squealed and then clung to him like a koala on a eucalyptus tree.

He put his arm around her and pulled her close so he could whisper, "Breathe. I've got you."

She did and he tightened his arms. Damn, she felt good—vulnerable and relying on him to protect her. Wes was learning more and more just how much of a protector he was toward the people in his life. And even if they couldn't be more than friends, he wanted her to be in his life—for good.

"Talk to me," she said, her face buried in his armpit. "Distract me."

"Like how I've been dying to tell you all day that I didn't know about the early opening."

She blinked up at him, looking at him through those dark lashes. "I'm sorry I jumped to conclusions."

"Don't be sorry. I've given you plenty of reasons to doubt me."

"I was so mad when Cleo told me. I felt like a fool. Like you were being nice to me to distract me from what was going on back home. Like you played me."

He took her hand in his and placed them in his lap. "I'd

never play you. Maybe once upon a time I would have done anything to win, but I'd like to think I've changed."

"So what did Harper say?" When he didn't speak, she said. "That was me being nosy. You don't have to answer that."

"No, I want someone to bounce ideas off of." And for some reason he wanted that someone to be her. "The board made a unilateral decision to up the opening knowing that it would be nearly impossible to make the date. They're doing whatever they can to sabotage Randy and me."

"I just don't get why the board would want you to fail. They still stand to make money with you at the helm. And you're so good they'd be at a loss without you. They make me so mad I want to slash their tires."

"Love, are you getting protective over me again?"

"Damn straight," she said, and something inside him warmed. "I hate bullies, and they're bullies."

"It's hard not to be conniving and cunning when there are billions at stake. I mean, just look at the tricks I played on you. I really was just having fun with it all, but I knew that it was messing with your head. And for that, I'm sorry."

"It was all fair play. I did my share of sneaky things to tick you off."

"Some of your pranks were ingenious. Like walking your dog through the wet concrete, leaving paw prints all over the pad near our front doors."

"Well, Princess Buttercup is very particular about her potty spots, and your land used to be a vacant lot. Potty Utopia."

"Uh-huh," he said with a grin.

"It took the crew two extra days to re-pour that concrete.

I had to pay a security guard to watch it overnight. And there is still a big print right in front of my door."

"Jeremiah was a nice guy. I bribed him with my nonna's molasses cookies and he let me get in one last word."

"I think it had more to do with the baker than the cookies. One look at that smile of yours and any guy would be toast."

He loved the way she got flustered when he said things like that. What he didn't like was that she didn't know how to take a compliment, as if other men in her life had deprived her of them.

He could tell by the way she stared off into the distance that it was topic over. He'd let her have this one. But at some point they were going to talk about how she deserved to be treated for when the next guy came around.

An unexpected flash of jealousy and anger raged through him and he felt his arms tighten, pulling her closer at the thought of some other douchebag holding her hand, kissing her, touching that amazing ass.

"You okay?" she asked.

He tucked her into his side. "I am now."

They were quiet for a long moment, but it was that comfortable kind of silence that only happened when two people had a special kind of connection. And he felt theirs growing every day.

"If it was that serious of a call, why aren't you on the road back to Ridgefield?"

"I'm heading that way tomorrow."

"I have to go back early too," she said. "I have a podcast to do."

"I have an idea, why don't we wake up early and drive together? We can get done what needs to be done."

"It would be nice to have someone to argue with," she teased, and he laughed.

The Ferris wheel came to a stop to let another party on, and she wrapped her arms around his waist and buried her face into his shoulder.

"Are we falling? It feels like we're falling. Oh god, we're falling, aren't we."

"Open your eyes and you'll see that we just came to a stop to let someone off."

"I want to get off. How do we get off?"

"I have a few ideas on that, but we're in public," he said in a sexy voice.

She elbowed him in the ribs but laughed. She was terrified to her bones and he'd made her laugh. It felt as if he were on top of the world. And they were. They were just a few feet from the peak of the ride.

The top of a Ferris wheel was like mistletoe, right? It came with a kiss?

He looked down at her shrink-wrapped around him and decided that while he'd love to kiss her, this was enough. Her trust was a treasure to hold close to his vest.

"What happens when the project is done?" she asked quietly. "I mean, when the store opens up, what happens to you?"

"I'll stay on for a few months to make sure it's solid, and then I'll head back to London and see if I can breathe my life into my own business."

She sat up straight, and he could see the shock on her face. "You own your own business?"

"A robotics company that specializes in building medical equipment."

"Was it successful?"

"It still is. I hired a good pal from university to be president in my absence. I'm still CEO and am very hands on from a distance."

"Where do you find the time?"

"I don't get much sleep."

"You gave up your country and business for a dad who sounds like a jerk?"

Even to himself he sounded resigned. "What was I supposed to do? What would you have done?"

She shrugged. "The same thing."

"Look at us, a pair who would do anything for family."

"So the Grinch does have a heart."

"Don't mistake my single-mindedness for the lack of a heart. It's just the single-mindedness wins out most of the time."

"Funny, my heart is always running the show."

"I know," he whispered, taking her hand once again. "It's why I pulled back yesterday. I don't want to mislead you so that when I leave you feel blindsided."

She laced their fingers together. "I know who you are, Wes. And I know what you're capable of, even if you don't."

His Grinch-heart didn't just grow two sizes that day, it nearly exploded out of his chest. He soaked up her praise like he was a dying man in the desert, desperate for a drop of acceptance. A sliver of connection. And she was giving him that without expecting anything in return.

It had been a long time since he'd had someone who had that amount of unconditional faith in him.

"And what is that?"

"You have the world in your hands, Wes. Whatever direction you choose to go you will find success. You just have to have the courage to make a decision that is good for your soul and not just the bottom line."

"Like this?" he asked, cupping her chin and tilting it up so he could see her face when he lowered his mouth. He went slowly, giving her time to pull away. And just when he thought he was going to make contact—*Houston we have a problem*—she said, "Wait."

He prepared himself for the "too little too late" lecture, but instead she took off her Cone of Shame and set it on the bench next to her. Then she wrapped her arms around his neck and whispered against his lips, "Even though it would make for a funny meet-cute, this moment calls for something that doesn't fit into a love guide. You deserve more than a Cone of Shame kiss. You deserve this . . ."

Before he knew what was happening, her arms had tightened around his neck and her lips were on his. Soft and tentative, as if she wasn't sure what his reaction would be. If he was into this. So he RSVPed immediately by threading his fingers through her hair to cradle the back of her head, while the other hand went around her back, pulling her so close she was practically on his lap.

That's when the kiss went from a sweet get-to-know-you to volcanic. The blast of chemistry and sexual awareness was heard around the world. She tasted minty from the gum she'd chewed and felt as warm as the sunny breeze.

She dug her fingers into his hair and tugged a little while she gently nipped at his lower lip. Just enough to let him know that beneath the sweet bookstore owner was a woman who liked a little kink when it came to romance. Wes wasn't normally a kink kind of guy, but with Summer he'd be whatever she needed. Especially when it felt like this.

He wasn't sure how long the kiss lasted—it was a single kiss that didn't even give them time to take a breath. Like they needed each other more than they needed oxygen. Then her hands were on the move, palms sliding down his chest, over his pecs and lower, to his abs.

"What happened to crossing the line?' she said against his lips.

"Love, we crossed the line that night in your store when you told me to get my ass out of your shop. I was just in denial."

She pulled back, her eyes sex-hazed. "Is this just a kiss or is it more?"

"I'm moving back to London, so these next few months are all that I can offer."

"So like a friends-with-benefits thing? Then we're just long-distance friends?"

"Lots of benefits. And yes. But before you agree, I really want you to think about it. I don't want anyone to get hurt."

"Friends with benefits is one of my favorite romance tropes."

And that was his fear, that she'd get caught up in the romance of it all, believe that they would somehow beat the odds and it would work out.

"This isn't a book. This is real life, and my life is jam-packed and chaotic and about the bottom line. And it's across the ocean. So before you answer, I want you to really be sure."

She opened her mouth to answer, and he could see the *yes* in her gaze. "Don't tell me now, when we're both worked up and hormones are running high." He brought her hand to his mouth and pressed a kiss to her knuckles. "You've had a lot of disappointment when it comes to men. I refuse to be another."

Chapter 22

FAKE BOYFRIEND

Summer didn't think about his proposition as their Ferris wheel car slowly lowered to the ground. Not when Wes held her hand as they got off. Not as he placed the Cone of Shame back on her head. And definitely not when he kissed the tip of her nose in such an endearing way her heart sighed.

She didn't even think about it as they walked hand in hand down the boardwalk, sharing a triple-scoop ice cream cone and watching the waves come in while the seagulls and harbor seals barked in the distance.

The gentle June breeze blew stray hairs against her lip gloss. The afternoon sun was at its highest, shining down on them and off the cresting waters of the Atlantic. But it was the smell of the cotton candy and wet wood from the pier that brought her back to when she'd been a kid.

"My dad and I used to come down here and fish when I was a kid," she said, noting that their intertwined hands were swinging as they walked.

"I can't imagine you fishing."

"Why, cuz my nose is always stuck in a book?"

He chuckled. "No, because I can't imagine you catching something and then killing it."

"Oh, we didn't kill them. Dad would catch them and then I'd run down to the beach and let them go. It was our thing.

Then, when we were done, we'd get an ice cream. I'd get vanilla with sprinkles and he'd get nutty coconut."

Wes stopped mid-lick and looked at her. "You didn't mention sprinkles when we ordered."

"I didn't take you for a sprinkles kind of guy."

"Come on." He tugged her hand and practically dragged her down the pier back to the ice cream truck. He didn't stop until they were in line and breathless.

"Really, it's fine just the way it is."

He looked at her in a way that made her belly flop. "Love, you deserve more than *fine*. You deserve the world. And your world includes sprinkles, so sprinkles you shall get."

"What if you don't like it?"

"Then I've tried something new and know it isn't for me."

Summer's heart stopped painfully in her chest. Was that how he was with relationships? He'd give it a try, and see if the woman in question was for him? And how would she feel if he took a taste and didn't like her?

Suddenly, she regretted all the food she'd scarfed down that day as it rolled around in her stomach.

"You okay?' he asked quietly.

No, she was not. Her mind was beginning to spiral into What-If Land. This thing with Wes could go three ways. One, she went for it and things worked out. Two, she went for it and was left heartbroken. Or three, she passed on the opportunity and regretted it for the rest of her life.

This was a WWNED kind of moment. And What Nora Efron Would Do was have the heroine risk it all for love. Not that this was love, but it was something. Something worth treasuring and exploring. She had her answer.

"Wes?" she began tentatively, nerves stringing her limbs tightly.

"Yes, love."

Oh, how she loved it when he called her that in that husky whisper of his. It jump-started all her spark plugs to life.

"About your offer—"

"Summer?" someone said from behind. A male blast from her embarrassing past. "Summer Russo?"

"Bryan?" she croaked, because who in the hell would want to run into their worst failed meet-cute ever, especially when wearing an orange parking cone, a smear of ice cream on her right boob, and smudged mascara from when she'd barfed on Wes's shoes.

"It is you!" He yanked her out of Wes's safe hands and into a giant hug. Her arms hung at her side as Bryan swung her back and forth. Unlike her, Wes was in his WINNING WITH HER shirt, pressed navy shorts, and not a smear of anything on his right boob. He was dressed like a Tommy Hilfiger ad, minus the tee.

Behind Bryan was another familiar face with flawless makeup, a sparkling diamond on her hand, and a little baby bump advertising that they had reached family-status. A status Summer desperately wanted to reach.

The second Bryan released her, his plus-one moved in for a hug. Summer shifted sideways so they ended up in one of those awkward side-embraces.

"Bryan, this is my uh . . ."

"Fiancé, Wes." All eyes fell to Summer's bare finger. "It's being remade. The diamond wasn't big enough. Only eight carats will do for my girl."

Summer nearly burst out laughing at the look on the other woman's face at the mention of the diamond's size.

"Nice to meet you." Bryan stuck out his hand to Wes, who shook it. "This is my wife, Candy. And this lady right here"— he playfully punched Summer in the shoulder like she was one of the guys—"is responsible for all of this." He put his arm around his wife and smiled. "If it hadn't been for Summer, Candy and I never would have met."

Wes must have sensed her discomfort, because he threw his arm around her shoulders and slid his hand into her back pocket, effectively cupping her butt. She tried to move but he tightened his grip. "You introduced them, love?"

"Kind of," Summer said, and suddenly she felt like that awkward teen all over again. She didn't want to tell him the truth because she didn't want him to know just how romantically cursed she was. And how pathetic her dating life up until this moment had been. Between humping dogs ripping her skirt, elbowing plumbers in the pipes, and a mime performance for a proposal, she'd had her fair share of meet-uglies. She was romantically challenged in the worst way.

Wes pulled her closer, against his chest. Whereas Bryan had a dad bod with a soft muffin top and a receding hairline, Wes was all muscle and sinew with a head of hair that was so thick and luscious that her fingers itched to tangle themselves in it.

"Define 'kind of,'" he said to her, but she knew he was glaring down at Bryan.

"On Fridays they bring in a local band and there's dancing. Bryan and I came here on a date and we walked onto the floor together and he left with someone else."

"That would be me," Candy said, wiggling her fingers.

"It was a date? I don't remember that," Bryan said, looking genuinely confused.

Summer's cheeks burned with humiliation. Had he really not considered that a date? He'd picked her up, had his arm slung around her the entire night, paid for their dinner. He'd even called her "babe." Plus, his best friend had been on the double date with Autumn.

She closed her eyes. Everything made sense.

Then she felt her hand enveloped by Wes's. His arms coming around her. "That's right, love. You told me about Bryan. Wasn't he the worst meet-cute of your life?"

"Well, there was this one guy who tried to have my car towed, but this is a close second."

Bryan's voice rose. "I wouldn't go as far as second-worst."

Wes puffed out his chest, reminding Bryan of their size difference, then stared him down.

"You didn't even know we were on a date," said Summer.

Bryan took a step back. "I'm sorry if I misled you. Your sister and Kent were going out that night and Autumn didn't want you stuck at home reading one of those romance books you loved. I mean, you were like one of the guys."

And how embarrassing was that? She'd been friend-zoned even before he'd asked her out. Once again she was the gate-keeper to her more popular, aspiring influencer of a sister.

Wes picked up on her disappointment and frustration. "Things clearly work out how they're supposed to." He kissed her fingers and then added, "We'd better get going, love. We have a reservation at the Wharf House to make."

They said their goodbyes, and as they walked off Wes still had his hand cupping her ass.

"You can stop with the show," she said, moving away from him. He gave her ass a little squeeze then let go. "How did you know my favorite restaurant is the Wharf House?"

"You're my fiancée, after all." He winked her way.

"I've been your fiancée for a whole five minutes, there's no way you could know that about me."

"Being your fiancée means I talk on the regular with your parents, so of course if I were to meet you at the boardwalk I'd know."

"You really asked my parents?"

"I did and our reservation is in twenty minutes. We're meeting Randy and Autum there."

She was having so much fun with Wes, she didn't want to involve Bonnie and Clyde, but this was Twin Day.

"You know," she said. "A good fiancé would hold my hand."

"A good fiancée would take me behind the funnel cake stand and give me a blow job."

"And a gentleman would say ladies first."

∽

Being around families and happy couples usually made Wes uncomfortable. He wouldn't know how to act, what to say, or how to feel when he saw people on some of the happiest days of their lives. Babies normally made him queasy, soon-to-be brides made him nervous, and he was confused at his reaction when Summer cooed and awwed every time they saw a couple with a stroller.

This was what Frank had been talking about. The hopeless-romantic side of Summer that wanted this kind of life. Usually in situations like this he'd come up with an excuse, something at the office that was time-sensitive, and bail. But not today.

Wes couldn't seem to stop touching her. Holding her hand, letting their hips brush as they walked, even tugging on one of her braids as they leisurely made their way toward the Wharf House. They passed families with tiny tots, kids holding balloons, and couples holding hands. And for the first time, Wes felt as if he belonged.

She was wearing a parking cone and had puked on his shoes and he couldn't seem to get enough of her. In fact, the closer they got to the restaurant, where they were supposed to be meeting his brother and Autumn, the more he dragged his feet.

Randy was a lot on his own, the loudest guy in the room who was into bro hugs, chest bumps, and an all-around good time. Autumn seemed to be able to match his energy. Wes didn't know if that was a good or a bad thing.

But he was here to support Randy, and that's what he was going to do. His brother had promised to slow things down, really think things through, and Wes was counting on that.

"I can't believe I'm saying this, but today has been one of the best Twin Days I've had in years."

That warmed him in several places. "Why do you say that?"

"It wasn't the Autumn show." She clapped her hands over her mouth. "Did I just say that?"

He grinned at the look of horror on her pretty face. "Yes, you did."

"I take it back. I just meant to say it was nice to have a low-key fun time with someone who enjoys dual-sided conversations over diatribes."

"I had a good time too. When your dad told me that Randy

had hijacked your day, I knew how important it was to you and I didn't want you to be the third wheel."

She stopped and her mouth fell open in pleasant surprise. "That's exactly how I felt. How did you know?"

He tugged a pigtail that was sticking out from beneath the cone. "I think I've gotten to know you pretty well over the last few days."

She gifted him with the sweetest smile, and he was certain she was made of everything sugar and sweet. "Me too."

"Today was a pretty epic meet-cute. It had all the tropes. Hero to the rescue, fake dating, Ferris wheel kiss—"

"That's not a trope."

"It is now. Just like puking on my shoes and wearing a traffic cone as an accessory." He lowered his head until his lips grazed her earlobe and his breath tickled her neck. "I especially liked the fake-boyfriend part."

"Only because you got to touch my ass."

He was about to tell her that it was more than that when he heard a frat boy. "Yo, bro! We had a bet if you'd make it. I guessed Summer would bail because of the cone and puking and all, but Autumn said she'd stick out." He turned to Autumn. "I owe you a downtown tonight."

"Thanks for having my back, sis. But eww."

"Always." Autumn placed her left hand to her chest, and that's when Wes saw it. The knuckle-sized rock on her ring finger, twinkling so bright in the sunlight Wes had to blink when he looked at it.

"What the fuck?" Wes said.

"What?" Summer looked confused.

"Guess what happened?" Autumn said, wiggling her finger

more dramatically, and Wes knew the moment Summer caught sight of the diamond Rose threw overboard at the end of *Titanic*. Her breath caught, and her hand, which was still in his, went completely slack.

⚬

"Does Dad know?"

Autumn's eyes narrowed. "Seriously? That's your first question, is if he asked Dad?"

"I just thought you'd want the traditional route," Summer said. "Then again, you said you never wanted to get married, so I guess I don't really know what you want."

"She wanted to be proposed to just like her grandma and grandpa. On the Ferris wheel."

"You did?" Summer asked Autumn, wondering how some guy she'd known for the blink of an eye could know more about her sister than Summer. Especially after how many times she'd told Autumn about her dream wedding.

"I did." Autumn's expression was crushed. Summer had taken what should have been the best day of her life and turned it into an argument. Made it about her. Autumn had just had the perfect proposal and she'd shit all over it.

"I'm sorry, Autumn," she said. "I was just caught off guard. Let me see the ring." Autumn's face lit up with glee as she held her hand out.

"It was my mom's," Randy said. "I got it reset to Autumn's style, but the stones are family heirlooms."

Autumn kissed Randy on the cheek. "Isn't he the sweetest?"

And he had to be sincere, because what kind of serial proposer would give her his mom's wedding ring? It was the act of a thoughtful man who was in love.

Plus, it was just an engagement—that still gave them months or, knowing her sister and her need to have an *event*, even years.

"I'm really happy for you, sis."

Emotion rimmed Autumn's lashes. "You are?"

"Of course I am. You're clearly happy and that's all I want for you."

Autumn worried at her lower lip with her teeth. "Do you really think Dad will be disappointed?"

"No," she said vehemently. "I was projecting my wants onto your moment. Everyone will be thrilled. They love Randy." She looked at her soon-to-be brother-in-law and smiled. "That was sweet of you. And I'm sorry for my reaction. I was just caught off guard."

"Well, you haven't heard the best news," Randy said, taking Autumn's hand, both of them standing tall like a unit. "We're eloping."

Summer looked at her sister for confirmation and her belly churned, like right before she'd puked on Wes. "I'm trying really hard not to react again."

"Did I do something wrong?" Randy asked, completely oblivious to the rising tension in the room.

Summer opened her mouth to say words she knew couldn't ever be taken back she was so mad, but then she felt Wes lace his fingers through hers, standing beside her like they were a team, just like Randy had done with Autumn.

"The Russos aren't like the Kingstons," Wes began. "Each

family member is connected to the next and they work as a unit. Like me, you don't have a lot of experience with that, but I would imagine if Autumn's family were cut out of the wedding it would break their hearts. It would also start off your new chapter alone. And haven't you and I had enough alone in our lifetime?"

Something spilled over Summer's chest at the vulnerable and open way Wes communicated, sharing his own demons to help Summer get what she wanted. And that was to be a part of whatever Autumn and Randy were planning. If she couldn't talk her sister out of rushing into a wedding.

Chapter 23

HAPPILY FOR NOW

Summer was lying on the top bunk silently scrolling through all the emails she'd missed that day.

Ever since the restaurant, Wes had begun to distance himself. It was as if he'd shown too much of himself and now he was retreating back into his cold world of one. He hadn't chosen the floor over her company, but he might as well have. He'd been in bed with his back to her when she'd come in the room.

He was so quiet, if it weren't for the suffocating sexual awareness, she'd have forgotten he was even on the bottom bunk.

She was torn between giving him his space and opening a much-needed conversation about what had transpired that day. Including him asking her to have a clandestine affair. One with an expiration date.

The old Summer would have shaken her little chicken ass out of there. But this new Summer, the one who was tired of putting herself last and was learning to meet things head-on, was telling her to go for it. To throw a stick of dynamite into the water and see what floated to the surface.

From past experience with Wes and water, it was desire and bone-deep honesty that rose to the top. And she wanted that again.

Suddenly, her attention was drawn to a particular email. It was about halfway down the screen with the subject line SLOAN CHASE BOOK SIGNING. It was from Sloan Chase's publicist!

She took in an audible breath, and with shaky hands clicked on the email. With every word the excitement and the reality of it all grew bigger and bigger. She got to the end and had to read every word just to be sure she had read it right the first time through.

"Ohmigod," she whispered, ecstatic. Then she slapped a hand over her lips. "Oh my freaking God!"

She heard a rustling below followed by a bang that shook her bed, and a "Fuck, that hurt!"

"I'm sorry." She leaned over the bed so that she was looking at him upside down. Like Spider-Man hanging from the ceiling. "Did I wake you? I really didn't mean to wake you."

"I lost at least three of my nine lives," he said, his voice sexy with sleep. "Are you okay?"

"Better than okay. I'm awesome!"

"Care to fill me in, since I won't be able to sleep for the rest of the night with this bump on my head?"

She didn't know what to say. She wanted to share the good news with someone—that someone specifically being Wes. But Cleo's video call played back in her mind on super speed, about the plan to be a disruptor. Their big strategy of landing Sloan Chase for a signing on the same day as Wes's new grand opening.

Telling him felt like she was betraying Cleo, but being silent was the same as being a coward. A lying coward.

"If I tell you, you are sworn to secrecy. I don't want my family to know until it's a for-sure thing."

He held himself up on his elbow, and with his other hand reached out and tugged her ponytail playfully. "I'm honored to be your confidant."

"You also have to promise not to get mad. It was Cleo's idea, not mine. I swear."

He lay on his back and stared up at her, a sexy smile on his face. "Did you put sand in the gas tanks of my work trucks?"

"No, but that would have been a good one," she said. "Do you know who Sloan Chase is?"

He snorted. "Love, I might not read romance, but I run a book empire. We've crossed paths a time or two at conferences."

This time she snorted. "Of course you have."

"Plus, I don't think there's a person in the world who hasn't heard her name or read one of her books."

"You read her book," she accused.

"Strictly for research reasons."

"You read it for the sex scenes, admit it."

He reached up and took her hand that was hanging over the side and laced his fingers through hers. "I may have read those parts more than once. How about you?"

"I went through a whole box of AA batteries."

"On what, love?" he said in a sexy voice that made her panties go damp.

"You know."

"Oh, I do. But I want to hear you say it."

"Fine. I broke my vibrator. There. Are you happy now?"

"I think there's another H-word that comes to mind first." He lifted his head and kissed the center of her palm, which hung next to his ear.

"Stop distracting me, because I have to tell you the good *and* bad parts. The good part is that Sloan's publicist said she'd consider having a signing for her new book at my store."

"That's amazing, it could be a game changer for you. Really put you on the independent bookshop map."

"You think?"

"I know."

"And you're okay with that?" A hint of uncertainty creeping in. "Because every customer I get takes one away from you and vice versa."

"I want nothing more than for you to be a huge success and I'll do whatever I can to help you."

"Even if the signing happens to coincide with your new grand opening?"

"It doesn't matter."

"I'd be a disruptor for your big day."

There was a long silent moment where she was certain that he was going to let go of her hand and say the war was back on. Instead, he said, "I am so proud of you. I wish you were down here so I could hug you."

This was it, her gut said. This was the moment when she needed to make her decision. Yesterday, she'd been ready to reestablish the battle lines of their war. Now she found herself in a situation where she needed to decide if they were going to cross those lines. Delicious, dangerous lines that there was no coming back from.

Good thing her hormones were in the driver's seat because she wanted him and she wanted him bad.

"*If* I came down, it wouldn't just be to hug," she said. "Because I have on Gumball Pink panties."

"That statement needs to be expanded on."

"According to Cleo, the color pink is important when trying to relay to a man just how interested you are in sex. Pastel Pink means I'm destined to missionary until the day I die."

"Please tell me you're not into pastels."

"I am not. Now, Wild Orchid hints at the fact that I own a red room and there's a ninety percent chance I have a hidden runway behind my lace that's ready for takeoff. Tickle Me Pink, well, that's self-explanatory. Then there's Gumball Pink, which means I'm playful in bed and don't mind a little blow action."

"So your panties are saying—?"

"Why don't you come up here and see."

∽

That was as clear of a green light as a man could ask for. Which made him one lucky SOB. The woman he'd harassed and hurt in so many ways with his single-mindedness, his desperation to win, was trusting him with her mind and her body.

Wes didn't waste even a breath with indecision. He'd been working hard all day to give her space so that when she agreed, and thank Christ that he had because it sounded like she was as sick of space as he was.

Without a second wasted he was out of bed, climbing the ladder and sliding up her body, running his nose up her bare thigh and bringing her nightshirt with him. He breathed in deep when he got to her thong. "Gumball Pink, my kind of girl. Although I think you have a little Wild Orchid."

"Are you saying I'm kinky."

"I'm saying I know you're kinky."

He nuzzled into her core, running his nose right up the center, and breathed in again, drinking up the scent of her.

"What are you doing?" she asked, breathless.

He rested his body over hers like he was a weighted blanket, lining up all the right parts, then nipped her lower lip. "Laying all my cards on the table."

"I thought that's what you did earlier today."

"Well, now I'm calling. What's your hand say, Summer?"

Summer lifted her hands over her head in invitation. "I guess you're going to have to see for yourself."

A hoarse groan left his lips at the sight of Summer lying beneath him with her hair fanned out across her pillowcase. She was beautiful. So fucking beautiful his steel rod turned into a tent pole in seconds.

"I was serious the other night at the lake. I don't want you to wake up tomorrow and regret this, or act like it's just some kind of blowing-off-steam situation where we're caught up in the events of the day kind of bullshit."

Her eyes went wide at the absoluteness in his voice. "What does that even mean?" she asked.

"I don't know, but I'm willing to figure it out if you are. But you'd better be fucking serious because I'm not looking for a friends-with-benefits kind of thing tonight."

"What are you looking for?" she whispered and, god, he wanted to be inside her—like now. But not until he got confirmation that he wouldn't be some insignificant screw in her life. He'd been insignificant all his life and refused to be that ever again. Especially with this woman.

If he took his dick out of the equation, he could admit to himself that if he wasn't careful he could easily fall for this woman.

Hard and fast.

His heart felt like it was on the Gravatron, spinning faster than gravity, and he'd lost control over his body and then suddenly the bottom dropped out.

You're encroaching on falling territory, you idiot.

Yet he wasn't running away. Nope, he was sliding his palm up her stomach and over her tits, and her nipples immediately beaded at the attention, as if begging him to lavish them with his tongue.

"Wes," she said on a moan, arching into his hand.

"What will it be, love?"

"We argue all the time."

"Thirty-nine times to be exact. Which means we have thirty-nine times of makeup sex in our future. We can bang out some tonight, right now. All you have to say is this isn't a one-time thing."

"This isn't a one-time thing. And I don't know what this is, but I want to figure it out. Together."

That was all he needed to hear. Neither of them was committing to forever, but they knew this wasn't some meaningless one-night stand. He'd had enough of them over the years, and in the months after his breakup, and now he wanted something real. With all the bullshit and deceit in his life, he needed a taste of something honest and sweet. Something pure that he could hold onto.

"Do you still hate me, love?"

"How could you ask that?"

"Because just last week you were leading a petition to get my business shut down and you called me a crumpet."

She cupped his cheek and he pressed into her hand as if he needed the reassurance. "A lot can change in a week."

He pulled her nightshirt up to the underside of her breasts and ran his nose through her cleavage, breathing her in, then met her gaze once again. "You going to tell me exactly what changed and where I stand so we can finally fuck until the sun comes up?"

As if of its own accord her groin arched up to meet his erection, and they both groaned at the sensation of the physical connection.

"I want to fuck until we shatter the sheetrock," she said, and in the slight moonlight filtering through the window he could see her blush.

"Even it if takes days?"

"Even if it takes weeks."

His heart pulsed so hard every limb went on high alert. She was talking like there would be some kind of future for them. A knot of panic and relief tied itself inside up in his chest. Of course she was speaking of the future—she wanted a fairy-tale romance. Something he couldn't offer her, even on the best of days. Not with the upcoming expansion and him moving his home base back to London.

"I'm still leaving in the next few months. Maybe even earlier now that the grand opening has been moved up."

"Wes," she said in the gentlest of voices, "I'm not going to fool myself into believing this is some romance novel with a happily-ever-after, but with you I can handle a happily-for-now."

"I just don't want you to confuse all of the meet-cutes and the heat of the day to give you unfair expectations."

"I think you're selling yourself short, but if anything I'm thinking clearer than I have in months."

"But be certain, that once I'm in you you're mine until this is over." Her eyes went wide with shock over his possessive talk. "Say it. You're mine."

"And you're mine," she said. "I wouldn't have it any other way. I like you, Wes. A lot. And I want you."

"How bad?"

She took his hand and ran it down to cup her core. "Can't you feel how badly I want you?"

"I've been so focused on not screwing this up I've clearly been neglecting this beautiful pussy."

He crawled his way down her body, taking her Gumball Pink panties with him—and, would you look at that, a landing strip came into sight. Damn, he was toast.

"Hell, I'm obsessed with you," he said, not caring if it freaked her out, which it did by the way her body stiffened a smidge. But he'd said he was laying it all out there. And it wasn't as if he was getting down on one knee. "I'm obsessed with fucking you, with kissing you, with arguing with you."

"You like arguing with me?"

"I love arguing with you. But I'm terrified that one time I'll go too far and it will be the last argument we have."

"You're not the only one with an obsession. I've read your profile a dozen times and scroll through the pictures you put up."

"The pictures my brother put up. And I already know you're a snoop because RoChance alerts you every time someone looks at your profile."

Uncertainty lit her eyes. "You haven't looked at mine."

"Hell yeah, I have. You have to look in the settings. I've also listened to your podcast. Every single one."

"You have?"

He rested his forehead against hers. "I love them. You're authentic and funny and endearing."

"I've listened to your podcast a few times. You're charismatic and really know a lot about business."

"I know about a lot of things," he said, and he ran his hands down her thighs and yanked them up until her legs were bent at the knee and she was completely exposed. She gasped with surprise. "And I think it's time to get down to business."

Her response was a long, lusty groan because he went straight in, using his entire mouth to suck her in. But it wasn't enough. He burrowed himself in her wet folds like a starving man, loving how her hips pushed up against him, riding his face.

He was drowning in her scent and taste. He'd imagined a million times what she'd taste like, and man his imagination must be lacking because this was the sweetest thing he'd ever devoured.

He found an easy rhythm, fast and deep enough to bring her to the edge but with enough restraint that she didn't quite make it over.

"Wes," she begged, her hips now moving against him so hard he thought he might suffocate. Then she clenched her thighs around his head and he was sure he was going to pass out. But what a hell of a way to go. "I've waited so long. Please."

He looked up at her through his lashes. "As you wish," he quoted from *The Princess Bride*.

That was all it took. She bucked once, twice, and then fell down the stomach-dropping start of a rollercoaster. Because that's what this night was about. Dips, turns, climbing, falling, even upside down and sideways. Front, back, and every position in between.

"Wes," she arched up all the way, thoroughly suffocating him in the best way possible. He let her ride out the intensity. Then he was off the bed, rustling through his bag for a strip of condoms, and back on top before the sex haze had even left her eyes.

"You ready, love?"

She nodded, as if she didn't have enough breath to speak.

"We're going to shatter that sheetrock."

"Big words for a big man."

"I always stand by my words, and 'big' doesn't even begin to describe it."

Her hand slid down his bare torso, beneath the elastic of his pajama bottoms and took him in her hand. She moaned.

"I can barely wrap my hands around it."

He kissed her nose. "I'll go slow, I promise."

"I don't want slow. I want you, intense and single-minded. I want the man who doesn't stop until it's done."

"Baby, I'm going to fuck you so hard we'll break the damn bed."

"Sounds like a long night." She stretched out like a sated kitten, her shirt pulled all the way up over her tits.

He licked one, then the other, then put his forehead to hers. "This bed doesn't have half the determination I have for you. We'll rock the foundation."

"Do I sense a wager?"

"Are you trying to start an argument when I'm seconds away from sliding all the way home and giving you the night of your life?"

"It's foreplay, remember? And who says I won't be the one giving you the night of your life?"

"God, I love it when you're feisty. And I know how much you love a good bet."

"We break this bed on round one and I host you as the King of Cocks on my podcast. If we don't, then you look over my business plan and give me sound advice on how to kick your ass in selling romance books."

Already wrapped and ready, he rested his erection at her opening and said, "Deal," then he slid in as far as he could to seal the deal. She gasped, and he was only halfway inside her. Damn, she was tight.

He gave her a moment to adjust to his size then slowly began pumping, in and out, side to side, until she took him inch by inch.

"You doing okay? he asked.

"There's more?" She sounded fatigued just thinking about it.

With the ceiling just above him he didn't have the room to flip her over or come at her from the side. He didn't have much room to reposition himself at all. But he could move her.

"Here." He caressed the gentle inner slope of her knee then slowly brought it up until it was by her side. "This will make it easier." And he slid in the final inch.

"So much better," she groaned. "So good. Don't stop."

She wrapped her arms around his neck and pulled him to her

mouth and they started making out. There was no other word to describe it. Lips devouring, teeth nipping, and her hands were everywhere. His hands made their way to her exposed tits and he loved on each one for what seemed like hours.

"Have I mentioned how insane your tits are. They're perfect." He sucked one in his mouth hard enough to leave a mark. But it wasn't dark enough, so he sucked harder, making sure to leave a mark on her pale skin.

When was the last time he'd wanted to leave his mark on a woman? Lindsey Hayes, grade eleven, in the back of his mom's Fiat after a school dance.

"Did you just give me a hickey?" she asked, amused.

"I wanted to put one on your neck so the entire fucking world could see you're mine, but I thought that might be a little too possessive too soon."

"I like possessive." Her words seemed to shock her as much as they shocked him. "Let me clarify. In this moment I'm feeling very possessive myself." Then she lifted her head and sank her teeth into his shoulder. So hard it bordered on pain and pleasure.

"Tit for tat," he said and she laughed at the innuendo. "And I still have one tit to go. But I'm thinking I like here better."

He nuzzled into the crook of her neck and found the perfect spot that she could hide if she wanted, or wear as a badge of honor, and closed his mouth around it. With every suck he pumped into her. Deeper thrusts, curling up to hit that glorious G-spot.

She wrapped her free leg around his waist, loosely resting it on his ass. Helping him set a rhythm that was pleasurable for her. He was going so deep she had to put her hands against the headboard to hold on and not bang the top of her head against the wood.

"Harder," she panted, moving her hips against him. When he thrust in she pushed up, creating a friction that had his balls tightening up to almost inside of him.

Soon the headboard was pounding the wall, and the bed was squeaking beneath them. There was no way the entire house couldn't hear them. And he didn't give a shit. He'd been anticipating this moment with this woman for months.

The bed was rocking and the springs were cutting into his knees and elbows as he held himself over her so as not to crush her. She wasn't a petite woman, but she wasn't any match for his size.

The squeaking intensified, as did the pounding.

"Wes," she breathed. "I'm about to . . ." She trailed off into a loud groan that sounded suspiciously like "Weston."

"Me too, love. Just hold on another second or two. I want to do this together."

"You want to win the bet."

"That too, but I want this to be like we're one. I need this to feel like we're in sync."

He wasn't in sync in anything else in his life, but there was an instinctual desire to be in sync with her. At least as long as it lasted.

His hand slid down her stomach to her pleasure button and he used his thumb to drive her higher. The bed hit the wall so hard he heard the wall crack. But he still couldn't seem to get deep enough. He rolled her onto her side and came at her from behind. Both of them being spoons while they forked each other's brains out.

His hands gripped her tits, which were bouncing with the aggressive thrusts, and pinched her nipples. And there she went. Flying off upside down and around the spiral curve of the coaster.

Her core was tightening around him, so he flipped her on her stomach, yanked up a leg and went all the way in. With a loud string of colorful words, which were surprising coming from the woman who never cussed, she clenched and began milking him.

Her face was pressed into the pillow, his into the slope of her neck, and they were both panting as they came back down to earth. Even though he'd blown every drop he had, he kept pumping until he couldn't move an inch.

Their bodies were slick with sex and sweat, but they didn't let go of one another. She turned in his arms and cuddled into his side. And he drew her to him so tightly he was afraid he might hurt her, so he loosened his grip—a fraction. But then her arms tightened.

Jesus, that had been amazing. Mind-blowing was more like it. He'd had all kinds of sex with all kinds of woman. Who knew it would take a bookish tyrant to tame his beast? And with her, he felt tamed. Calm and safe. Two things he always viewed as a weakness but today it had made him feel as if he were on top of the world.

"We didn't quite break the bed," she said in a languorous way. "You have to help me come up with a business plan to take on the big tycoon next door."

He lazily ran a hand down her spine. "I would have helped you no matter what."

She looked up at him through her lashes. "Really?"

"We can't have you losing to the crumpet twice in a row, now, can we?"

"What do you mean? I won."

"Just keep thinking that." Wes flipped her onto her stomach again and came down on her body like a man on a mission. "I'm still hard as a rock." He showed her just how dire the situation was. He'd come, yet he was still hard.

"So this is still round one?"

"Exactly. Now lift those hips and put your hands on the headboard. You're going to need something to hang onto for this."

"What are you going to hold onto?"

"This." He wrapped her ponytail around his hand and tugged her head to the right, exposing her neck and holding her in place. She moaned in pleasure and they fucked until the bed collapsed onto the bottom bunk.

Chapter 24

THE MORNING AFTER

Summer stepped out of the shower with a grin on her face. Not surprising since Wes had just taken her up against the shower wall, and then down on the shower floor.

"If you're still able to walk then I didn't do my job correctly," he said, snaking his chiseled bicep around her stomach and pulling her and her towel back into the shower, where he planted on her a loud, long, languid kiss that had her body revved to go like it was the final light at a Formula 1 race.

They'd crossed the finish line four times last night and three this morning. One more turn around the track and she wasn't going to be able to move, let alone walk.

"You got my towel all wet," she accused with no heat.

"Sorry about that. Let me dry you off with my tongue."

His other arm came around her and he pulled her against him so that his erection slid between her ass cheeks. He was rock hard.

"Impressive," she said, turning her head so she could give him a kiss.

"I'll show you impressive." He walked her under the hot spray of water and then placed her hands on the wall. Using his foot he spread her legs apart like she was being frisked, but in the sexiest way possible. With one arm still around her waist, he pushed her over so that she was bent at the waist.

"Damn, love, you're a walking wet dream."

"A wet dream who needs to be a dry reality so she can load up the car and make it back to Ridgefield on time."

"Five more minutes won't hurt," he said and her heart beat until her head was spinning. What happened to the all-work-no-play tyrant who would have been up at five a.m. to drive back to Ridgefield to give his board hell?

"You said that thirty minutes ago."

"What can I say. A job worth doing is a job worth doing well."

His hand slid down her slick stomach to her go-button and began making lazy circles with his thumb. His other hand cupped her right breast, which was still tender from his love mark. And teeth marks.

"Weston," she sighed. "You're not playing fair."

"There is no fair in love and war."

She knew he hadn't meant to say that four-letter word in reference to her, but hearing it fall from his lips made her heart do stupid, dangerous things—like want things that weren't possible.

Brain scrambled with pleasure and confusion, she tried to reverse into his embrace. He stopped her—not that she gave up much of a fight.

"At least let me make you come," he said with determination in his voice. "With my mouth. I want you to be the first thing I taste in the morning."

How many mornings was he talking? Six? Sixty? And she didn't want to ask because she was afraid of the answer. He'd been clear about what he could offer and she'd been clear in her agreement. Then she'd woken up with his arms wrapped around her, like a protective bubble, his lips delivering gentle open-mouthed kisses down her neck, and all that clarity and common sense went out the window.

Which was the only reason she could think of why, when he turned her around and dropped to his knees, instead of letting him part her legs, she straddled him, taking him in one long, luxurious slide home.

He growled and grabbed her hips, moving her up and then back down. He was on the third pump when she stopped. "Condom!"

He froze and went white as a sheet.

"I'm so sorry. I was just so caught up in you and this that I didn't think." How many women had tried this same ruse with him to trap him for his money? Had she just expired their already expiration-dated relationship? "I swear it was a mistake. But if it helps I'm clean and have an IUD."

She went to slide off of him but he held her firmly in place, with him all the way inside her. "Love, I believe you. And I'm clean too. And you feel so fucking good I'm good just going bareback. But only if you are."

"I am," she whispered against his lips.

"Good, because I'm starting to like having nothing between us. No walls or barriers. Just open"—he thrust inside her—"honest"—another thrust—"us."

She knew he was talking about this moment, but her heart wanted it to be about more. Her throat tightened and her eyes began to sting, so, embarrassed, she buried her face in the curve of his shoulder. The last thing she needed was for him to see her crying while they had sex.

But as always he sensed the shift in energy. "You okay?" he whispered into her hair.

"I was just thinking that five more minutes won't hurt."

∽

Summer strolled down the stairs with a goofy smile on her face. She couldn't help it. A sex-a-thon with a sex god could do that to a girl.

She was packed and ready to say her goodbyes and head out. Goodbyes were hard for her, especially now that she was going home alone. Normally, she'd be heartbroken and in near tears, but she couldn't seem to muster up even a one. Because she wasn't alone. She was riding back to Ridgefield with Wes.

Last night had been life-changing. And it wasn't a one-night stand—a romance trope she was more than happy to skip. So it wouldn't last forever? It was a happily-for-now, and if that meant more time with Wes, she could handle it. She'd have to handle it. Wes was right when he said long-distance was hard. And between their responsibilities she just didn't see how it would work. Not without someone getting hurt in the end. Because it would eventually end.

Still, here she was, smiling like a fool.

"You need to talk to your sister before you finalize this." Her father's voice echoed from the kitchen. The last time she'd heard him this stern was when Autumn agreed to go to prom with Summer's long-time crush.

"I will, Dad," Autumn said defiantly. "When the time is right. I need to see if they even have an opening."

"You will tell her today. Do you understand, young lady. I won't have her blindsided. Not about this."

Summer assumed they were talking about the elopement, but even that news couldn't get her down. She didn't think anything could sink her mood. Not today. Not after last night.

She was in a relationship.

You're mine.

Just thinking about him growling those words last night, as if he owned her body and soul, made her panties damp. Schooling her features, she walked into the kitchen. It wasn't as if anyone who didn't hear them last night wouldn't figure it out when they saw the broken bed, but she still wanted to play it cool. "What do I need to know?"

Guilt filled the room, making the air so thick Summer could barely breathe. Another ball was about to drop. She could sense it using her twin powers. Autumn was carrying another secret. One that would make getting engaged look like child's play.

"We were just talking about the proposal and . . . Oh my god! Is that a hickey?" Autumn pulled Summer's hair to the side. "It is!" A bright smile overtook her face. "I knew it. I just knew it. Watching you two fight was like watching Skinamax. The day of the kayak race, the heat nearly singed my eyebrows."

"Summer Marissa Russo," her mother scolded. "What have I told you about your body being a temple?"

"That you only get one," Autumn inserted, ever so helpful.

Blanche wasn't talking about sex, she was talking about marring her skin. Hickeys, sunburns, piercings, and tattoos all fell into the same category: sinful.

"I'm twenty-four, I'm pretty sure I can—"

"That was my doing, Mr. and Ms. Russo," Wes said from the kitchen's threshold without an ounce of apology in his voice. Then his hands rested on her shoulders in support, and she melted back into him. It wasn't a conscious reaction, but a feeling leftover from their night and morning had her nearly burrowing into his big capable arms.

She felt his possessiveness, which normally she wouldn't like. But he wore it well. It also made her feel as if she weren't about to have a bomb dropped on her alone.

Plus, he was making a statement to her family. At this moment in time, they were a team.

"And the bed?" Cecilia asked, and when Wes looked at her with a *how the hell did you know about that?* look, her aunt said, "My guides told me."

"You walked past their room," Blanche said, outing her.

"Only to see if what I was shown was true." She looked at Wes and Summer with a mischievous smile. "And it was. Was that you too, sonny?"

"I'd like to take the credit, but Summer might fight me for the title."

"Can we stop talking about this? Please?" Summer said. She'd turned to Wes to apologize for her family's behavior when she stopped short. No longer was he wearing cargo shorts and T-shirts, he was in a full suit with a tie and cuff-links. He was clean-shaven and looked like the cover of GQ magazine. The difference was so stark her heart leapt—and not in a good way. She was reminded of the kind of man he was when he wore a suit. One who didn't smile or laugh—a man who put the bottom line first.

As if reading her mind, he gave her a playful wink and her heart leapt into triple-time. He was back. That easygoing, fun-loving man who gave mind-blowing orgasms, kissed like a pro, argued like a lobbyist. The man she'd dangerously started to fall for.

"What did I tell you, dear," Cecilia whispered loud enough for everyone to hear. "Your guides said they'd bring you home a good Italian man. In a tall, dark, and sexy suit." She waved a hand in a very Vanna White-esque manner and said, "Voila."

Summer remembered the first day he'd met her family and how uncomfortable he'd been. But now it was as if he felt part of the pack. And that made Summer love her family all the more.

"Hate to burst your bubble, but I'm British," Wes said.

"Not everyone can be perfect, dear." Cecilia patted Wes on the shoulder.

Summer could see where this line of questioning was going, so she interrupted it before it began. "Before everyone starts speculating, we are just seeing where this goes. It's new and fun and Wes is moving to Los Angeles in a few months and then he's going back to London."

She felt his hand loosen just the tiniest bit, as if he didn't like her answer. But she wasn't going to let herself think that this was more than they'd agreed to. Her head was determined to keep her heart out of it for once. Because she hadn't pushed things, hadn't turned a regular meet into a meet-cute, hadn't gone in with expectations, and look at her now. She was spending time with a great man and on the way toward mastering the *Kama Sutra*.

Boldness swept through her and instead of hiding her

hickey behind a cascade of hair, she pulled her hair over the opposite shoulder, wearing it proudly.

"Now, what did everyone think was so important that it required a family meeting without me?" Summer asked.

All eyes went to Autumn, who plastered a big, bright smile on her face. "Randy and I have been thinking about how no one would be there if we eloped, so we've decided to have a wedding."

Summer walked over to her sister and gave her a big hug, lifting her off her feet. "That's the best news! What changed your mind?"

Autumn pressed her forehead to Summer's. "You guys did. I can't imagine a wedding without you as my maid of honor."

"Or you as my best man," Randy said to Wes, who had to clear his throat before responding.

"I'd be honored."

Summer's eyes began to tingle with glee. Her sister was becoming her sister again, putting the family first, respecting their bond as twins, and thinking past her impulsive nature. And Randy and Wes were starting to connect like brothers were supposed to.

"Autumn," her dad prodded.

"Right." Autumn snapped her fingers. "We've decided to keep it small, you know, just a few friends and family. Private and intimate. VIP only, if you know what I mean. And we've already found the perfect place."

"Where?"

Autumn spread her arms like Julie Andrews in *The Sound of Music* and spun around the kitchen. "Right here."

A lump lodged itself in Summer's throat as the betrayal of

it all pounded in her head, causing her eyes to throb. "Like, in Mystic?"

"No, silly. We want the reception here, at the beach house. Of course the wedding would take place at the Church by the Sea. Isn't that a great idea?"

Summer had to force the sound past the growing lump to form actual words. And even then, they sounded strained. "Of course it is. It's my idea."

"Well, kind of. I mean, I'll have a different color scheme and the vibe will be more luxe, but how great would it be if we both shared the same wedding venue? We share everything else," Autumn added when Summer just stood there with her mouth gaping open. "What's one more thing?"

"How can you even ask me that? I mean what am I supposed to say? 'Oh, you know the wedding I've been planning since I was eleven, the one that I have a hundred-page scrapbook on, well, my sister is stealing it.'"

"I'm not stealing it! I'm just using it as inspiration. Imitation is really a form of flattery. You should feel flattered."

"Well, I don't." Summer began walking out of the kitchen. "I don't have time for this. I'm already late getting on the road. I need to pack the car, get Buttercup, and head out."

"Don't leave mad, Summs," Autumn said with so much sugar in her voice it turned Summer's stomach.

"I'm not mad." She was crushed. "I'm just late for work."

∞

Wes considered beating some sense into his brother, but it was clear Autumn was the showrunner in the relationship.

Randy was just along for the ride. Plus, he wanted to get to Summer as soon as possible to see if there was anything he could do to make the situation better. Other than buying the church and not letting his brother get married there.

He was still considering that when he walked out the kitchen door and saw Summer crouched down on the balls of her feet, her head in her hands. Her shoulders were slumped over and shaking slightly with emotion.

In all of the times they'd gone head to head, he'd never seen her cry. In fact, he didn't know what to do with tears. But seeing them fall from her beautiful brown eyes was apparently his kryptonite.

He walked straight toward her, and instead of the empty platitudes he'd usually use on a woman in distress he went for actions over words.

He took Summer's hands and lifted her into his arms. She clung to him as if she would never let go and he allowed himself to imagine for just a moment what it would be like if she didn't. Strangely, it didn't rouse the terror and the cornered feeling he'd imagined it would.

It felt right.

"Do you want to talk about it?" Wes asked, pressing his lips into her hair.

"Nope."

"That's not how this works now. So we can have a conversation or you can just listen."

She swallowed.

"I think what your sister is doing is bollocks. And I think that no one but your dad is standing up for you is shit. I know how it feels to be you against the world, and I want you to know that you're not alone. You have me. I think I made that pretty clear last night."

She tightened her grip.

"I take that as a yes. Were you about to take off without me?"

Silence.

"Another yes."

"What do you want me to say? I'm crushed that my sister is being so selfish and keeping secrets. And not just from me."

Wes froze. "What does that mean? Is she lying to my brother?"

"That's between them. But let's just say they have a lot to talk about before this wedding happens."

"If I have it my way, they will have a long engagement followed by a destination wedding."

She looked up at him with red-rimmed eyes. "My family can't afford that, and neither can my sister."

"But I can."

"Did you just offer to pay for my sister's wedding so that she won't steal mine?"

"Yes."

"You make it sound so easy. Like money can fix everything."

"Not everything, but it can fix a lot." He pressed their foreheads together. "Let me fix this for you?"

"Why? You hate weddings."

"But you don't. And when you find that right man, I want you to have the wedding of your dreams."

Even as he said it, a rush of jealousy pulsed through his body. His hand fisted at the idea of some other man kissing her, getting down on one knee, sharing her bed. Putting a ring on that elegant finger. That lucky son of a bitch better appreciate—no, worship—what he had.

"Thank you." She went up on her toes and delivered a gentle kiss. "But this is my family's problem, and I don't want to drag you into the drama."

Normally he'd thank Christ for a clean exit from family drama, but for some reason her comment didn't sit right. Not after the time they'd spent together, and the warm welcome he'd received from her family.

"Plus, I could never take your money."

This truly flabbergasted him. "Why? I have it. You need it. Problem solved."

"I think a lot of people come to you for money, and I don't want to be one of those people. You deserve more from me and more from whatever this thing is between us."

"This thing between us already involves your family. It took everything I had not to flatten my brother."

"It isn't Randy. It's Autumn, and I see that now. And she'll see it when she's ready too."

"'Sorry' doesn't even begin to cover how screwed up that was. And I wish I could take you back to this morning in the shower before the world interrupted."

"Is this what's going to happen to us? We'll go back to Ridgefield and the world will interrupt what time we have together? Will the reality of owning rival shops put up a roadblock that's impossible to cross? And please be honest, I don't think I can stand another person I care about playing me."

He cupped her cheeks so that her gaze was locked on his. "As far as I'm concerned, that rivalry ended the second you kissed me in the water that night."

"You kissed me."

He smiled, then brushed the tears away with the pad of his thumb. "Whatever you say, love."

Chapter 25

SMALL GESTURES

"So, that's her final decision? She doesn't even need to talk to me first?" Summer asked, so much emotion bubbling up to the surface, first from the ride home and then from this amazing news, she was afraid her cork would pop.

"Nope. Her mind is made up," Cleo said. She was kicked back in the office chair, with her feet on the desk, cleaning her fingernails with a pocket knife. "Her decision is final."

"I thought she'd at least want to talk to me first, discuss the details."

"I guess your email did all the talking she needed because Sloan Chase is going to be signing her new release right here, at All Things Cupid."

"Oh my god!" Summer clapped her hands over her mouth in utter disbelief, excitement causing her to bounce on the balls of her toes. "It's really happening?"

"There are a few terms and demands in her contract," Cleo went on.

"Contract?" That sounded so official. She'd never signed a contract with an author before. Then again, this was Sloan Chase.

Summer had just made an agreement with Wes that she wanted to desperately amend. Now, the idea of signing on an official dotted line for her career was so overwhelming her body didn't know which emotion to feel. What if she regretted the terms she agreed to? What if Sloan wanted to change them but it was too late?

"Are you going to puke on me? I know how your gag reflex just loves to fuck with my life. So, I'd like to remind you I'm wearing my new biker jacket. If you puke on me, you're puking on the whole biker gang, and they don't take lightly to outsiders blowing chunks on their property."

"I'm not going to throw up."

"Ah shit. Then it's tears." Cleo scratched the inside of her wrist like she was breaking out in hives. She stood and puffed her chest out. "Here, puke on me instead. It'll be less painful. For the both of us."

"I'm not going to puke or cry. I just want to know what I'm agreeing to."

"Little things, like she needs a green room to relax in between events."

"Events? As in plural?"

"She agreed to do the podcast with a live audience first, take a break, and then come back for the signing."

"My podcast?"

"Just think of how many listeners it will bring. We're talking maybe ten thousand."

That's what Summer was afraid of. Not the new listeners and potential slew of new customers. That would be a dream come true. It was the pressure to be perfect that she'd battled her entire life that was making a tsunami in her stomach. What if she blanked? What if she was so star-struck she babbled on? There were so many what-ifs her brain went into overload.

"Nope. Don't you dare spiral on me," Cleo said firmly. "Do you know how much time I've spent on this event?"

"Um, exactly five minutes, because that's how long we've known about it." Cleo remained mum on the subject. "Right?"

"I may have called her publicist's assistant, and from one assistant to another we had a long chat. Where I may or may not have brought up the fact that there is a customer who is terminal."

It was the truth. Every Wednesday the Bosom Buddies, all women with breast cancer, met at the shop for their book club and support meeting. But to use their disease as an ace up your sleeve? "Cleo, that's low even for you."

"FYI, I asked the group if they minded that I used their struggle and support to help attract such a big author, and you know what they did? They preordered the woman's book and said use away. But Sloan's assistant told me in confidence that they were already going to say yes to the event."

"So locking down Sloan was all on me?"

"All on you, sister. Your email must have really touched her. Because she could sign anywhere in the world and she chose here."

Summer felt a burst of pride and gratitude in her belly, making her dizzy with excitement. "I had a friend help me," she said, thinking back to the car ride home, when she'd drafted the email and Wes had encouraged her to go personal, really encouraging her to pull from her personal life and go with emotion not facts. Although, being the consummate numbers guy, he did throw in a few hard numerical facts about their customer base and the store's long history in the romance community.

Summer scanned the contract and it was like reading an encyclopedia—extensive and complicated. Then she got to the last page and nearly hyperventilated.

"She wants me to spend five thousand dollars of my own money promoting this?"

"Which wouldn't be a problem if Autumn had paid you back."

"It's a problem either way." She'd never spent more than a few hundred bucks promoting an author signing. She mainly hung flyers around town, mentioned it on her podcast, and sent out an email to her loyal customers. "I'd have to dig into my wedding fund." More like drain it.

"Before you keel over on me, let's focus on the solutions not the problem. First off, the green room will be easy."

Summer plopped into the chair facing the desk as if she were the guest in this situation and her mind was racing with solutions. "We can just use the staff room and turn it into a spa-like haven. As for the podcast. We'll have to sell tickets ahead of time to limit going over the official capacity and having someone call the fire marshal."

"You mean like Sir Crumpet?"

Summer's face heated. She couldn't believe she used to call him that. Of course, it was before she knew him, but still. How prejudiced she'd been, assuming that he was the bad guy in what was just a shitty situation. "He would never call the fire marshal on me, and we should probably stop referring to him by that name."

Cleo studied Summer with narrowed eyes. "You slept with him. You actually slept with the enemy." It was a statement not a question. Summer was about to deliver a speech she'd prepared on the way over to defend Wes and herself when Cleo said, "Was it hot? Oh, yeah, that sex-dazed look tells me it was. Did he get the job done?"

Summer just smiled a mischievous smile.

"Yeah, his BDE is so big he nearly made me toss out my vibrator the first time I saw him." She leaned forward on the desk, resting on her elbows. "We talking home run or grand slam?"

Summer actually heard herself sigh. "Out of the ballpark."

"The vibrators of the world thank His Royal Highness. He has no idea how many vibrators he's prevented from working in a sweat shop."

"I'm not that bad," Summer said defensively. Cleo lifted a brow. "Okay, fine, maybe I had a little problem. But sex with men never felt like they write about it in novels."

"And he's novel-worthy?"

Summer leaned forward. "Babe, he's *Guide*-worthy."

"Then why do you seem so conflicted? I mean, don't get me wrong, your hair is sticking up in the back, you have no foundation on around your mouth, and your eyes seem a little crazy like you had a quickie in the parking lot, but you also seemed lost."

Summer released a dreamy breath. "He's moving back to London and doesn't believe in long-distance relationships."

"And new boy Asher last night didn't think he had the core strength to do the Betty Rocker, but he lasted nearly an hour. Men just need the right stimulation and, *pow*, they're on their knees begging to give you what you deserve. And last night I deserved a little Face-Off 69 action. What do you deserve, Summer?"

Wasn't that the question of the hour. A month ago she would have said she deserved a quiet, dog-owning man who was into stimulating conversations and walks on the beach. Now she wanted a straight-laced, alpha male with Big Dick Energy who drove her crazy—in and out of bed.

Now that they'd opened the floodgates, they couldn't seem to keep their hands to themselves. They'd even pulled over on an abandoned road and done a little rocking action of their own—twice. But then they'd arrived back in Ridgefield and he'd given her a quick peck and disappeared into his lair. She hadn't seen or heard from him since.

"Okay, if that's too hard of a concept—not surprising after the dickheads you've dated—then what do you want?"

"More than a quick sendoff smooch before he heads into work, but not so much that I get distracted from my goal of making this the most famous romance bookshop in the world."

"What did he say he wanted?"

"About the same."

"Then what's the problem?"

Summer dropped her head to her hands. "I'm pretty sure he's already distracting me." She took a deep breath and met Cleo's gaze head-on. At least she had the courage to face her friend after she'd thrown her under the bus. "I told him about the signing."

Cleo shot up to a stand. "You did what? Why?"

"Because it felt wrong to keep it from him. And if I win I want to do it the honorable way. Not by playing some kind of game."

"But the element of surprise is the only thing we had on our side, she says to David concerning Goliath."

"That's not true. We have enough grit and determination on our side."

"I'm sure he's sitting in his five-thousand-dollar ergonomically correct chair, checking the minutes on his Rolex until your shop goes under."

"He's not like that," she argued. "Maybe once upon a time he was, but that guy is gone. He's really an amazing, caring, reliable, and honest man, Cleo."

Cleo sank back into her chair and exhaled slowly and painfully. "I had a feeling he was."

Summer placed her hand over her heart. "He called me *his*."

"Damn, I love a possessive streak in a man. But this ruins my entire story I made up about his silver-spoon childhood."

"He isn't that either, and his story is heartbreaking."

Cleo rolled her eyes so hard her brow piercing nearly popped out. "If you say so. Just don't fuck this whole thing up with getting you feeling so involved you stop putting yourself first. Because when you agree to this signing you are putting it all on the line."

Weren't those Wes's exact words to her?

"What do you mean?"

Cleo pulled out a file with a fifteen-page printed contract in it with sticky notes, highlighted lines, and notes in the margin. "I looked it over a time or two, had Asher look it over, but his specialty is real-estate law, so you need to read it before you get back to them. Maybe even hire a third party."

Summer's stomach went sour with uncertainty. She didn't know the first thing about contracts, and hiring someone meant spending money she didn't have. Then Wes with all his podcast wisdom popped into her head, and she knew he'd understand the document. Or if he didn't, he'd definitely refer her to someone who would.

"I know a guy," she said without revealing said guy's name.

"Does he look like the dark, dangerous Duke of Loafers? Because if so, he's the first guest to arrive for the podcast."

Summer turned around and her breath caught. Standing against the back wall, leaning on his big shoulder, was Wes. He'd lost the tie and suit jacket, and his shirtsleeves were rolled up above his elbow. His hair looked mussed, like he'd been running his hands through it, and his eyes looked tired. She knew he'd had a meeting with the board today and hoped it had gone in his favor. But his drawn expression told her that it hadn't.

Without saying goodbye to Cleo, Summer raced out the office and over to Wes. Before he could get a word out she kissed the hell out of him. It made Autumn and Randy's exploits look like hand-holding.

He let out a long sigh and his hands slid over her ass and into her back pockets, jerking her against his hard body. They didn't stop until they both needed oxygen.

"How did the meeting go?" she asked.

"I don't want to talk about that right now. Right now, I want to say good luck on your podcast and just know I'll be here cheering you on."

"You left work early to see my podcast?"

He cupped her cheek. "I left early to see you." His eyes went over her shoulder. "And why is your employee pointing a switchblade at me?"

"That's her way of saying hi."

"Somehow I didn't expect tonight's topic would be based around the feminist view of *Jane Eyre*," Mable said.

"Cleo kind of hijacked the podcast," Summer said. "She wanted to do a parallel book talk."

"Well, it worked. Everyone was entertained and felt like they were a part of everything going on."

The podcast had been packed. Not a spare seat in the house. And Cleo had been right, not only had the entire audience bought both books and read them, they'd been excited to compare the two books and talk about what Bertha in the attic symbolized. They'd also bought other books while they waited for the podcast recording to start.

Summer had strategically placed Cleo at the front door, organizing them in a line that zigzagged through the aisles, so people could peruse while waiting to be seated. Summer had walked up and down the aisle welcoming everyone and inquiring about what kind of romance they liked, then coming up with a suggestion to match their favorite trope or genre. It was a genius idea and it had been all hers.

The excitement from hearing back from Sloan Chase's publicist had given her a bump of confidence she hadn't felt in a long time. And maybe it also had something to do with the handsome, noble man who'd stood in the back, smiling at her as if she were the most entertaining and beautiful woman on the planet. He'd even winked at her once or twice, which had made her belly flutter.

She hadn't expected him to stay for the entire thing, but he'd stood there, stoic as ever, a proud smile on his face. And all that pride was for her—jump-starting an emotion that felt new and refreshing and something she wanted to experience every day.

He'd even waited until she'd locked up the shop so he could walk her home. Even though the stairs to her apartment were around the back, they walked slowly, making the most of every second.

The night sky was inky with a silver glow from the full moon. A gentle breeze spun around them and he slid his jacket over her shoulders.

"Thank you," she said, looking up at him through her lashes. "That's very sweet of you."

"No one's ever called me sweet before."

"That's because no one knows the real you." She took his hand. "Not like I do." She started swinging their arms as they walked up the concrete steps side by side.

Summer's apartment was a small three-bedroom, one-bath, with all of the original floors and fixtures from the forties when it was built. Black-and-white tile laid on the diagonal, arched entryways, and a reading nook in the front window—which was all leaded glass and cast rainbows across the room, filling every cranny with brilliant colors.

This was the apartment her grandparents first moved to when they'd bought the shop. It was the place where her mom was born, where Autumn and Summer had spent part of their childhood. And it was the place where the two had moved into when they'd graduated high school. There were so many memories and so much history tied to this place, Summer never wanted to leave.

She'd thought Autumn felt the same, but that had been wishful thinking. What was the reality? That they could both get married, have kids, and still share the apartment? It was nothing more than a silly plan made by a silly little girl who'd never imagined a reason good enough to be separated from her twin.

Well, that wish would be snuffed out as soon as Autumn packed her stuff and moved down to New York to start her new life with her new love. A reality Summer was trying really hard to come to terms with.

Wes gave her hand a gentle squeeze. "Thinking about Autumn?"

"A little." He raised an eyebrow. "Okay, a lot. How did you know?"

"I guess I know you better than you think I do. Which makes us both lucky."

Summer pulled her key out of her purse and put it in the lock, but couldn't seem to turn it. She dropped her head against the wood and felt tears fill her eyes. "I was just thinking that this is the first time I've come home alone and Autumn won't be here. Like ever again. It's a lot to take in, you know?"

His arms came around her from behind and he pulled her against his chest and whispered, "I know. When my mom died I dreaded going back in the house because I knew it was the first page of my new chapter. A chapter without her in it."

"How old were you?"

"Eighteen. A first-year at university."

"And your dad didn't offer for you to come out and live with him?"

"I didn't want anything from him. And I still don't. If it weren't for Randy I would have let the board have the company. But now that they're trying to take it away, they've awakened the beast. I will maintain control of BookLand until I decide I've done what I need to do for Randy. Plus, it was my mom's dream for me to get my birthright, so I think she'd be proud of me moving here and what I'm doing." He curled his body around her. "You'll find your way too."

"It's not the same. I mean, I'm not losing her forever like you did with your mom," she said quietly.

"But it's the death of a dream, of how you imagined your future."

She turned in his arms and didn't bother to hide the emotion in her eyes. And when she looked up at him, her first tear fell. "Thank you for understanding. My family is so over the moon about the engagement my dad is the only one who took the time to think of how it would affect me. And I don't want to sound selfish, this is a big moment for her—I guess I just dreamed I'd be more a part of it. At least meet the guy before they became official."

He took his thumb and caught a tear with the pad. "Not to sound selfish, but if it had gone down any other way I wouldn't be standing here with the most beautiful woman in my arms."

She wrapped her arms around his waist and rested her cheek against his heart and let the calm rhythm soothe her. He rested his chin on top of her head and let out a deep, contented sigh.

"I know you have your doubts about my brother, but I have seen him grow so much since meeting Autumn. He might not be the most responsible guy and his follow-through is questionable, but I really think he is deeply in love with your sister."

"Thank you for that," she said, releasing him to unlock the door. Once the key turned she opened it and stepped one foot inside the entry and took his hand. "Do you want to come in?"

"And see where you live? Yes."

"I was hoping you'd want to see where I sleep. Although I don't think we'll be getting much sleep tonight."

Chapter 26

FALLING HEAD FIRST

"Sleep? Hell, love, I don't think we'll make it to your bedroom," Wes said, and Summer's nipples reached out to high-five him.

"How far do you think we'll make it?"

"Let's put it this way. I've been staring at you in the denim skirt with those thigh-high boots all night, imagining if you have underwear on. And if so, what style and color. So we'll be lucky if we make it through the doorway."

"Well, why don't we see what's behind door number one," she said and very slowly pulled her blouse up over her head, letting the silky top pool at her feet. "As you can see it's Wild Orchid."

He ran his hand through his hair. "And see-through."

He took a step forward and she took a step back, holding her hand out for him to stop. "Not yet. We still have door number two." She slowly unbuttoned her skirt, teasing him as she went, then pushed it over her hips and onto the floor. Then, in her boots and lace, she did a little turn for him to see the entire view.

"Are you ready for door number three?"

"As long as the boots stay on."

"Always the negotiator."

She reached behind her and unclasped her bra and let it slide down her arms onto the pile of her clothes.

"Door three is definitely my favorite. But if you tell me there's a door four, you'd better fucking believe I'm partaking in the moment."

She crooked a finger at him and gave him her best come-hither look in the history of the world, and he wasted no time in being an active participant. He was on her in a second.

She prepared herself for his mouth to come crashing into hers. For him to grab and tear and rip her thong right off. But she should have known better. His lips were soft and languid, a gentle exploration.

His hand traced her jaw to her cheek, then threaded through her hair at the base of her neck. As the moment went on so did the neediness in her body, spiraling in her core and curling at her toes. He was taking his sweet-ass time, and she was already revved and ready to go. Just ask her nipples. And the hot juncture between her legs, which was already vibrating with need. He'd barely touched her and her body was responding as if she were in the middle of a Face-Off 69

She would try to pick up the pace and he'd slow it down.

"Are you trying to tease me?" she asked as his lips trailed down her throat.

"Isn't that what you're doing in nothing but a Wild Orchid thong and fuck-me boots?"

"I was giving you a taste of what was to come."

"Love, the only thing I care about coming is you." And with that he pulled her nipple into his mouth and sucked until she was sure she'd pass out. Then he moved to the other breast and this time her legs did buckle.

Not that she needed to worry. He lifted her up and walked

down the hallway and into Summer's room and set her on the mattress, and that's when she remembered that she'd emptied her closet looking for something to wear, in the hopes she'd see him tonight.

"Looking for a special outfit?" He dropped to his knees and scooted between her thighs. "Were you thinking of me when you did?"

"Yes."

"And before you went down to the shop, did you masturbate while thinking of me?"

Her face flushed fully, but she answered honestly. "I wore out the battery thinking of you."

"Well, you won't need a vibrator tonight. Unless you want me to use it on you. Because you're mine, remember."

"I remember."

"Clearly not enough." He dipped his head and licked her straight up the center. Then he pulled the Wild Orchid pink lace aside and began to feast. Unable to hold herself up, she fell back on the mattress with a thud. Hands gripping the sheets, legs over his shoulders, he continued until she felt that churning in her stomach, the coiling in her core.

She was there. Right on the precipice, ready to fall, when he pulled back.

She sat up. "Are you stopping?"

"You've come enough without me today. This time when you come it's going to be with your pretty tits bouncing from the force and that sweet pussy clamping down on me. Understood?"

What was she supposed to say to that? Nothing but a "hell yeah" would suffice. She grabbed his face and kissed him until their bodies were like a match thrown on gasoline. She pulled him on top of her.

He pulled her thong down and off her legs, then crawled his way up her body, which was more than primed.

"You ready?" he asked, and she shook her head. "Wrap your legs behind me, love. This is going to be one hell of a ride."

She had no sooner locked her ankles behind his lower back when he thrust into her. One long thrust that stung as much as it pleasured.

"Christ, you feel like a dream. A wet, hot, sticky dream."

"I've been like this since I saw you at the shop."

"I've been like this since you dropped me off at my office."

"Then what was up with the drive-by peck?"

"Love, anything more and I wouldn't have been able to stand straight. And it would be difficult to run a meeting and intimidate people who needed a little intimidation in their day with an erection the size of a telephone pole."

"And did you intimidate?"

He gave a hard thrust. "What do you think?"

"That if you don't start moving I'm going to lose my head or grab the nearest BOB."

"Not in this century."

"Then you'd better get moving, big guy."

"Arguing even when you have my cock inside you."

"Are you surprised?" she teased.

He withdrew and slammed back in, making her gasp. "I think you're the surprised one."

"Surprise me again. And again. And again," she moaned.

And surprise her he did. He took her fast and hard until

she'd reached the pinnacle, then he surprised her again by slowing down so she could feel every thrust, every withdrawal, and every emotion that was arching between them.

Their bodies were slick with sweat, gliding over each other, and his mouth was gently nibbling at her lower lip, then her upper one. One hand was at the base of her neck, the other cupping her ass like he owned it. And he did, she realized.

But that wasn't all he owned. He owned her heart and soul. Somewhere between him trying to have her car towed and them kissing in the lake, she'd fallen. Hard. Fallen for a man who'd given her the best meet-cutes ever, who kissed like a god and made love like it was a religious experience.

But he's leaving, her head reminded her.

Love can conquer all, her heart argued.

But could it withstand three thousand miles and an ocean between them, with a man who didn't believe that long distance could work?

It was something she was willing to try. Now all she had to do was get him onboard. She knew he felt deeply for her. She could feel it in every stolen look and touch. In the way he spoke to her, caressed her. In the way he stood by her side.

"Stay with me, love," he whispered against the curve of her ear.

She looked him dead in the eye and this time it was his turn to be surprised. "I am so with you my heart is synced to yours. Can you feel it?"

She took his hand and placed it over her heart, and the sweet smile he gave her made her belly flip over and over and over again. She was in deep trouble. Summer had fallen head over heels in love with a man who didn't believe in love, romance, or happily-ever-afters. She knew it was because of his traumatic upbringing filled with abandonment and rejection, but she wanted to show him what the other side felt like.

He gradually sped up his pumps, faster and faster. His lips never hardened, but remained gentle and loving. His hands moved up and down her body, everywhere all at once, creating a frenzy of feelings—all the feels in her body.

His thrusts became more intent as he rolled his hips, hitting all the right spots. And in those final moments before they both fell he looked into her eyes and held her gaze, never once breaking contact, and what she saw there gave her hope.

"It's too much pressure," Summer said, and Wes rolled onto his back and she cuddled into his chest.

They were both still naked and exhausted from their all-night sex-a-thon. She might not have a red room, but she was definitely part of Team Wild Orchid. He had the scratch marks on his back to prove it.

"These kinds of requests are common with bigger authors. Usually they're three times the ask," he explained, but he felt like an asshole. Five grand was a drop in the bucket for him. In Summer's world that was an entire month's budget.

She rested her chin on folded arms on his chest and looked up at him with so much trust he felt like he was ten feet tall. He'd earned that. The only person in his world who completely trusted him and what he brought to the table was lying on him fully exposed and open, with nothing between them, not even air.

He knew how important this event was for her and he knew how to promote this so it could be huge.

"So you think it's worth it?"

"I know it's worth it. Plus, there are tons of thing you can do to promote that don't cost a penny."

"I was going to send out newsletters to my subscribers, post flyers around town, and mention it on my podcast next week, which will have a sexy bookstore legend as the guest."

"You mean the King of Books," he corrected.

She nipped his nipple—hard.

"Just remember, payback is a bitch," she said, and he chortled.

"You can also have bookmarks made up and leave them by the cash registers of local shops. I know that I'd put them by my registers."

"You would?" She sounded so surprised he wanted to kick every asshole who'd come before him.

"Of course." He ran his hand up her spine, and then back down until he was cupping her ass cheek. "You can also run a discount. Bring a friend to the signing and get twenty percent off. You can join forces with other book retailers and ask them to do a newsletter swap. It will cross-pollinate your audience."

She cleared her throat. "Mister CEO of BookLand, would you want to do a newsletter swap with me?"

"You didn't even have to ask. I was going to do one already."

"Even though it's a disruptor that's meant to take away from your opening."

"Even then."

"Then I will send one out announcing the opening of your new bookstore."

"You don't have to do that."

She slid up his body until their lips were aligned. "I want to," she said against his mouth, and then gifted him with a kiss that was hotter than the fucking sun. His Summer didn't disappoint when it came to brightening the day of everyone she came into contact with, including a pessimist like Wes. She was like a fresh ray of sunshine in his world of darkness and betrayal.

"As you wish," he moaned against her, drinking down every last sip she was willing to give him. When she pulled back he nearly cried.

"Anything else I should be aware of?"

"Besides the erection that's pressing against your stomach?" She smacked his chest. "I meant the contract."

"It's a pretty standard and straightforward contract."

"Would you sign it and agree to five thousand dollars?"

He studied her for a long moment and saw the desperation in her eyes, the lack of confidence, the uncertainty. It made him want to go into fix-it mode, but he wasn't sure that was what she needed. And if he'd learned anything over the past couple of weeks, it was that sometimes she needed him to just listen. "Are you looking for a sounding board, or advice?"

She thought about that for a moment. "I think both."

"Five grand is a steal. I know it seems like a lot right now, but you will triple your revenue, gain new listeners, and expand your customer base. If it weren't for the money, would you hesitate?"

"No," she said immediately.

Well, that was an easy fix. "Let me give you the money."

She cupped his cheek. "I can't take your money, Wes. I

know that most people would jump at your generosity, but I need to do this my way. Plus, I'd feel like everyone else who's taken your money over the years."

This was new. The people in his world came up to him practically with their hands out. He always picked up the tab when he went out, even with his co-workers, women like his ex had always expected lavish presents, and the board was always trying to undermine him and get a bigger chunk. And here was a woman, torn between parting with what seemed like the last of her cash and hosting the event of the year, and she wouldn't take a cent from him.

He pulled her into his body, until she was on top of him like a comforter. "What if it was a loan and you paid me back after the event?"

"Wes, I like you and I don't want to confuse that with money. I already have a relationship that is strained over money."

"Autumn?"

She opened her mouth in a perfect O of surprise. "How did you know?"

"I accidently overheard your dad taking to Autumn that she had to come clean and then pay you back the loan. Come clean on what, and how much did you lend her?"

"I told her she had to tell Randy about the loan and her finances before they moved in together or I would. Then I gave her an extension on paying me back." Summer studied his chest and played with the light dusting of hair there. "I lent her ten grand from my wedding fund."

He chuckled. "Of course you have a wedding fund."

"Why do you say it like it's a bad thing? I didn't want my

parents to have to pay a cent for my wedding, and I'd never ask my fiancé to pay for what the bride should pay for, so I started my own fund when I was eleven, which I can borrow from for the signing. I just hate taking more money out of it."

"I mean it in the best way possible. I love that you're a romantic and how you view the world. I love that you knew what you wanted at such a young age and made steps toward achieving it. But I hate that Autumn put you in this situation and that you have to borrow against one dream to make another come true."

"Well, if your predictions are accurate, I can pay back my fund in a single day. Anything else I should be aware of?"

"There is a cancelation clause, which allows the author to cancel the signing within seventy-two hours."

"She can stand me up?"

"Yes. But it's more like if she's ill or an emergency comes up. It goes both ways; you can cancel too. I've seen the clause on many contracts that go through my company."

"Thanks for making me feel better. Now that I've spilled my guts, how did your meeting go?"

"Terrible. I can't change the date because it's already been advertised."

"The sneaky bastards."

"Exactly. Which is why I hired a third crew to get it done. It'll be tight but it will get finished."

She wrapped her arms around his waist, and it was as if luck had finally turned his way. He wanted more of this. Not the sex, although he could make love to her forever and still want more; he wanted the vulnerable moments where they were sharing their struggles and successes. He'd never had that.

"Can you fire them?"

"I wish, but no." That got him thinking about what he'd said to Summer about the upfront money being worth it in the long run. "But I can threaten to buy out each and every wanker who waited for me to be distracted to hold an emergency meeting to vote on the early opening."

"Can't you sue them for potentially costing the business millions?"

He gave her a big smack on the lips. "I can and I will. Tomorrow morning, first thing. I just need to get my brother there."

"Promise you won't tell Randy about Autumn. Give her a chance to tell him."

"It's her story to tell. Plus, I don't want our families or businesses to come between us."

"Really?" Her excitement was like sweet music to his ears.

"Really." Then he rolled her over and pinned her to the bed. "You think we can break this bed?"

"Do I hear a wager coming on?"

Chapter 27

BAD GUYS CLOSING IN

"Good morning, gentleman," Wes said, stalking into the room, the inner lair of BookLand, like he owned the place—and he did. Today would determine if that were still the case. He was dressed to intimidate in a navy blue Armani suit with matching vest over his crisp French blue shirt, polished off with a power tie and cufflinks that cost as much as most people's weddings. It was a suit that was tailor-made specifically for a moment like this.

It was a power-play number and every eyeball in the room knew it, since they all looked up at his six-foot-three-inch frame and turned toward him with fear in the whites of their eyes. His desired response to what was about to transpire.

Oh, how hell was about to rain down and scorch the earth. He didn't like cowards, and the board had made a cowardly play. Not just last week, but today as well.

"What are you doing here?" Mr. Harper, the president of the board, said.

"I heard there was a secret meeting today to decide if I should still be CEO."

"This isn't a secret meeting," another board member said, a quiver in his voice.

"Then why weren't Randy and I included in the email? What? No one has anything to say? Not a word? Well, and since *I am* the agenda, I figured my brother and I should be here. And we have a few words to say."

On cue, Randy walked in looking like a grown-up business-man with an ace up his sleeve. There was no ace, and his sleeves were a bit too long, but he finally looked more like a VP than a Swiftie—a direct result of Wes dressing him today and lending him a simple black suit for the meeting.

Wes walked to the head of the boardroom table, followed by his brother, looking each and every traitor who'd tried to undermine them in the eyes. It wasn't hard to tell who'd voted against them; their faces were white as paper the agenda was printed on. After carefully reading the secretary's notes from the last meeting, Wes also learned that the board was to vote this morning on strengthening their power and firing Wes, citing that he wasn't performing up to task.

If it hadn't been for a few loyal members who'd believed in upholding his father's will, he would never have known that this meeting was happening.

"According to the will, you and your brother have to make this opening a success. Nowhere does it state you have to be CEO," Harper pointed out, his chest puffed, accentuating his spare tire, which was waging war with the bottom button of his vest.

"How is he supposed to make the impactful and strategic decisions from the mailroom?" Randy asked, resting a hand on Wes's shoulder. The sign of brotherly support touched Wes.

Harper crossed his arms over his chest. "That isn't our problem."

"Well, it will be the second I file a lawsuit against you for using the emergency clause as a way to skate around the rules of having all voting board members present. Especially two of the shareholders who own a collective forty-one percent of the company."

"You were out of town."

"But I was reachable, so the proper procedure would have been to have notified myself and my brother. Oh, and if you go ahead and relinquish me from my current position, my attorneys assured me that we'll be caught up in litigation for years."

"You can't do that," Mr. Harper said. He was so outraged spittle had collected in the corner of his mouth. He was the one who was gunning for the CEO position. "You'd destroy the company."

Wes looked at Randy for confirmation. Randy nodded. "My brother and I are ready to burn this company to the ground rather than go against my father's wishes," said Wes.

"Your father didn't even have faith in his own son," Harper said, and it was as if all the oxygen had been sucked out of the room. "Which is why he called you in to babysit Randy. For god's sake, the kid took off on a world tour to follow some teenager around for a few months after his father passed. What kind of VP does that?"

"She's a grown woman, and what the hell do you mean 'babysit' me?" The second question was addressed to Wes, but Harper kept harping on.

"Didn't your big brother tell you that your dad wanted you nowhere near running the business, so he called his bastard to run the show? Do you really think he'll give you the reins when his year is up? Because he doesn't have to, he can go on forever keeping you from your birthright."

Randy looked at Wes as if pleading with him to discredit

Harper. To tell him it was all a lie. But Wes was done lying. Summer was right, he was a different man than he'd been a couple of weeks ago, and he was about to prove the trust and pride she felt for him.

"I wanted to tell you but there was an NDA preventing me."

An NDA Harper had just broken, making replacing him even easier.

"We're brothers," Randy said quietly. "That trumps any NDA. It trumps everything. Is that why you went with me to Mystic? To keep me away from the business?"

"I went with you because you said you needed a wingman and I wanted to get to know you better. As a brother should. Dad kept us apart for years and I didn't want him to win with us being estranged."

Wes knew the minute he said the word "win," a word the old Wes would have used and the real reason he had gone to Mystic if he were being honest, that he'd lost his brother's respect.

"Well, I guess Dad won, because no real brother of mine would view our relationship as a game to be won. If you knew me at all, you'd know that I hate liars. I spent a lifetime with liars as parents, girlfriends, friends, coworkers, all underestimating me and using me for whatever they could get from me. I thought you were different. Guess I was wrong."

And with that Randy left the room. Wes wanted to follow but there was a vote to be held.

"You're a bloody wanker, you know that, Harper? And you're excused from your duties. I am using the ethics and morality clause, not to mention breaking the NDA, to buy your shares back."

"You can't do that. I've been with this firm since before you were born!"

"I ran it by legal this morning and they said I can and I will. Breaking the NDA was just the icing on the cake. You can go quietly or you can go to court. Either way I will bury you and you know it." Wes faced the room. "Does anyone oppose me?"

Not single hand was raised.

"As for replacing me as CEO, do I hear any yeas?" Not a one. "Nays?"

Every other board member raised their hand.

"Now since that's settled, I'm going to find my brother and then look closely at each one of you to see if I need to buy back your shares as well."

⌒∞

By the time Wes located Randy, he was in his office already packing up his personal things in a box. Wes noticed that the framed photo of them on a skiing vacation when they were little was in the trash.

"So that's it? You're just going to leave?" Wes asked, standing at the threshold, not wanting to push himself on his brother, even if his heart was breaking over someone else walking out on him.

"What do you expect me to do?" his brother asked without looking up from his desk.

"Fight. Prove them wrong. Dad didn't leave you this company, because he wanted to start a war between us, make the rift bigger. Don't you get it? Even from the grave he's trying to get in the last painful dig. Keep us apart. Remind us of our place."

"Well, it worked. I can't even look at you without thinking everything was a lie."

"You were right back there—brotherhood trumps any NDA. I was more worried about the state of the company and keeping it in the family than I was about my brother. Now that I've stopped viewing things through success-driven eyes I see how much this must hurt you. I betrayed you, brother."

Unsure what to do next, Wes pulled a play from Summer's handbook and went to the heart of the matter, with honesty.

He crossed the room and placed a hand on his brother's shoulder. "I might have omitted the truth, and yes for a time I worried if you could handle running the company, but I was wrong."

Randy looked up. "So you think I can?"

"The question is, do you want to?"

"Hell no." Randy collapsed in his seat. He looked so lost and hurt it reminded Wes of one summer back when they were kids and Wes had been there for a rare visit, and he'd found Randy sitting on the curb outside the property gate crying. He'd had a tennis match and lost. But he was crying because he'd overheard his dad say to the winning parent, "You must be so proud of your son. I know I'm not with mine."

And their dad had done it again, and Wes had played a part in the scam. And for that he was livid—with himself.

"There's nothing wrong with wanting to carve out your own path."

"I want to do something that I'm good at."

"You have so many talents. One of them is connecting

with people. Which would make you the perfect head of business development."

"You think?" Randy's excitement actually broke through his insecurities.

"I know. You'd be able to make partnerships with publishers, authors, vendors like Starbucks. I watched you seamlessly slide into the Russo family like one of their own. You have a god-given talent for making people feel comfortable, a part of the action. I could never do that."

"You can and you did. Look at you and Summer. You two are the perfect match."

Wes was a little stunned at his brother's observation. He'd been trying to hide just how deep his emotions were for Summer, but clearly he hadn't convinced anyone.

"I'm leaving when this project is up and running, don't forget."

"Are you leaving for the next project, or are you running away from the possibility of being happy?" Randy asked. "I know you had the rug ripped out from under you and that happiness isn't your usual state of being."

That wasn't true. This past week he'd been happier than he could remember. Even when he and Summer were arguing he was happy. When they were sharing dark secrets and discussing difficult topics from childhood he was happy. God, and when they kissed he could barely contain himself, which was why a kiss usually led to sex. But not all the time, and even then, with blue balls and all, he was happy.

"I have to oversee the next project," he said. "You know how hands-on I am."

"We took care of that today; it won't happen again. So

maybe it's time you go hands-on with another part of your life. You can work from here. You've been managing your company successfully from Connecticut for nearly a year, why can't you keep doing it long-distance? Hell, move corporate headquarters here if you have to. If she's worth it, then fight for it. Isn't that what you just told me to do?"

Summer was more than worth it, and that was the problem. When it came to her he was punching out of his weight class. She wasn't just beautiful; she was captivating and a breath of fresh air. What you saw was what you got. Only, where she was happy-go-lucky, Wes was jaded.

"Do you love her?" Randy asked, as if he already knew the answer.

"Love?" Wes choked. "We've only known each a few weeks."

"You've been circling each other for months. And when you know, you know."

All that Wes knew was that the thought of getting on that jet and never seeing her again made an ache the size of a golf ball form in his throat. But he didn't want to string her along when he couldn't see marriage in his future. Once upon a time he'd imagined marriage and kids, the whole thing, but he'd never seen that kind of love growing up. Hell, his own dad hadn't even wanted him.

He'd thought he'd found it in his ex-fiancée, but then she'd left him when his company went through a rough patch and he wasn't worth millions, and it had further tainted that dream. Then his dad had passed and both of his companies had needed all of his attention. They still did. So no, he wasn't sure he wanted to reopen that box.

"I'd still be gone two weeks or so every month. Summer deserves more than a drive-by husband."

"Summer deserves to be loved by the man she loves."

Wes's stomach crammed into his chest, nearly choking him, which was fine since his lungs stopped working. "She loves me?"

"Of course she does. You'd have to be an idiot not to see the way she looks at you," Randy said. "That woman is crazy about you."

There was no way in hell that a sweet and joyful woman like Summer could ever fall for a man who chose his job over love. Although looking back, he and his fiancée hadn't been together so much for love, it had been compatibility and convenience.

What if she actually, somehow, magically was in love with him? Was he stupid enough to walk away from that?

"Man"—Randy clapped him on the shoulder—"welcome to the club. It only gets better from here."

Chapter 28

FRIENNIES WITH BENNIES

Summer's phone pinged the second the front door to the shop burst open. She looked up from the window, which was a collage of all Sloan Chase's backlist books. The publicist had sent an advanced copy of her new release, which was highlighted in the display.

Someone had already offered her a thousand dollars for the book. But Summer had politely declined, explaining that in her contract no one was allowed to read or purchase the copy. And Summer wasn't about to do anything to jinx this signing. She had followed everything to the letter.

She had read the book herself to prepare for the interview and it was Sloan's best work to date. She'd reread it three times—the juicy parts five.

The five thousand dollars had been painful to part with, and her bank account needed some serious CPR when it all was said and done, but it was going to be worth it. She could feel it in her bones. The podcast had sold out in under ten minutes, they already had over a thousand preorders of the hardback, and every single shop on the street had put a flyer in the window and a free bookmark by the register. She'd sent out two emails already and had a sixty-five percent open rate, and had done an email swap with twenty-two different book-shops in a three-hour radius—which was phenomenal.

Even more phenomenal was the person who was stalking toward her. A six-three wall of muscle dressed like a GQ model and looking like a powder keg ready to explode—with excitement. What a change from the man who'd tried to have her car towed. What a change indeed.

He glanced around the store and then his eyes went immediately to hers, as if she were the beacon he'd been looking for. His gaze raked her body up and down and she felt like prey about to be pounced on.

She slid her hands down her jeans and remembered that she was in her uniform she wore when dealing with stock. A work shirt, tattered old jeans, and tennies. No makeup and her hair must look like a squirrel's tail, and she was covered in a fine layer of dust from moving around boxes in the back room to make space for the insane amount of Sloan Chase books that the distributor had sent out for the signing.

As he stalked toward her, he heard a collection of *Oh my's* and *I wouldn't kick him out of bed for eating crackers*, come from the Smut Club who had gathered around the reading section of the shop. Every eye followed him as he strutted toward Summer, shoulders back, chest puffed out, gaze set to *I'm going to eat you for dinner.*

Summer's thighs began to tremble and her core became a furnace, radiating out to her limbs and covering her neck and face. She wasn't blushing, she was preparing for the attack.

Without a word he slung her over his shoulder like caveman, walked her down the hallway into her office, and kicked the door shut.

"Babe," she scolded. "Put me down."

He gently set her on her feet. "Call me that again."

"Babe?" she whispered, and it was as if she had unleashed an animal.

A primal look came over his features and his nostrils flared. He took her hands and pinned them to the door above her head. "I like it when you call me that."

"Why?"

"Because it's your name for me. It's a statement that I'm yours." He moved his body against hers and she could feel his erection pushing into her belly. "Am I yours, love?"

"Yes."

His mouth came crashing down on hers and the way he kissed her made her knees go weak and her heart stutter to a stop. It was as if she were too afraid to move for fear that it would break the moment.

He ran his hands down her arms, over her breasts, gently cupping her hips.

"You're shaking," she said.

"It's the adrenaline," he said, and she felt a stab of disappointment.

"From the meeting?"

He pulled back. "From seeing you. Whenever I see you, especially when you're smiling and doing what you love, it's like I need to feel what you're feeling. Be a part of it. Be a part of you. How does that make you feel?"

"Desired." She unbuttoned his jacket. "Sexy." She slid it down his arms and let it fall to the floor. "Precious." She went to work on his vest. And when she had his tie undone, she yanked him toward her. "Yours."

Then it was her turn to blow his mind with a kiss that led

to another and another until there was no oxygen left to spare. His hands were everywhere, then suddenly she was magically shirtless and his mouth was giving her a love mark in her cleavage.

Summer's head fell against the door.

"What does blue mean?" he asked, and she was a little confused.

"Blue?"

"The bra. It's blue."

"Oh," she chuckled. "Blue is for bold. A Boardroom Barracuda who knows their worth. I wore it for you."

He stopped, his hands gentling, almost worshiping, and his gaze met hers. He kicked out her office chair, took a seat, and pulled her onto his lap. "For me?"

"So you wouldn't be alone in that meeting. How did it go? Did you kick ass?"

"By the time I was done they were pissing themselves. I'm still CEO, the man behind the push to get me out is gone, and Randy and I even talked through our differences. He found out about the NDA."

She clapped a hand over her mouth. "Oh, no. How did he take it?"

"Hard at first, but instead of walking away and playing tough love like I would usually do, we talked it out. And he is officially the VP of business development."

"That's a great job for him."

"I know. His first assignment is to get more sponsors for our grand opening."

"That's only a week away," she said.

"He can do it," Wes said confidently. "And I will be with

him every step of the way." That confidence slipped a little and his face flushed. "Speaking of steps."

Oh no, she thought, this was it, the this-isn't-going-to-work conversation. Something had felt different last night when he'd dropped her off at her door and chosen to sleep at his penthouse rather than stay with her. For that matter, he'd never invited her to his place. They'd always stayed at hers.

"I felt like last night we took a step backward," he said. "Maybe it was because everything was going too good or I was so focused on the meeting that I retreated, but I didn't like how it felt."

"And how did it feel?" She cupped his cheek, on which a five o'clock shadow was already forming even though it wasn't even lunchtime.

He wrapped his arms around her middle and hugged her hard. "Lonely. So fucking lonely and I hated every second of it." His mouth wandered down her neck. "I was up all night thinking strategy and about you and what you'd feel like beneath me. Next to me. Jesus, I can't think when your tits are out." He grabbed her shirt off the floor and stuffed it over her head.

"That bad." He pushed up against her and it was rod-of-steel bad. "I can take care of that."

She started to fumble with his buckle and he placed his hand over hers. "What I have to say is important. I need to be working on all cylinders." She wiggled her ass. "You aren't helping."

"Because you won't let me." She batted her eyes.

"Summer." His tone was serious and her heart dropped painfully.

"Is everything okay?"

"I'm not sure," he said, and panic and fear knotted inside her.

"Is this about the meeting, or us? Because you said the meeting went great. So then it must be about us. God, it's about us?" That knot tripled in size and constricted her chest because he seemed uncertain and uncomfortable like when someone was about to break her heart. "Did I do something wrong?"

The tiniest of smiles creased his lips. "No love, you did everything right. So right I can't imagine going back to London and leaving you here."

She blinked—twice. "Are you asking me to move to London? What about my shop?"

Love was worth every sacrifice—wasn't that what she'd said?

"I'm asking if I were to stay here, make this my home base, how would you feel about that?"

Ecstatic. Overjoyed. Deliriously happy. "That depends."

His face went blank, as if holding a raw emotion in check. "On what?"

"Why you want to stay."

She knew it had only been a few months and they'd argued most of them, but she needed some reassurance that he was heading in the same direction as she was. He didn't have to be in love with her right now, like she was with him, but there had to be a possibility. What was the point of dating, uprooting his life, if marriage wasn't the endgame?

"Because Randy helped me see that I can have it all," he said, and that wasn't what she really wanted to hear.

"All what?" She tried to keep her fragile control.

He ran a hand down his face. "I'm overcomplicating things." He cupped her cheek. "Bottom line, I love you. I'm in love with you and I want to be with you. Every night and every morning. I want to share my day with you and listen to yours. I want to make love to you all the time." He ran his hands down her sides, his thumbs brushing her breasts. "Like now. You drive me crazy, in the best kind of way, and you make me feel like I finally have a place. You're my place. I just hope I'm yours."

"Of course you're mine." She brushed a gentle kiss on his lips. "You've been mine since the first time you called me love."

"Thank Christ," he said and fused his mouth to hers.

When they came up for air she asked, "If you're wanting to spend every morning and night with me, does that mean you're asking me to move in with you?"

"I'm asking to move in with you."

She stammered in bewilderment. "Why? You have a beautiful penthouse overlooking downtown. My bed is tiny, my place is small, and old and—"

"Home. It's your home, and I want it to be mine. I know how much the apartment means to you, so it means something to me. Unless you'd rather . . ." He said the last few words tentatively, as if maybe he'd gotten it wrong.

"No. I love my apartment and it just so happens I'm looking for a roommate."

"You mean a bedmate, because there's no way you're wearing Wild Orchid and I'm sequestered away in the other bedroom. Although we will have to get a new bed. A sturdy one that can fit my large frame."

"Deal." And she sealed it with a kiss. Then another and

another until her shirt was on its way over her head. Just then, there was a banging at the door.

Then another.

"Not sure what you guys are doing in there," Cleo said. "But I will be honest and say there's a poll going on with the book group and, man, can romance readers get creative. Do you have any cucumbers in there?"

"Um, no," Summer said, covering her mouth to keep from laughing.

"Sorry, Mable, no cucumbers involved."

A chorus of disappointed moans echoed through the door.

"I wouldn't be interrupting if it weren't important, but there's a very beefy and tattooed man in a construction hat here for Wes saying that a pipe burst and he has some major plumbing problems."

"When Aunt Cecilia said that, I thought she meant your—" She looked at his lap. "But you'd proven that wrong."

"My downstairs plumbing is in Olympic shape, which you will see tonight after we get off work."

Cleo opened the door, one hand covering her eyes, but the pointer and middle finger were parted so she could see through the slit. When she saw they were both clothed she dropped her hand with a disappointed sigh. "He says it's flooding the storage room and has the potential to ruin your book inventory."

"Go," Summer said, standing up.

"But—"

"Go, we can finish this later." She kissed him on the lips and smacked his butt.

❦

Summer was tying a bow around the gift bags that held a bookmark, pen, and magnet for the first thousand customers when the front door of the apartment opened. Thinking it was Wes, she turned with a big smile, which fell the moment she saw Autumn.

Her twin looked as if she'd just come from a photo shoot. Her hair was perfection, her makeup was flawless, and her outfit was runway-ready. She looked like a bona fide influencer.

The two hadn't spoken since the beach house and Summer had refused to make the first move. She'd always been the one to go to Autumn, apologize for fighting even when she hadn't been the cause or initiated the disagreement. Well, this wasn't a disagreement, it was a battle of moral compasses, and she didn't know how to navigate that.

Wes had taught her her worth, and she wasn't willing to be a doormat anymore. Not even for her sister. Which was why she didn't run over and embrace Autumn, even though that was what every cell in her body was telling her to do. Autumn seemed disappointed that Summer hadn't made her usual first move.

"Hey," Autumn said tentatively, her face clouded with uneasiness.

"Hi." *Don't you dare move! This is her doing. She needs to come to you.*

"I went to the shop to see if you were there and Cleo told me to go eat a bag of dicks. So I figured that meant you were in the apartment. And still mad at me."

"I'm not mad, Autumn. I'm hurt and devastated and, yeah, angry. But mostly I'm just sad. You lied to me, broke a promise to me, and blindsided me. That's not how sisters treat each other."

"I know, and I'm sorry. I put my dream above yours. Which is why I have this." Autumn held out an envelope that was so stuffed it barely closed.

Summer looked at it like it was a scorpion ready to strike. For all she knew it was a letter explaining all the reasons why Summer couldn't be in the wedding. "What's that?"

"Me paying off my debt." Autumn took out a wad of cash and fanned herself with it.

She walked over, but the island was between them. She set the money on the tile counter.

"It's all there. Ten grand plus interest."

"Where did you get this?"

Autumn smiled. "I listened to my really smart twin sister and came clean with my fiancé."

"He just gave you ten thousand dollars?" Oh, to be a Weston.

"No, I wouldn't take his money. But I did take his help. He co-signed my loan that will give me enough breathing room to go after my dream the way you've gone after yours, and really make it as an influencer. I already have a photographer and lighting guy set up. They come highly recommended. One even worked for the Kardashians for a bit. And I made a business plan, a real one that you would be so proud of. I'm going to make this work. I promise."

"That's great, Autumn," Summer said with no emotion. Once again, her sister was making it about herself.

"But what I really came to ask is if you're okay. I know you're with Wes, how is that going?"

A little brick of her emotional wall crumbled at the sound of his name. "He said he loved me."

Autumn took a step closer. "He did? I knew you two were a match when you made the bet for him to pack up and leave."

"You knew about that? How?"

"You two were talking so loud the whole house heard. That's why we all voted for him to win."

"So you rigged the game?"

"Yup. And it worked."

They were both smiling but still neither of them moved. It was as if they were on opposite sides of the Grand Canyon, reaching out to each other. But both were afraid to fall in and get hurt.

"I've missed you," Autumn said. "Like my soul has a Summer-sized hole in it, and no matter what I do, or how I try and distract myself, it won't heal."

"Me too."

"Did you know that we've gone nine days, six hours and fifty-two minutes without talking. That the longest we've ever gone without speaking to each other."

"I know. It feels like a part of me is missing too. I've had all these amazing things happen and I haven't had anyone to talk to them about," Summer said. "And it sounds like you have too."

Autumn hopped on the island counter and crossed her legs like she was a little kid. She patted the tile next to her for Summer to join. So she did.

They sat like that, knee to knee, silently staring at each

other and looking for any differences. Any new scars, pimples—residual anger. There was none. They were still the mirror image of each other. And something so right filled Summer's chest.

Completeness.

"I heard you landed a mega author," Autumn said.

"I did. Sloan Chase," Summer said with pride. "Wes helped some, but I used our family history to win her over."

"I'm not shocked. You've always been great at connecting with people."

"No, that's you. I have my nose in a book."

"But when you look up there is this genuine quality to you that makes people want to be near you. You're like a warm summer's day."

"Ha ha," Summer deadpanned.

"Seriously, why else would Mom and Dad have called you Summer?"

"Because I was born on the last day of summer and you were born on the first day of autumn."

"There you go, holding that big-sister thing over me again," Autumn teased and Summer laughed, a real, from-the-belly laugh. Autumn joined in, and before they knew it, they were forehead to forehead, their hearts synced.

As it should be.

"I heard you went wedding-dress shopping," Summer said, trying to hide the hurt she'd felt when her dad told her. The hurt she still felt.

"I did, but the second I walked into the store I walked right back out. It wasn't the same without you by my side."

Summer's eyes blurred with emotion. "Really?"

"And I'm not having my wedding in Mystic. I'm having it in Paris under the Eiffel Tower. Randy is flying everyone out."

"You didn't have to change your mind because of me." Even though she was touched that she had.

Autumn took Summer's hands. "It wasn't my wedding. It's yours. And I only wanted it because I wanted the day to be perfect and you are the queen of romance. So who better to plan the perfect wedding?"

"That's why you wanted to get married in Mystic?"

"I wanted to be like my older sister who believes in love and destiny and magic. I wanted to be like you. But let's face it, I need a glamorous affair for my big day. Something nobody else has done. The event of all events."

Summer didn't bother to tell her that when it came to the Eiffel Tower, many had come and gone before her, because all that mattered in her sister's mind was that she'd found her perfect venue.

"Do you know what your color theme will be?" Summer asked.

Autumn shook her head. "I couldn't pick that out without my romance guru by my side."

"Barbie pink," Summer guessed.

"That was at the top of my list!" Autumn said with enthusiasm. "But before we talk about me, I want to hear all about you."

Summer pulled her twin's hands into her lap and locked eyes like they used to when they were kids.

"Oh, I think we're going to need some chocolate ice cream for this talk."

"You can tell me while we finish tying up these swag bags."

"God, I need the help. I have four days to finish a thousand and I just started."

"Well, I'm the queen of swag, and now you have her at your service and she already can tell you you're doing it wrong. The bookmark goes in first, then the pen, and lastly the magnet. Now at the top, a pretty bow." Autumn demonstrated, and it looked a hundred times better. "I will commend you on choice of bag color. Wild Orchid. How risqué." Autumn waggled her brows.

"It was a no-brainer."

Chapter 29

THE DARKEST MOMENT

The next day, Wes was still dealing with his plumbing problems. By day it was either Old Faithful or the Mohave. But by night? By night his personal pipes were working overtime. As Summer could attest to.

He and Autumn had essentially swapped houses, with Randy and Autumn in the penthouse – deciding to defer their move to New York for a while—and Wes at the apartment. The switch seemed to suit each couple to the tee.

"How much do you think there is in damage?" Randy asked, walking toward him. He was dressed in business casual, perfect for his new job, and he had the bling of an engagement ring on. Autumn said it was to tell the other ladies he was off the market. Wes preferred his love marks and nail scratches to a material item when it came to ownership.

"Tens of thousands in water-damaged books alone. Then there's the concrete they had to dig up to find the pipe and fix it. Insurance will cover most of it, but it's a headache."

"At least we'll still make the grand opening," Randy said. "Right?"

"All of the damage is in the basement. Had we not found the leak when we did it would have overflowed into the stockroom and then, no, we would not make the grand opening."

As it was, he had six industrial fans going around the clock, an interior designer and her team finishing the decor, ten stockers stocking shelves with books and toys, and a partridge in a pear tree. And Wes was trying to oversee it all, but cutting his hours from ninety a week down to a sensible sixty so he could spend time with Summer wasn't helping.

He was a master delegator, but this opening was too important to leave even one detail to someone else. He and Randy's professional lives depended on it. The only person he trusted to do his thing was Randy. It was a way to let him stand on his own two feet and gain confidence in his new position at the company. Which was why Wes had felt comfortable canceling their most recent update meeting.

"Well, we'd better make it, because I've been putting all my time and energy into this opening. The other night I was lying in bed with Autumn—"

"I don't need to hear the rest of this."

"Not like that. Although ten minutes before it was going on, if you know what I mean." Wes rolled his eyes. "Anyway, I had an ah-ha moment and it hit me. Instead of opening at ten a.m., why not open at one minute after midnight?"

"Who the hell is going to show up at midnight?"

"Oh, just every Sloan Chase fan in the surrounding three states."

Fear, stark and vivid, registered in his gut. "What the hell do you mean Sloan is coming here?"

"It worked out perfect, man. Her book comes out on the day of our grand opening and her publicist thought it would be a perfect pairing to host a mega signing. I have eleven sponsors donating things for swag bags, a DJ"—he mentioned the name of some masked DJ who was world-famous—"and I even got a red carpet with photographers for super fans for a meet and greet with Sloan to get their photo taken. We're talking red carpet event. *Entertainment Tonight* is going to promo it tomorrow, I've already sent out newsletters to our subscriber list, which is now over a million by the way thanks to Autumn helping with social media outreach. Our publicity team is working with another company that has access to another three million romance readers."

Wes's head began to pound. "Does Autumn know?"

"Not yet. I wanted to see if I could pull it off first. I was going to run it by you the other day at our meeting, but you had to bail to meet Summer for lunch, remember?"

Oh, he remembered. They'd skipped lunch and made love until they both collapsed breathless on the bed.

"I wanted to talk to you first, but tonight I wanted to ask Autumn to host live on our social media feeds."

Randy was clearly not reading the room, because while Wes's heart was jackhammering against his chest, and the excitement and pride Summer had carried around the past couple weeks played over and over in his mind, his brother just went on and on about how much he'd done, who he'd signed contracts with, the endorsers he'd partnered with, the verbal agreements he'd made, all in the company's name—with the kinds of people you didn't default on without getting sued.

"Why do you look like you're pissing yourself—and not in a good way?" Randy asked.

Wes started getting blurry around the eyes and he felt like

he was going to puke. He bent over at the waist. He breathed in through his mouth and out through his nose while counting backwards from ten. When he reached one, he felt not one ounce better.

"Did I do something wrong?" Randy asked, as if Wes's reaction had aroused old fears and insecurities.

"No, you did everything right."

It was Wes who'd got it wrong. Randy had tried to meet with him several times, but he'd been in a rush to get his work done so he could get home to Summer. He'd been so distracted by what was in his right hand he'd lost track of what was going on in his left.

"I told you to run with it, and you did," Wes said.

"Then why do I feel like I fucked up?"

"You didn't. I did, and I don't know how to fix it. This screws up Sloan's signing at Summer's shop."

"No, I made it clear that Sloan was going to do both signings and the podcast. She just wants a bigger venue for the release. We have that venue."

But Summer had the heart and passion. Hell, he'd convinced her to put the last of her savings into this signing. And now he was essentially throwing the party of the year twelve hours before her event.

"Who the hell is going to buy a book from Summer after they've already bought one from us?" he asked. Randy's face went blank as if, in all the excitement, he'd forgotten that detail. "Who's going to go to some hole-in-the-wall bookshop when they can party like it's New Year's."

"I didn't even consider that. I just ran with it and . . . What the hell do we do? We can't cancel."

"Hell no, the board would have me replaced."

"What about Summer?" Randy looked up at the ceiling for divine intervention. "This is my mess."

"No, I should have made time for you, but I've been so distracted with Summer, I dropped the ball."

"A distraction," a broken female voice said from behind. "Is that how you see me?"

Wes slowly turned his head and what he saw tore his heart right out of his chest.

Summer was standing there in a pretty blue summer dress with her hair braided and her glasses on her nose. Her arms were around her stomach as if they were the only thing holding her together. Her eyes were bloodshot and the tip of her nose was pink from crying.

"I didn't mean it like that."

"Then how did you mean it?"

He took a step closer and she backed away. "I just meant that I have so many balls in the air one was bound to fall through the cracks."

"So, I'm something you have to juggle. That doesn't sound fun." She held up a BookLand flyer that made hers look like the PTA had designed them. "So is it true? You're having Sloan at your grand opening?"

"This is all new news to me. I'm just finding out about it now."

"It was me," Randy said, holding up a hand. "I swear it was all me. I just told Wes about the event."

"You mean BookLand's event. It sounds like it's going to be a blast," she said, and her voice cracked.

"We'll cancel it," Randy said.

Wes looked at his brother as if he'd sprouted a unicorn horn and was farting rainbows.

"The solution isn't that easy, Randy. We'd be sued by everyone we contracted with, verbal or contractual. Not to mention Sloan. The signing in is three days. We've missed the seventy-two-hour clause. It's going to be on *ET*, for Christ's sake."

Summer started gently rocking back and forth as if holding a baby, like the motion would soothe the pain. "I remember you telling me that you had a team of lawyers who could get you out of anything. 'Shred,' I believe was the exact wording."

"This is different."

"Why? Because I'm a hole-in-the-wall bookshop who doesn't have the money to fight back?"

"Love, I would reverse this if I could, but we'd stand to lose millions," Wes pleaded, needing her to understand.

Her lips turned into a sour grin. "I might not have millions on the line, but I have my dream on the line." Her face was stark with emotion. "And my heart in your hands." She closed the distance and intertwined their fingers. "I know that for you, everything is about the bottom line, and I know you should choose love every time, but I'm tired of being the only one choosing love. You taught me that."

"And it's true. You deserve to have someone who gives you everything. I promise I will make this up to you."

"Or you can move the event to the night of the grand opening, after mine." And damn, the emotion in her eyes finally spilled over her lashes. It shattered his chest and punctured his heart, which felt as if it were made of ice.

"The board would have my ass."

"Well, we wouldn't want to disappoint the board."

"Love," he whispered, because he knew he was losing her. He knew the minute she dropped his hand that she was gone. Out of his life.

"I promised myself a long time ago that my partner would love me as much as I loved them. So the perfect meet-cutes, the funny tropes, the rising tension—none of it matters. All that matters is what happens in the next few seconds. Do you love me enough to walk away from the event, because I love you enough to walk away from mine." And he could see the conviction in her eyes. All he had to do was say he chose love and she'd change her signing. "I love you enough to cancel my contract, cancel my signing, and pick you over anything else."

"It's out of my hands," he said.

A quiet sob escaped her lips. "Then so is my heart. I love you so much, but I can't be with someone who can't prioritize my love over a contract." She went up on her toes and gave his cheek a chaste kiss. "Goodbye, Wes. And good luck with your opening."

Chapter 30

THE GRAND GESTURE

Summer hadn't had many lonely days recently, not since Wes had come into her life. But last night had been hell. He'd come and collected his things, which she'd boxed up and put on the porch so she wouldn't have to see him. In fact, she'd been dodging him since the breakup. Avoiding his calls, texts, visits to the store, flower deliveries. He'd even sent a hundred heart balloons to her shop which had been *Guide*-worthy but too little too late. They were over, a fact that had spread like wildfire through the town.

Summer rolled over in her tiny bed, which seemed gigantic now that she was sleeping alone again. It was cold too. And a reminder of what she'd lost.

Her store had seen more customers than she knew what to do with, but they'd sold very few books. They were there to check in on her. Which was sweet and very embarrassing. A good chunk of them had also come to cancel their orders for Sloan's new book.

It was the first sign of the new normal. The second sign was when the property tax bill came in and was double last year's because of the appreciation due to the new behemoth store next door. The third sign was when a real-estate agent—Mable's niece—had approached her to say that if she ever decided to sell, to please give her a call.

Even her most loyal customers knew it was game over.

Autumn and Cleo hadn't left her alone, hovering around her like she was a fragile snowflake falling in the dead of summer. Even her parents and auntie and uncle had flown out from Florida. But instead of being there for her big event, they were there for moral support.

Wes had been right when he'd told her that love was fiction, because if it were the amazing, magical thing she'd thought it would be, it wouldn't hurt this much. Right?

The rest of her family had made it work, so maybe she was defunct. She was a mirror twin, meaning her heart was on the wrong side of her body. Maybe she had been destined to be loveless from birth. Not that she wasn't loved by her friends and family, but she wanted the everlasting, romantic kind of love. And she'd found it, then lost it.

Maybe love wasn't enough. At least not for everyone. Because she'd put everything into Wes, and he'd chosen a piece of paper over her. Then again, he'd always been honest with her that when it came to his life it was all about the bottom line. Which meant her worth was beneath a signature on a piece of paper.

And the last sign was when the music started thumping next door at BookLand's version of Burning Man. She had avoided looking out the window, but curiosity won out and she nearly yelped at what she saw. When she woke up at six, there were people sitting in lawn chairs at the entrance to BookLand. By noon the line had grown around the block. And by four the line had nearly doubled around and ran the length of both sides of the streets.

That was when Cleo sent her up to her room for the day.

When she'd looked around the shop and spotted not a single customer, she'd obliged. Her dad tried to teach her to knit. Her, her auntie, and her mom made lasagna from scratch, and Autumn took her shopping to buy a new dress for the signing and podcast because apparently, they were still happening.

Autumn had told Randy that she would not host the event and that her loyalties lay with her sister, and she even went on a sex ban in support of Summer. By the time her family was done distracting her she was exhausted, so she turned in early just so she could breathe.

That night there was a tap on her bedroom door. She rolled back over to check her phone. It was nearly midnight so she decided to ignore it. But the tapper wouldn't stop tapping.

"Ugh! Come in," she grumbled. It wasn't like she was sleeping. Even her ear plugs couldn't keep out the thumping bass from BookLand's Mardi Gras.

"Did I wake you?" her dad asked quietly, as if he hadn't just tapped himself onto her shit list.

"How can anyone sleep through this?"

"Your mom. This doesn't even match my snoring."

"If you're coming in to check on me, I'm fine. Fine. Fine. Fine."

"Well, now that I know you're fine, I came to tell you a story."

Frank crossed the room and Summer sat up against the headboard, leaving room for him to sit on the side of the bed. "Did you know that your mother left me?"

"What?" Not only was this shocking, it was clearly fiction. Her parents were so in love with each other that sometimes it was hard to look at them without feeling like you were interrupting an intimate moment.

"When you girls were little."

"I don't believe you."

He chortled. "Trust me. It was the worst week of my life."

"Oh, Dad." She took his hand in hers. "What happened?"

"I wanted to grow my company to keep up with the competition."

"I know."

"What you didn't know was that I didn't have the money, so I put the house on the market without even asking her. She came home to find a FOR SALE sign on her front lawn. She tried to talk me out of it, but I wouldn't listen. I wanted to provide everything for my family, not just be an average man. For my family, I wanted to be Superman."

"Did you sell it?"

"Yup, and in less than a year we'd lost the company. Your mom took you girls and moved back into this apartment, and I stayed in a motel. Nine days we were apart. Nine days I thought I'd lost the best thing in my life. All because I was trying to be a big man, taking on all the responsibility. I forgot that love goes both ways, and if I had just listened to her fears and concerns she probably would have let me chase my dream, but I made a unilateral decision that tore my family apart."

"Dad, I had no idea," Summer said, raw and tentative grief overwhelming her.

"But it wasn't just your dad," Blanche said from the doorway. "I was to blame too."

"How?" Summer wanted to know. Her mom hadn't sold

the house out from under her family and put business over love.

"Because I ran. When your dad needed me the most I was a coward and ran." Blanche sat next to Frank and took his hand in a loving and tender way. "Worst of all, I took his babies away from him."

That's when Summer realized she was shedding silent tears. Her parents' story didn't follow the traditional romance novel plot. Or did it? They'd reached their darkest moment, and instead of working it out together Blanche had fled. And Frank hadn't gone after her.

It was just like how Summer had fled. At the first sign of trouble, she'd broken things off and run, even though she loved him. So no, love wasn't enough; you had to have the courage to make it work.

Wes was the most courageous man she knew. And he hadn't let her run, he'd tried and tried to reach her, but she'd turned him away time and time again. Just like his family.

Oh god, what had she done? She'd done exactly what Wes had done—she'd let the bottom line define their love.

She threw the covers back and kissed each parent on the cheek. "Thank you for sharing your story and for having the courage to put love first."

She hopped out of bed and put on her robe.

"Where are you going?" her dad asked.

"I need to see Wes."

"At least let's put on some foundation and a smidge of mascara," Blanche said, but Summer was already sprinting down the hallway. "Lip gloss?"

Wes didn't need makeup or a pampered princess, he

needed her. She was sure of it. She burst through the front door and ran down the back steps, the concrete cold on her heels, little bits of gravel digging into her toes.

She rounded the corner to the alley and came to a dead stop. In front of her doorway was a red carpet with gold ropes zigzagging back and forth. Between them were hundreds and hundreds of people who had made it to the front of the line. And standing next to the door was Sloan Chase herself, surrounded by a team of security that could rival the secret service.

"Thank god you're here. I'm getting mobbed."

"Sloan?"

"Summer." She shook hands. "Nice to meet you. Now can we get this party started."

"Shouldn't you be next door?"

"Yes, but the owner informed me that they no longer carry romance and that Romance Central is All Things Cupid."

Her heart did a little flip of disbelief while a flutter of butterflies took flight in her belly. "He said that?"

Had he really put her, put love and emotions, before his work? Was there a small bead of hope for them?

"Then he moved the party over here. Now that you're up to date, would you mind opening up shop so I can be ready to sign the first book at 12:01 a.m.?"

"Of course." She reached into her robe pocket and came up empty. "My keys are back in the—"

"They're right here," Cleo said, looking like she'd just gotten off her motorcycle and hadn't had time to remove her helmet. Behind her were twenty-plus Harleys rumbling and creating a spectacle, which only drove the crowd crazier.

Cleo unlocked the door and led Sloan to a table that was

already set up, with a pink chair, books ready to sign, and decorations surrounding the store. There was a tablet at the front of the store, right at the door, where people could sign up for their newsletter, and to Summer's surprise nearly everyone was.

From there the line went up and down the aisles and, just like they'd hoped, customers were picking up stacks of books to buy.

"We'll never get them all rung up," Summer whispered to Cleo. "We don't have enough staff."

"Already taken care of." Cleo pointed to three men, each built like a beast, each with a handlebar mustache, each probably carrying a warrant to appear in court, and each running their own tablet with a credit-card slide.

Thank god biker romances were the thing, because the ladies were eating it up. Their winks, their flirting, even the permanent frown on the third one.

She turned to Cleo. "You knew. All day you knew, and that's why you wanted me out of the shop."

"It was all Wes's idea. He showed up at six a.m. on my porch. Lucky I didn't shoot the bastard. Then he told me his plan."

"But he'll get sued."

"I'm willing to take the risk," a familiar voice said from behind her.

Summer turned around and felt her heart ping through her chest like it was a pinball machine. Wes was dressed in low-slung jeans, an ALL THINGS CUPID shirt that said STAFF across the back, and sneakers. He looked like a harbor in the storm that had been building the past few days.

She pushed her way through the crowd as he started walking toward her, people automatically moving to the side for him. When they were close enough that she could smell the fog machine vapor on his skin, she released the first full breath since she'd walked away.

"I'm sorry," they both said at the same time, and a smile touched each of their faces.

"What are you sorry for?" Confusion collapsed his forehead.

"That I walked away. You told me you loved me, you showed me you loved me, and at the first sign of trouble I ran. I ran because I let my insecurities and prejudice get the best of me," Summer said. "I never should have left. I should have stayed and worked it out. I know that people have walked out on you your whole life, but I refuse to be one of them. I love you, Weston Kingston."

"How? I put my needs over yours, hung you out to dry, and wasn't even open to other solutions. I chose pride. I hurt you and I hate myself for that."

She looked at the shop full of customers who were going to get her back in the black. "You came up with a solution. Look at this place." She went serious. "You aren't going to get sued, are you?

"Nope, I sold them on the idea of a local bookshop with generations of romance and smut. I explained that as a romance author, how could she stand in the way of love, and she agreed." He cupped her hips. "But I would have done it even if they'd threatened to sue."

Her heart bubbled up like a bottle of champagne ready to explode. "You would?"

"I have a team of lawyers who can get me out of anything, remember? Plus, the board knows I'm the best man for the job. And they're scared of me. Just somewhere along the way I forgot that the power of love is stronger than the power of fear."

"I'm not scared of you."

"I know, and that's part of the reason I love you. You call me on my shit, are honest to a fault, and know how to argue like it's dirty foreplay. Plus, we've had more perfect meet-cutes than you have in this store. And I hope those outweigh the darkest moment."

"Every romance has its darkest moment," the biker with resting kill face said, and the crowd voiced their agreement.

"They're right. And it's what the couple decides to do that matters."

"What are you going to do, love?"

She cupped his cheek. "How can you ask that after giving me the best grand gesture a girl could dream of?"

"I love you, Summer. Today, tomorrow, and in fifty years I'll still choose you. The question is, do you still love me?"

She threw herself into his arms. "I will love you until my heart takes its last beat. You're mine, remember, babe?"

"And you're mine, and I look forward to reminding you about that tonight."

"My parents are staying with me."

"Then we get a hotel. For them. I just want to come home.

She tightened her arms. "Then hold me tighter."

"As you wish."

Epilogue

A NOD TO NORA EPHRON

Six months later . . .

Summer pushed through the side door of her bookstore into Between the Chapters, the new coffee house that connected BookLand to All Things Cupid. The warm aroma of roasted coffee mixed with the spicy scent of pumpkin muffins wafted around her.

It was nearly closing and still the place was hopping. If you asked Wes, he'd attribute the shop's unprecedented success to quality products and exotic coffee beans, but Summer knew it was the welcoming atmosphere of buttery leather sofas, barrel chairs, local art hanging on the walls, and framed bookcases filled with that week's bestsellers, which whispered to sit down with a great book and stay a while.

In addition to the main door, there were two additional doors to the café—one led to Summer's shop and read HAPPILY EVER AFTER, while the other led to Wes's and read LET YOUR ADVENTURE BEGIN.

Tonight was Tuesday, which meant it was date night, and every date night came with its own unique meet-cute. Tonight, they were going with a nod to Nora Ephron with a blind date, so Summer had come with a book in hand—*Pride and Prejudice*, the enemies-to-lovers, opposites-attract classic by Jane Austen, to be specific.

Summer smoothed down her fuzzy sweater, took a seat at the furthest table, opened her book and delicately laid a single daisy on the spine, and waited patiently. She was ten minutes early, but she couldn't help it. Even though they'd been doing this every week for the past six months, she always got nervous butterflies in her belly the day of. It was the surprise and sweetness of it all, because Wes planned every detail of every night. He said that he wanted to check off every meet-cute and romance trope in her *Cupid's Guide to Love*. So far he'd checked off so many boxes she could barely believe it. He'd even come up with a few she hadn't thought of. He was as creative out of the bedroom as in.

A double Cupid's ping echoed as a familiar British voice asked, "Excuse me. Is this seat taken?"

Summer couldn't believe she'd ever thought his tone to be stodgy. It was smooth and silky as velvet.

When she looked up, she had to blink twice. Not only was he holding a book in his arm that held a single white daisy acting as a bookmark, but he was wearing a tuxedo. Cufflinks, shiny shoes, and all. And it wasn't a rental either, it was too fitted to his muscular frame not to be custom.

His lips tilted up at the corners. "Unless I got the wrong table. You are Summer, aren't you?"

He was going with the whole role-playing thing. He knew how much she loved a little role-play—clothing optional.

"Oh, you got the right table. I was just thinking I got the wrong memo. I seem to be underdressed." She smoothed her hand down her fitted jeans.

He looked her up and down and flashed that mega-watt smile of his that had the power to make her panties melt off. "You look ravishing to me."

"That's a bold statement for a blind date."

"According to my app you could be my soulmate."

"Do you believe in soulmates?"

He hooked his foot around the chair and in a very manly way pulled it out and took a seat. "I do now."

"Is that just the app talking? For all you know I could be some crazy-stalker chick."

"For all you know I'm into crazy-stalker chicks," he said with a wink.

"What did you think of the book?"

"I think that Darcy was misunderstood. I felt for the guy. It took Elizabeth three hundred pages to realize that he wasn't some stuck-up prideful wanker."

Summer gasped. "He was rude to her."

"It was a bad first impression. To be fair, the poor guy didn't want to be there with all those women wanting him for his money. So they had a meet-ugly—you have to cut the guy some slack. We've all been there."

"Okay, you have me there. And he did figure it out first that there was something between them."

"Oh, I think it was love at first sight for him."

And there went those butterflies again. "How do you know?"

"Because a man knows these things." He took her hand in his. "It might take him some time to figure these things out, love. But when he does, he is certain."

"Give me another example," Summer whispered breathlessly, as he wove their fingers together.

"Okay. When I walked in here tonight and saw you sitting at the table, before our phones even chimed I knew you were my soulmate. In fact, if I weren't being such a stubborn wanker, that first time I met you I would have admitted it was love at first sight."

"I didn't think you believed in things like love at first sight."

"I didn't until you. With you I believe in a lot of things I didn't used to. For example—"

Wes got off his chair and knelt in front of her on one knee and she clasped her hands over her mouth, while her heart did a nosedive straight into her belly then shot into her chest like a champagne cork.

"I never truly believed that forever could really exist for a guy like me. That someone could see past my arrogance and pride to the man beneath who wants nothing more than to be loved."

Summer cupped his cheeks. "You deserve all the love in the world."

"You also make me believe that. And I want to give you that, even more, in return. Which is why . . ." He pulled the daisy out of his book. "You have made me happier than I've ever been and I can only imagine how happy the rest of our days together will be. So, Summer Russo, will you marry me?"

He held out the daisy and that's when she saw it, the glittery square-cut diamond in an antique setting and surrounded by dozens of smaller diamonds. It reminded her of the stars in Mystic's night sky.

He slid the ring off the stem of the daisy and held it up to her finger. "Will you be my wife?"

"Yes! With all my heart yes!" she said.

He slid the ring all the way on her finger and, just like them, it was the perfect fit.

ACKNOWLEDGEMENTS

To my incredible editors Katherine Pelz and Allison Moore, for their enthusiasm and insight, and to the entire team at 8th Note Publishing whose dedication and amazing contributions are appreciated.

I'd love to thank my all-star agent, Jill Marsal, for her constant support and devotion to my work and career. This journey has been amazing, and a big part of that is due to Jill.

Finally, to my husband Rocco who became Mr. Mom for the weeks leading up to my deadline, never complaining when I fell asleep spooning my laptop, or when I was still in my pajamas come dinner time. You were my first and last perfect meet-cute and I would follow you anywhere.

For exclusive excerpts sign up to be a VIP reader at
MarinaAdair.com/Newsletter

© Tosh Tanaka

ABOUT THE AUTHOR

Marina Adair is a *New York Times* and #1 Amazon bestselling author whose fun, flirty contemporary romcoms have sold over a million copies. In addition to the Sierra Vista series, she is the author of the St. Helena Vineyard series, which was turned into the original Hallmark Channel Vineyard movies: *Autumn in the Vineyard, Summer in the Vineyard,* and *Valentines in the Vineyard.* Raised in the San Francisco Bay Area, she holds an MFA from San Jose University and currently lives in North Carolina with her husband, daughter, and two neurotic cats. Please visit her online at MarinaAdair.com and sign up for her newsletter.